Unlikely Prophet

L.S. King

Copyright © 2018, 2020 L.S. King
All rights reserved.
ISBN: 1-7356188-3-7
ISBN-13: 978-1-7356188-3-8

Cover Design: Miblart Copyright © 2020
miblart.com

Loriendil Publishing
loriendil.com

DEDICATION

In memory of my late husband, Stephen King, for all his support and pride in my writing for so many years.
I miss you!

CONTENTS

Acknowledgements

Thanks to:

Dr. Jonathan Crofts - My Very Own Physicist™ who has patiently waded through my questions and tried valiantly to keep me from breaking the laws of physics. Without him, the technology of this world would be much diminished, although to be honest, his brain would probably be in a much better state if he didn't have my stories twisting his mind into knots.

Sarah Hulett, Johne Cook, James King, Talibah Chikwendu, Shannon, Corrie, and Troy McNear for their feedback and support.

And as always:

Johnston McCulley and Guy Williams—for my love of capes, swords, and brave deeds.

Map of Elyria

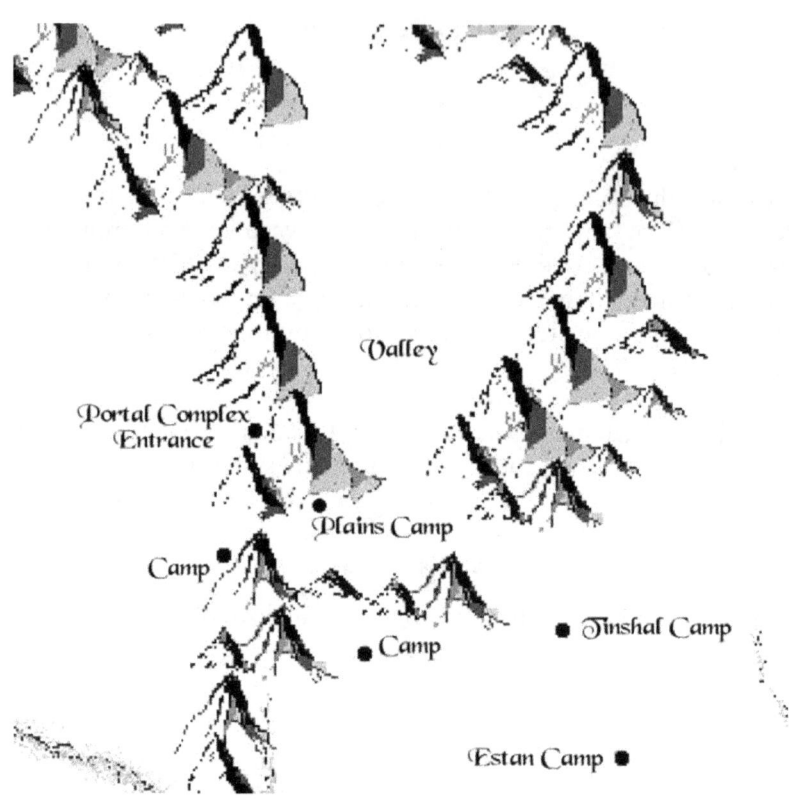

PRONUNCIATION OF NAMES

Teldheri:
- ' indicates a glottal stop except when used after ch, in which case it indicates the ch is a hard sound (as in Scottish lo**ch**)
- dh indicates a fricative **d** (as in mo**th**er or **th**en)
- a is **ä** (as in f**a**ther), except in an accented syllable, in which case it is short
- e is short as in **e**gg
- i is short as in p**i**t, except as final vowel, then it is long **e**, as in Teldheri (or when followed by double consonants, such as is common in female names)
- ai is a diphthong, with the separate vowels pronounced as given above: **ä** and long **e**
- ei is a diphthong, with the separate vowels pronounced as given above: short **e** and long **e**
- o is long **o**
- u is long as in r**u**le
- gh indicates a soft g (as in **g**eneral)
- jh indicates a sibilant s (as in mea**s**ure)

Male names:
- accent is on the first syllable except when it is a three syllable name beginning with a vowel with a closed second syllable, in which case the accent is on the second syllable, therefore *El'adhrel* but *Alcan'dhor*

Female names:
- in names such as *Sarinna*, or *Colinn*, the i is pronounced as a long **e** and carries the accent, as indicated by the double consonant after the vowel
- in names such as Amara or Aleta, the accent is on the second syllable
- in names such as Sherel, accent is on the first syllable

"enh?" used at the end of a sentence to indicate a question does not carry a long **a** sound, but rather the nasal enh sound similar to "hein" used by the French.

UNLIKELY PROPHET

The door of the maglev opened, and Avadhron emerged to semidarkness. Behind him, the railcar slid past along the guideway. Before him, the platform and boarding area appeared vacant, as did the street that led away from the tube station. Not too unusual, for this dome anyway, as the world cycled toward the end of day, but still...

His eyes narrowed, Avadhron stepped down slowly, checking the few spots capable of hiding assailants. He thumbed the comm behind his ear. "Elites. All clear for now, but be ready."

"Right, Chief."

His team had wanted to travel in the same railcar, but the two clan thanes would suspect a trap. He ordered them to follow in the next car.

Thanes Linsar and Camven had both agreed to a secret, peaceful meeting to put an end to their clans' feuding. Trusted men from each clan should be at the station. This did not bode well. If he found no one at the first common area, he would withdraw.

The diffused reddish-orange glow of the dome faded to indicate to its inhabitants that sunset yielded to night. One hand on the half-staff on his hip, Avadhron strode down the narrow, trash-strewn street between the two tall buildings, glancing about and listening. Lights should brighten as night fell, but most of the ones along this street did not work at all. The clan thanes blamed the government—and the king—for such problems, citing lack of funds provided, even though each dome's council was allocated proportionate amounts based on size and population. The problem could not possibly be dome council mismanagement, no.

He slowed his pace as he reached the small common area at this first intersection. A few people lounged near the working lights, talking and laughing, and several hurried along with carry bags, probably heading home after work.

One man stepped forward, jerking his head to indicate Avadhron should follow, then turned toward a side street. He had seen this man before with Thane Camven of Rach'adar clan, one of his chiefs. With another glance around the area, he started across the commons.

Two men stepped forward, arms crossed, to block the clan chief. "And where are you going?"

"None of your business."

"Think you're so much, Rach'adar?" the one sneered.

"More than your pathetic clan, you Galadar scum."

Avadhron caught up to the three and stepped between the members of the two clans. "Enough. Back away. All of you."

The second of the men from Galadar clan spat, "You've sunk lower than low to be with a Ch'shalna Sec. Betraying your kin, are you? Or our whole dome?"

Men in the common area now walked toward them, and more appeared from side streets, shouting rude names and hurling insults at each other.

Avadhron thumbed his comm. "Elites, I need you on site. Possible riot imminent."

"On our way, Chief."

More people swarmed into the bare stone of the commons—too many gathered too quickly. This was not spontaneous. Had Camven and Linsar been detained, victims of their angry clans, or had they been on the planning of this tumult? Blast it, all their intelligence had ensured this meeting was legitimate! He swung his half-staff onto his shoulder, not believing his weapon might cause these men to think twice, not if they didn't already respect the security jerkin he wore, or the emblem of his rank.

A man in front bellowed, "Out of the way, Sec!"

Both sides took up the cry, shouting threats to each other and Avadhron, waving their fists, and shaking their various ersatz weapons, mostly long-handled tools. So their grievances appeared to be with each other, not necessarily against him; he just happened to be in the wrong place at the wrong time. Or was he?

Avadhron planted his feet, eyeing the crowd in the dim evening light cast by the dome and the few working streetlights. Shadows blurred their angry faces, and their cries echoed off the glimmering, silent stone of the surrounding buildings. Blackened windows hid onlookers. Not willing to be involved, but willing to watch, out of curiosity, boredom, to cheer their clan, or perhaps eager to see a Ch'shalna security chief go down.

He shifted the grip on the half-staff, his mind whirling. So much was at stake; if this situation came to blows, the fighting could easily spread into a riot. King Janadhan would use that as an excuse to make an example of these clans and seal East Valley Dome Six to contain the violence. If that happened, too many would die.

The clamor grew until the sound was deafening.

He thumbed the activation switch, and the tip of his half-staff hummed, emitting a blue glow. Swinging the business end first at one clan, then the other, he ordered, "Disperse."

The two groups approached, closing the distance, faces angry, snarling. He whirled the staff in a tight circle as a warning, leaned forward slightly onto the balls of his feet, and waited. He knew he wouldn't be able to take them all down before they overwhelmed him, but that wouldn't stop him from trying.

The nearest man swung a crudely made metal baton at Avadhron's head. He ducked the blow and spun the half-staff in, striking the man's forearm with a sharp *crack*. The assailant grabbed his arm, dropping to his knees with a cry.

Avadhron twirled the security weapon again. The half-staff was effective against individuals, but wasn't designed for crowd-control. Secs did not use any projectile weapons in-dome, due to unlikely-but-potential damage.

Three men bore down on him at once with tools held high. He ducked one and kicked the other in the knee. He lunged at the first, swinging his staff into the attacker's midsection. The man fell with a howl. He took out the third with a kick to the ribs, then a staff-strike to the man's head. Four men now lay sprawled at his feet, groaning. That should have been enough to give most people pause, but this was now a mob, whose only goal was pointless, thoughtless, stupid violence. Growling and shouting threats, they closed in.

Avadhron remained in a fighting stance. "Disperse!"

Several attacked him at once. He swung his weapon, shocking one after another. Some fell to their knees with cries of pain or wailed, writhing on the ground. A pile of bodies grew around him, the aggressors not caring if they stepped on the downed men to get to the Sec Chief. Hands grabbed his shoulders and arms from behind. Two men, fists clenched, dove at him. He lifted both his legs and kicked, falling backward, pulling his attackers down atop of him.

Lights flashed, and the air crisped with the smell of burning ozone. Screams of pain from the rioters echoed in his ears. The crush of bodies relaxed. Armored hands stretched down toward him and hauled Avadhron to his feet. His Elites clouted him on the back.

Avadhron sized them up with a critical eye, hiding his relief with a scowl. "Took your time, you lazy louts."

<>

Avadhron glowered as he strode down the corridor toward his office, Paldhran on his heels, ranting more like a father than head of security. The fact he was both seemed inseparable to the man; he treated his son more like an errant stripling than a highly trained security chief.

"What were you thinking letting yourself get caught in the middle of a riot? Aren't you smart enough to sense a trap? I expect better from the Chief of the Elites. Have you detained that scoundrel Camven? He's ever plotting something."

"My Elites are investigating the incident, including the possibility Thanes Camven and Linsar were involved, sir," Avadhron said over his shoulder.

"Hopefully they'll do a better job than you did!"

Avadhron whirled. "Do you believe I was remiss? Are you going to file charges and relieve of me duty?"

"I didn't say that."

"Then what?" He was too exhausted to care about being disrespectful—to his father or his superior. "I'm Chief of the Elites, by vote of the First Table. If you think I'm incompetent, you should call Question. If not, suck sand!"

"Don't you address me in that manner!"

"Are you speaking as my superior or my father?"

"Both."

"You can *both* suck sand."

Paldhran snatched Avadhron's jerkin with a snarl. Avadhron struck the outside of his father's arms just above the elbows with the heel of his palms, breaking the grip, then quickly stepped back, hands raised. "We're both tired. I'm going home."

"I'm not finished speaking to you!"

"Leave off, *sir*."

"This is what I'm talking about. Your constant disrespect. It broke—"

"So starts another tirade of how I broke Mother's heart."

"You did—"

"She was ill long before I announced I was going to marry a commoner."

4

"Chief!" Avadhron's second in command, Galadhan, sprinted toward them, his face lined with worry. His Second saluted Paldhran, fist over his heart, then turned to Avadhron, data-paper in hand. "Pardon my interruption, sirs, but I need you to review this interrogation."

His father snorted, whirled, and stalked away

Avadhron took the data-paper and walked into his office, thumbing it on. Requisitions for replacement gear for the Elite One Team. He touched the upper right corner for the contents. The paper blinked and listed various requisitions for his department. He frowned at Galadhan. "Wrong data-paper?"

His Second's his lips pursed, hiding a smile.

Avadhron flipped the data-paper onto his desk. "What if he had decided he wanted to review the interrogation?"

Galadhan's eyes widened with facetious innocence. "'Oops?'"

"You're a devious scoundrel."

"It's why I'm your Second."

"Bold too. How is the investigation going? Have all the participants in the incident been interrogated?"

"Not yet. They should be by the time you return in the morning."

Avadhron glared at his Second.

Galadhan jabbed a finger at his face before he could say anything. "Go home, Chief. Get some rest."

"Not while my men are still here processing—"

"You've been here since first shift, these men are third. And this was a minor disturbance, we stopped it before it went to a full riot. Let your men finish investigating whether it was pre-planned. Go home."

"You've been here since first shift as well. Are you going home?"

Galadhan stared at his feet, letting his breath out slowly in lieu of answering. Avadhron grinned and poked his Second's chest. "Got you."

"You have a wife to go home to. I have an empty cot in a barracks."

"A wife has nothing to do with needing sleep, Second. If you want me to go home, I'll demand you do the same."

"Extortion, Chief."

Avadhron straightened, peering down his nose at his friend. "Is it working?"

Galadhan hesitated, then sighed and nodded.

Chapter Two

The door slid open and Avadhron stepped inside. Only the dim base light near the entrance gave any illumination to his home. Jhendill must already be asleep. He hoped she hadn't waited up long, but knowing her, she probably had. His wife wasn't one to dramatize her worry, thank the Elders, but worry she did.

He tossed his security jerkin across the chair by the desk console in the small living area. Rubbing his aching neck, he hesitated, peering into the dark toward the kitchenette at the other end of the room. No. He was too tired to eat. He dragged into the bedroom, let his clothes drop into a pile, and stepped into the sonic shower. His eyes barely stayed open long enough to stumble out and fall into bed.

His muscles ached. He sat in that desk chair too much lately; he needed to exercise more. And get involved in dome patrol more often. His wife sighed and snuggled against his back, murmuring her relief he was home safe. Ah, more so than work-outs, he could do with more of this. He smiled and let sleep overtake him...

A cool breeze caressed Avadhron's face as he inhaled the tangy, fragrant scent of the bushes. The sound of birds singing and chattering filled the air. To one side rose a tall mountain, and he squinted as the sun edged out from a billowy white cloud in the blue sky. A brown and grey bird streaked overhead. He turned to follow its flight and saw the downhill path in front of him. Majestic trees lined the descent. One hand strayed to touch the rough bark of a tree trunk as he ambled by—

Avadhron's eyes snapped open, and he gasped despite himself. After taking deep breaths to quiet his aching heart, he rose and dressed, sleep driven from him. He stumbled through the dark to their living area and fell into the chair, feeling for the switch to the desk lamp. He pulled his data-paper toward him and thumbed it on, then recalled his private file. Staring at the wall, he tried to make sense of his thoughts.

> *The night winds do call*
> *And I must away*
> *To search for my heart*
> *Before it's full day*

Oh, I long for light
For warmth from the sky
For fresh fields of grass
And birds that do—

"What are you doing?" his wife's voice asked through a yawn.

Avadhron thumbed the close button. A flurry of nonsense characters flitted on the page as the file self-encrypted before disappearing. He spun around in the chair. Jhendill stood in the doorway of the bedroom, blinking sleepily, fetching even in the loose robe.

He gave a small shrug. "Just going over some things. I–I couldn't sleep."

"Never stop working, do you, Ch'shalna?"

Avadhron smiled at her use of his clan's name. It had been an insult when they first met: a low-born commoner with no use for anyone related to the high-and-mighty king. And it hadn't helped that he'd been in charge of an investigation in her research department. Now however, Ch'shalna was an endearment, her pet name for him.

Yawning again, Jhendill pushed her long, dark hair behind her ears and walked over. "Just can't sleep, or do you have cases bothering you?"

He shot her a wry grin. "Oh, various things." The dream wove across his sight, and he stood, willing himself to dismiss it. His jaw clenched against the despair of knowing his dream could never be a reality. In this foul mood, he couldn't stay. He snagged his black Sec jerkin off the back of his seat. "I need to leave." He shrugged the long, sleeveless garment over his shoulders and belted it.

She crossed her arms across her robe, her eyebrows lifted. "Already?"

"I..." He looked at his hands as he pulled on his black gloves, avoiding her eyes. "I thought of something. I want to check it out."

"You are nothing if not dedicated." She rose on tiptoe and kissed him. "Be careful."

He wrapped his arms around her slender waist and drew her close, returning the kiss. Her arms threaded around his neck, her fingers tangling in his long hair. Mm, perhaps she could help drive that blasted dream from his mind. But slowly, she pulled away with an apologetic pout. "I need to get to work early myself, but I'll make it up to you tonight. Promise." She gave him another kiss, a long one: a down payment. He was definitely not working late today.

When they finally ended the kiss, he brushed a strand of hair out of her face and asked, "So what are you doing that has you going in so early?"

Her eyes lit up. "We're testing the new atmospheric scrubber modules.

They're promising."

Avadhron nodded and, with reluctance, let his arms drop from her. Between both their jobs, they spent too little time together. And he dare not tell her that her life's work of trying to clear the atmosphere didn't give him hope. He understood little of it, and possibly her enthusiasm and optimism weren't misplaced. Perhaps in some future generation Teledhar's surface might truly be habitable again. Perhaps. But without the biodiversity of flora and fauna necessary to populate it and create a proper ecosystem? The agri-domes had saved only a fraction of plant life, and most of that was, naturally, food crops and herbs, not many flowers, or trees for that matter. No animal life or insects lived, save the vermin thriving in the sewers and underground areas of the domes and some small types of pets.

He murmured goodbye, dropped a quick kiss on her forehead, and left. As the lift took him down to ground level, his thoughts sank as well to a deeper depression.

Palace Dome, besides being the center of their government's administration, housed all the families of Ch'shalna, the royal clan. The king lived sumptuously in a large suite of rooms which took up an entire floor in the palace complex itself above the council chambers and security headquarters.

With only the illumination of the walkway lights, the residential buildings loomed darkly on each side as Avadhron walked toward the rail station. The shadowy structures housed level upon level of families, each one living in a tiny abode similar to his, two rooms plus sonic shower and priv.

In some clans, whole families lived in cramped one-room quarters; in the older domes many were even housed underground. Avadhron could not comprehend such an existence. Obviously neither could some of the more unfortunate clans, or they wouldn't be revolting. But what could be done? Domes were difficult to build and maintain, especially with the increasing frequency of earthquakes. Their world continued to spiral down into a whirlpool of despair.

The opaque dome slowly illuminated, signaling the start of another day. The synthetic stone of the walkways and buildings began to shimmer as the light grew. Avadhron found no beauty in the glittery surfaces, only a sense of confinement. Greenery in raised beds graced these narrow streets, but no insect or animal life flitted or scurried.

What would it be like to feel wind? Rain?

As he took the rail-tube to the nearest agri-dome, he stared out the window at the forlorn ash-grey wasteland, tinted red with the rising of the sun. What would his wife think of his amateurish attempts at poetry? No,

Jhendill didn't even understand his obsession with nature; he had better not let her see that side of her tough, Sec-guard husband.

The rail stopped, and Avadhron stepped onto the platform inside the edge of the enormous agri-dome. The guards nodded to him in recognition and allowed him to enter. He breathed in the humid air, his eyes sweeping the greenery. What had it been like when their whole planet had looked like this? He walked among the plants with reverence, touching leaves, memories of his dream—always the same dream, of the same place—flooding back over him.

The path of flat stones wound down, taking Avadhron to a small clearing. A stream trickled into a pool, then bubbled away downhill. Little yellow flowers with elongated petals curving into slender cups sprouted among the rocks and grass, their dark leaves rising from the ground. An aromatic shrub grew all around, filling the air with sweet perfume...

With a sharp inhale, Avadhron shook off the reverie. He leaned over and closed his eyes, breathing in the fragrant scent of a blossom, trying to ease the torment of knowing he would never experience such things while awake. Why did his mind torture him so?

He turned and strode back to the rail-tube. Time to get to work.

Avadhron tapped the update pad on the data-paper, and the surface blinked as the day's reports downloaded. He gazed at the paper, trying to not hear the inane chatter of Petill, Merdhil, and Emadhrel nearby, discussing their rankings in one of the more popular Grid-games. He didn't blame them for spending time in some imaginary world accessed through holographic and sensory inputs; many of his people did. A way to escape, like his forays to the agri-dome.

His gaze flicked to them, and he asked in a low tone, "Are you Elites on duty?"

They scattered, which answered his question. He returned his attention to the data-paper. Last night's riot was still in the investigative stage. Two other reports, however, flagged orange.

The first, an earthquake had hit East Valley Domes Three and Four with minimal damage. Avadhron paused to breathe a sigh of thanks to the Maker; he remembered all too well the devastation of the South Plain earthquake—every dome demolished, thousands of lives lost, entire clans all but eradicated.

The worst damage to East Valley seemed to be a few of the rail-tubes. Some of the residents had, in a dangerously foolish move, used the ones still in service to try to escape to other domes. Wisely, most stayed, either in their homes with enviro-suits at the ready, or at hastily erected mini-dome shelters.

Neither dome had been breached, although Four's had minute cracks, for which repair crews had already been dispatched. Evac teams and their shuttles waited in preparation for any aftershocks. Under control then. Good.

Avadhron continued to the second report and stiffened in alarm—an attempt to plant bombs in the Palace Dome within the last hour, thwarted by his own Elites. Three suspects had been apprehended.

They could not have carried the bombs in-dome intact. Either they were repeat visitors who smuggled parts in, or they had conspirators within the dome. And did that trio have the knowledge themselves of where to place the bombs to fracture the dome, or had someone instructed them? Their positions when captured were frighteningly accurate.

His eyes widened as he read their backgrounds; the three were from Jonasel clan. Why would one of the noble clans stoop to do their own dirty work? Were they that desperate to destroy the king? Palace Dome? His kin?

Avadhron rubbed his eyes. Much of the dissension was directly the fault of King Janadhan, as well as his advisors in both their own clan and in Viltara clan. Greedy sand-suckers. He dared not say it aloud, but he despised his supercilious scoundrel of a cousin.

He needed to increase security measures to keep insurgents from gaining access to the dome in the first place. This could not be allowed to happen again. He punched in codes to give his men new orders, his thoughts still racing. Yes, it was his job to protect the king, but just as important—and to his mind even more important, although he dare not speak such treason—he had to protect Ch'shalna's dome.

"Daydreaming, son?"

Avadhron gave a cursory glance up at his father, then tapped the data-paper. "No. Sir. Just thinking about this attack by Jonasel clan. Such an overt strike is alarming." He paused and made certain his face and voice didn't betray his disaffection for Janadhan. "Has the king been notified?"

"Yes. He's expecting a report." Paldhran nodded toward the console. "You had better get busy. Increase security and perimeter patrols—"

"I know my job!" he barked. Other guards in the office turned, and he modulated his voice. "I have taken care of all that already. Sir."

"I hope so. I don't want Janadhan breathing down my neck." His father glared at him, grey eyes flashing. "He's going to visit the prisoners and wants us along." He spun and marched out.

Avadhron suppressed a sigh as he rose.

Chapter Three

"I am not impressed by your son's efforts, Paldhran." The king stared straight ahead as they walked down the dim, narrow hallway. Avadhron eyed Janadhan as he and his father trailed behind. Their monarch turned, tilting his head to gaze up at him with a scowl. "Sloppy. You should dismiss him from service. Let him putter among flowers instead, or play with his commoner wife."

He unclenched his jaw. "I am present, Your Majesty. If you have a complaint about me or my men, say it to my face."

"Those traitors got into our dome, didn't they?" Janadhan's blue eyes closed to feral slits. "And you watch your tone with your king."

"He meant no offense, Sire," Paldhran interjected. "He merely desires clarification of your dissatisfaction—"

"Don't claim to know what I mean!"

"Bicker amongst yourselves later." Janadhan stopped in front of one of the cells and spun to face it, making his blue and silver robes whirl with a dramatic flair. "Let me see the prisoners."

The guard opened the door, and Avadhron stepped inside behind his father and the king, his stomach churning.

When new to Security, he had nearly been executed for his outrage and outcries of how prisoners were treated. His first cousin, the king's half-brother, Zaidhron, begged Janadhan for mercy. And convinced Avadhron that martyring himself would be of no benefit. The prince insisted Avadhron bore a unique, intense will and could help strengthen the voices of those trying to make a difference. That to live, and try to lessen injustice and bring about changes, was a worthy goal.

He still often wrestled with that rationale within himself, but he had to admit, he had saved victims, and been instrumental in modifying how prisoners were treated most of the time, unless the king personally got involved. He and Zaidhron did all they could to hinder Janadhan, but nonetheless, Avadhron had limited ability to stop his depraved liege.

The attempted-bombing suspects sat manacled to chairs in the small, bare room. From their similar appearance, he would have guessed the two were brother and sister even without having seen the identity check: red hair and high cheekbones. The third, a ruddy-faced blond man, was a cousin.

Janadhan lifted his head slightly and took a step toward the girl.

"Bring her to my chambers. The others, take out-dome and leave them there."

"You filthy beast!" the brother spat.

The girl and cousin both yelled obscenities at them all, cursing Ch'shalna clan.

Avadhron stepped between the suspects and his king. "Your Majesty, these are not some low-born or clanless. You cannot do as you please without repercussions. They must stand trial."

"And if they were low-born," retorted the king, "you would be crying for mercy due to their pitiful status and lack of opportunities."

Ah no, he would not be diverted from the topic. "Jonasel clan is too powerful to ignore. If you—"

Janadhan shoved his lined face up into Avadhron's, his long teeth bared. "Don't go too far, puppet. Your father can't protect you if you irritate me overmuch. And neither can Zaidhron."

Paldhran pulled on his son's arm. "These rebels are not worth it. They tried to kill the king, destroy our dome. They want to murder us all!"

"Regardless, they should stand trial." He raised his voice to be heard over both men's protests. "They are Jonasel clan! High nobility!"

Shouldering between the two, his father held his hands up in a warding motion. "Your Majesty. Avadhron, please!"

Ignoring his obsequious parent, he locked eyes with the king, willing himself to not show his hatred of the man, or his anger, as Paldhran whispered for him to calm down.

Their monarch pulled himself up and straightened his robes, glaring at Avadhron. "Then we shall have a trial." With a disdainful smirk, Janadhan stomped out.

The outcome of the trial was automatic, since any attack against a dome was considered an attempt at mass murder, but at least while in his custody, it appeared, the prisoners would not be mistreated. He took long breaths to bring his anger under control as he and his father left the cell.

Paldhran gripped his shoulder and whirled him around. "Wake up, son. Strip that idealism from your eyes. Live in the now and learn from me, or you will never survive politics."

<\>

"I hear the king had at you again," Prince Zaidhron said.

Avadhron pushed away the interim report of the ambush/failed meeting of the night before and sat back in his chair with a glower at his cousin.

Zaidhron sauntered over and perched on the edge of the Sec Chief's desk, his eyes mocking. He adjusted his royal robes, then flicked his blond hair over his shoulder. "I hear he called you your father's puppet to both your faces, too."

"He tried to treat the prisoners as refuse. Jonasel clan! Dome above us, can you imagine the results?"

"I know." The prince frowned. "But you did succeed in getting them a trial."

He snorted but refrained from replying; Janadhan had listening devices in his office. He wouldn't be surprised if he had Ears in his home too, although he did periodic sweeps to assure his privacy. Jhendill didn't deserve to be preyed upon.

Did Zaidhron ever suppose their king might spy on him? He never acted as if he did. He seemed too naïve, but in spite of that stood in charge of most administrative duties. One could be intelligent yet ingenuous.

"Well, you can tell him you talked to me and set me straight." Avadhron picked up the report and thumbed the corner to switch the page on display. "Now I have work to do."

The prince bent close, his face earnest. "Just a reminder that you have an ally."

"Thank you. But beware of our king if he knows you are too good a friend to me."

One side of the prince's mouth twitched. "He already knows, cousin."

Avadhron frowned. "You can find humor in what would make most men quail? Few stand close to me, much less claim friendship."

"The king knows my fealty rests at the foot of his throne."

Avadhron met his cousin's eyes, wondering, as he had many times, about the relationship between the half-brothers. Zaidhron, the loyal subject of the king, and Janadhan who relied on Zaidhron so heavily. "Does he really?"

Zaidhron's genial expression faded. "He does, and it does. Don't worry about me."

A vibration by his ear stopped Avadhron before he could reply. He thumbed his comm.

"Yes?"

Paldhran's voice filtered through the earpiece. "Get battle and surface gear. We have detected power fluctuations emanating from the Elders' mountain."

"Elders' mountain? What sort of power?"

The prince stood, his expression anxious.

"A high amplitude, periodic electromagnetic pulse," his father said. "Take Zaidhron with you. He's studied that place and knows it better than anyone."

Avadhron rose with a scowl, thumbing off the comm. "You're to come with me to investigate."

His cousin's face lit up.

He shook his head. "This could be dangerous. You stay back and obey me." He headed out the door, his cousin following on his heels.

"You can't order me. I rank you."

Elders, he sounds like he did when we were children. "I can if it poses possible danger."

The prince seized his arm. "You know I am as keen about our history as you are about plant life. If someone has broken into the complex and destroyed anything, I want—"

"There's nothing left to destroy. That place was breached long ago. It's an empty shell." Avadhron spun to his stubborn cousin and stabbed a finger in his face. "You listen to me while we're out there!"

Zaidhron blinked innocently.

Avadhron pressed his lips together and turned away. "If you don't obey me and get killed, at least I won't have you nagging me anymore!"

"Who could be out there?" Avadhron muttered, hunching his back in a futile effort to relieve the insistent itching between his shoulder blades that plagued him every time he wore full body armor. He glanced over at the second skiff as they both skimmed toward the foothills in the north.

The Elders' mountain grew nearer and darker as the minutes ticked by. Bare ground stretched to the horizon at Avadhron's left and right, dotted by dull red gleams as shallow pools of dead water reflected the sky, and the two skiffs occasionally changed course to swing wide of fumaroles, an ever-increasing navigational hazard.

"I don't know," Zaidhron said, his voice slightly muffled through the breathing gear in his face mask. Avadhron had suggested armor for him as well, but the prince merely donned an enviro-suit used by scientists when working out-dome. If this wasn't a false alarm, the environment wasn't what his cousin would need protection against.

"Only scientists and Secs are normally allowed out-dome," Zaidhron continued, "and then they require clearance. What could anyone want at the Elders' mountain?"

"You tell me. I think it's an error, equipment malfunction, perhaps caused by a recent earthquake. The mountain is too far away to reach on foot, even with the best gear. And no skiffs are checked out or reported missing. Who would have any interest in that forsaken site?" Avadhron cut his eyes to his cousin. "Except history fanatics with strange theories."

Zaidhron sniffed. "You truly think the Elders just dumped our ancestors on this planet and left? As if we were criminals or outcasts?"

"Teledhar: this planet's name means 'Abandoned.' You have a better explanation?" He held up a hand. "Never mind. I don't want to get into an argument about your precious Elders." What else did make sense though? Why leave thousands of children with only a handful of advisors—Elders—to give minimal guidance on an unstable planet, then forsake them?

Zaidhron pointed ahead. "We're here." His voice cracked, betraying his elation.

Fallen rock scattered here and there, but for the most part, the huge landing platform before the ruined entrance to the Elders' mountain remained clear.

Avadhron pulled his skiff along the other one, and his Elites piled out in full gear, weapons at ready. He snagged the prince's arm as his cousin started toward the smashed door set into the stone wall. "Let my men go first."

Zaidhron hesitated, frustration apparent in his frown. He obeyed though, hanging back as the guards positioned themselves on each side of the entrance. Avadhron gazed up at the sheer face of the mountain as he approached, bare, dark rock, tinged with red from the sun glowing through particulate matter in the atmosphere.

He took a deep breath, adjusted his visor, and thumbed the activation switch on his rifle. A quick glance at the display assured him that the magnetic acceleration system functioned normally. He nodded at his men.

The broken doors would not slide, and one of his guards kicked at the glass to make enough room for them to enter. Another joined him, using the butt of her weapon. He carefully stepped through, as did each of his Elites, and he cautioned Zaidhron to be certain he avoided any contact with the jagged edges which could damage his enviro-suit. Avadhron's boots crunched on the black glass as he peered into the darkness, everything turning green as his visor automatically switched to night-vision mode.

Nothing. Avadhron straightened slightly as he scanned the huge, domed chamber, rifle still at fore. No movement. No noise save their own breathing. On the far side of the room three doors faced them. A small light flashed beside the center one. He took a step toward it, and the place brightened. His visor switched modes again, and he blinked, heart thudding. Sconces high on the walls had lit up. *Must be sensors—the lights go on when motion is detected.* He let his breath out in a sharp exhale and strode forward again.

The center door slid open, and a man stepped out of what appeared to be a lift. One of the guards gave a small gasp. Avadhron's held up an arm to halt his people from any action, although if any of them had been the type to shoot without cause, they wouldn't be a member of his Elites.

This man wore what Avadhron assumed was an enviro-suit, but it fit like a clear second skin allowing one to see his loose-fitting clothing—a tunic and pants made of an off-white, open-weave fabric. Short, straight black hair swept back from his forehead, and his rich, dark complexion was like nothing he had ever seen. Only a small breathing apparatus covered his nose and mouth. He spoke, but Avadhron couldn't understand him.

Did the man's sudden appearance, strange looks, or short hair shock him more? A man's long locks were a sign of his strength. What did the lack of length signify then?

Zaidhron stepped forward and said something slowly. The man answered.

"What's going on?" Avadhron eyed the stranger. "Who is he?"

The prince grinned, his eyes shining with tears. His voice wavering slightly, he whispered, "He's an Elder."

Avadhron opened his mouth to laugh, then reconsidered. "He's a what?"

Several of his Elites gasped or snickered. He waved an arm to silence them. "How did he get here?"

His cousin cleared his throat. "Our legends say they can walk through air from world to world—"

Muttering a short, crude opinion of that theory, he replied, "I want to see where he came from. Are there any others here?"

Zaidhron and the stranger talked back and forth with some stammering and gesturing; then the dark-skinned man waved for them to come toward him, into the lift. Avadhron pointed at two of his guards. They joined him and the prince in the small circular chamber, and the door slid shut.

A slight vibration and his stomach both indicated they had shot downward. Avadhron kept his rifle ready, his teeth clenched so tightly that his jaw ached. Zaidhron still wore a silly, stunned expression.

When the door opened, he nudged the "Elder" with his rifle. The man stepped out and turned to point. On the far side of the large room, a glowing, pale blue ring took up the wall from floor to ceiling, and the inside shimmered and had a...a depth to it, as if stretching beyond the frame into a vast blackness. Avadhron had to stop his mouth from dropping open.

"What is it?" he asked, even as the stranger began talking.

"He says they call it a door—no, a portal," Zaidhron said.

"Like a wormhole?"

"I suppose. We can't communicate well enough to ask technical questions." The prince smiled. "Yet."

He resisted the urge to grab his cousin and pound sense into him. The man was just too trusting. He kept his mind on his job. "How many could come through? Are they here to invade?"

Zaidhron again talked to the alien, then frowned at the reply. Avadhron quelled his impatience as the two tried to communicate. After several minutes, they smiled and nodded at each other.

"I think he's saying he found coordinates for this planet—I can't understand much. He says he has friends, but they are not invaders. They will not visit unless invited."

He snorted. "Who invited him?"

The alien spoke again. Zaidhron quirked a wry smile at Avadhron. "I cannot be certain, but I think, I think he wants us to take him to our leader."

Chapter Four

As he piloted the skiff, Avadhron listened to the halting discussion between this 'Elder' and Zaidhron. Occasionally, he heard what seemed to be a familiar word or phrase.

"What's he saying?" he asked. "What is the language you're speaking?"

"It's actually an ancient dialect of our clan's language. He seems to speak something similar. We're just trying to work on communication. His name is Mattan, by the way."

Avadhron let his gaze slide to the dark stranger, his doubts growing. He couldn't get a fix on this alien, but some *thing*, some desire, pulled at him to want to like the intruder, and perhaps it was merely Avadhron's own contrariness, but that desire drove him to suspicion and increased distrust instead.

Mattan's deep brown eyes met his with a knowing look, then said something that seemed almost understandable, words familiar yet not familiar, scratching at the edges of Avadhron's comprehension.

Zaidhron chuckled and answered before saying to Avadhron, "He says you don't like him. I told him you don't like anyone."

Avadhron sniffed and turned his attention back to piloting. Wait until this "Elder" and the king met. The thought brought a small smile to his lips.

Janadhan swept into the audience chamber with pomp and seated himself on the throne without regarding anyone in attendance. When he looked up, his gaze lit on the alien, and his mouth gaped. Avadhron hid a smirk. For once, the king was speechless.

No one could speak at a formal audience save by their ruler's permission, so they all merely bowed and waited. Finally, Janadhan's lips peeled back from his teeth, then he spoke. "What is this? Who is he?"

"Your Majesty." Zaidhron bowed a second time. "This is a visitor to our planet. His name is Mattan, and he came through a portal in the Elders' mountain."

"Portal?" The king's long face scrunched with confusion. "What are you talking about, man?"

Zaidhron hesitated with a bemused expression and spread his hands in apology. "I am not a scientist, Your Majesty, but from what I understand this portal allows one to walk from world to world."

"Walk from world to..." Janadhan blinked. "So this is some alien?"

"An Elder, Sire, come back to us." Zaidhron held a hand out toward the newcomer. The dark-skinned man stepped forward and spoke, bowing deeply from the waist.

"His name is Mattan. He says he is most honored to be in the presence of our king."

Avadhron rolled his eyes.

"You understand him?" Janadhan's gaze darted from Zaidhron to the alien.

"More or less. Our languages seem to have a common root, and as Your Majesty knows, history and ancient tongues are a hobby of mine."

The king sniffed. He stared at Mattan with a blank expression, probably trying to find some personal gain in this situation. Avadhron got the impression his monarch was truly baffled and sucked at his cheeks to keep from grinning.

"What is this Elder's intention?" Janadhan asked.

"He is an explorer and wishes to be friends, Sire. I have suggested that, with your permission"—Zaidhron inclined his head—"he and I first try to learn more of each other's languages."

Janadhan hesitated. "Hm, yes, a sound idea."

Avadhron knew the king well enough to know his thoughts: it would give him time to discover ways to use the alien to his advantage, likely a dangerous advantage.

And who knew the dangers this alien brought? Avadhron stepped forward, bowing. When his liege nodded permission to speak, Avadhron said, "Your Majesty, as a security precaution, I suggest that two of my Elites be assigned to accompany the al—Elder."

Zaidhron spun with rounded eyes. "You think he poses a threat?" He flushed and turned to the king with a bow. "Apologies, Sire."

Ignoring his cousin, Avadhron addressed the Janadhan directly, as dictated by protocol. "I think that erring on the side of caution is wise."

"Mattan is no threat, Your Majesty!"

The king rose. "Save your bickering for each other. Let Avadhron have his way, or we shall have to endure his brooding and grumbling." He swept out of the chamber.

Zaidhron glared at Avadhron. "We have to endure that, regardless."

Magnanimous in his victory, Avadhron inclined his head at his cousin with a smile. He pointed at two Elites who stepped forward and took positions near the alien.

Zaidhron spoke in slow, stumbling words and Mattan replied with a shrug. His cousin gave a sigh of relief and said, "Despite your lack of circumspection, he doesn't seem insulted by your suspicion. That's one good thing, anyway."

Avadhron met Mattan's placid gaze with a hard look. "Then I'll have to try harder next time."

<<>>

The data-paper blinked as reports downloaded. Avadhron scanned the list. Three days that alien had been here, and his men could give him no solid intel. He ground his teeth. He glanced at the file Galadhan submitted and frowned. He called out to his Second, who ambled over.

"I see that Lewsin has an engineering background, and his was definitely the mind behind the attempted bombing. Does it appear there are more involved? An ongoing conspiracy or merely those three?"

Galadhan hesitated. "Considering they are of Jonasel clan, I would not rule out a wider circle."

"'You would not rule out?'" Avadhron frowned. "That's no answer, man!"

"It's all I can give you. Chief Paldhran took over their interrogation on orders from the king."

Avadhron cursed under his breath, and Galadhan lifted both hands. "Prince Zaidhron is attending." His Second pursed his lips in amusement. "He...stated bluntly that he wanted to ensure the prisoners were alive for their trial."

"I would have loved to have seen my father's face—wait. If Zaidhron is with my father in interrogation, then where is that alien?"

"In the Prince's office, reading on his console."

"That console is unmonitored and has the highest security clearance."

"Chief." Heavy chastisement filled Galadhan's voice.

Avadhron tipped his head in apology. Yes, he should trust his men to know what to do. "I want a list of every file, every document that alien accesses."

A smile spread on his Second's face. "Already taken care of, sir." He crossed back to his own console station.

Avadhron read over the various reports and sat back, smiling. "Have you seen this morning's *Beyond the Domes* nonsense?"

Galadhan rolled his eyes. "Which story? The one which states we created the report of an Elder to take the populace's sights off the real issues of our domination, or the one which states there really is an Elder, and he's working with us in subjugating the people?"

"At least you'd think they'd choose one theory and stick with it," Avadhron said, grinning.

"I don't know why you let these kooks publish on the media Grid in

20

the first place."

"Oh, I'll shut them down in a few weeks, so they'll think we're chasing them down, then hook up to wherever their new hack is. The occasional intel we get is good, as is the humor."

Galadhan shrugged. "You're the Chief."

"You're just still incensed over that one report."

"The one which stated I wear a leash tethered to you?"

Avadhron chuckled. "Don't you?"

Galadhan glared, but the glint in his eyes betrayed his amusement. "If you'll loosen the tether a bit, I'll get to my duties. Sir."

Avadhron waved a dismissal, chortling, and turned his attention to the morning's reports. His men had concluded their investigation of the incident in East Valley Dome Six. The mob appeared to be malcontents of various clans who didn't want their thanes to meet and resolve differences. For once, Camven wasn't involved. Linsar, despite being told to keep the meeting secret, had told all his clan's chiefs, one of whom in turn had spread word. The king had threatened if there were more disturbances, he would seal the dome. Avadhron sighed.

The rest of the reports were minor; overviews of events from various domes. Nothing requiring the attention of his Elites.

He leaned back in a spine-cracking stretch, rose, and crossed to the dispenser. He punched the code for his favorite hot drink, a strong blend of teas, well, a synthetic version, since none of those plants actually existed any longer save in the agri-domes, but those weren't used for bulk food preparation.

He sat back down at his console, a new report blinking for attention on the report data-paper. Avadhron ticked the corner to download it. A fight just erupted in East Valley Dome Six resulting in significant injuries, and three deaths. One of the Secs was in Medical with a broken collar bone. Avadhron slammed his fist on his desk with an explosive oath. They'd sealed their fate, figuratively and literally. Wait, maybe if they worked fast enough—

"Galadhan." Avadhron downloaded the newest report to his Second. "Get on this. Find the cause for the fight and which clans were involved. I want details and the guilty parties apprehended, if not already. We have to act quickly to forestall a dome lock-down."

"Yes, sir."

Galadhan shot out of the room, data-paper in one hand, barking orders into his ear comm.

Avadhron sent a query to Medical asking for updates on the Sec. It wasn't someone he knew personally, but it didn't matter. She was clan, and in Security.

The hopeless frustration hit him afresh in the stomach. Regardless of his efforts, what difference could he make? This was all futile. He let his breath out in a hiss, then flipped the data-paper onto the desk. It whisked across the smooth surface, and a hand caught it as it tipped off the edge. Zaidhron set the offending object back on the desk with a grin.

Avadhron glowered at him. "I thought you were in interrogation."

"We are through. For now."

"And how did you enjoy keeping my father in check?"

"I do much more with the king, thank you."

"You may have something new to stay."

"Oh?"

Avadhron nodded at the data-paper. "Violence in East Valley Dome Six. Three deaths."

Zaidhron groaned, closing his eyes. He gave a long, slow exhale and said, "My thanks for the warning."

"I doubt we can forestall the dome being sealed. I have Galadhan working on finding the instigators of the riots. If we can apprehend them, perhaps we can..." Avadhron stopped and leaned back in his chair, rubbing his face.

His cousin eyed him, his expression one of compassion and empathy. After a long pause, he said, "You, my friend, need respite. Dinner at my home tonight."

"With that alien there? No, thank you."

"Mariss has already talked to Jhendill, and they won't be happy if you refuse."

Avadhron glowered at his cousin. "Conspiracy. Of the blackest kind."

Zaidhron smiled and turned to the door. "Don't be late."

Chapter Five

Jhendill's hand shook in his. Avadhron's taciturn responses kept her from bubbling with talk about Mattan, but it didn't dampen her own awe at meeting an "Elder." He sighed in resignation at spending several hours with the intruder as they approached the building housing Zaidhron's home. This was "respite"?

His cousin lived in a modest two-room abode the same as the rest of his kin. He could, as half-brother of their monarch, live in the palace. But although heir, since Janadhan had no children, Zaidhron called himself liegeman and servant of the king. His lifestyle reflected this.

The two Elites assigned to the alien saluted as Avadhron and Jhendill exited the lift and crossed to Zaidhron's door. He nodded to them. "Your monitors are active?"

"Yes, sir." The one guard, Petill, touched the tiny, curved rod that ran from the comm at her ear around to her eye. "His Highness Prince Zaidhron is not happy about it."

He snorted and thumbed the chime.

The door slid open to reveal a smiling Tarnill, her long blonde hair falling in curls about her face. Her head was shoulder high to Avadhron. Dome above, that child was almost a woman now! In not too many years she would be of Age and Confirmed as her father's heir. Would the planet still support life by the time Janadhan and Zaidhron were gone? Would there be a throne for his young cousin to inherit?

Her blue eyes danced. "Come in! Come in! Have you met Mattan?"

Mariss rushed forward, all smiles, and took over, introducing Jhendill to the intruder.

The alien stood and bowed. "You are involved in the planet reclamation project. You design atmospheric scrubbers, I understand." His voice had only the slightest tinge of an accent. "I'm anxious to discuss this with you. We may be able to offer ways to help."

"That would be wonderful!"

Tarnill hung on Avadhron's arm as Mattan and Jhendill went to the two chairs in the small living area. "He's amazing, Avadhron! Don't you think so?"

"Cousin, I'm the one who ordered those Elites outside to accompany him everywhere to monitor his movements. What do you think?"

Her face fell. "Oh. I thought they were to protect him."

As naïve as her father. At least she had the excuse of youth. Tarnill mumbled something about helping her parents and left him standing alone.

The prince's home was identical to his own: a living area with padded chairs and a desk console on one end and kitchenette at the other, and dividing the one wall, the door to the bedroom and priv. Six people allowed little room to move. Zaidhron, Mariss, and Tarnill set up a small table and pulled chairs around it.

The formed protein cutlets were only a slight extravagance, but rest of the meal was exorbitant: two kinds of real vegetables, which probably used up a week's worth of their kitchenette's garden wall, and tea steeped from actual plant leaves, not synthetics. The confection served was one of the rare, expensive ones that Avadhron had only seen at the palace gatherings for the high nobility. Yes, Zaidhron could easily acquire such a delicacy, but this was not the fare Zaidhron's family would normally eat. Was it acquiescing to demands of the intruder, an attempt to cultivate his favor, or some other reason?

As they ate, he tried to keep abreast of the conversation of his cousins while listening to the animated discussion between Jhendill and the alien. Most of it involved technical terminology about atmospheric scrubbers that flew above his head. So, was Mattan a scientist then? He claimed to be an explorer.

Avadhron paused for a moment as something else occurred to him, the alien conversed fluently with a scientist, not only in her own language, but in the nomenclature of her profession. He didn't hear one slip in grammar either. Such proficiency in only three days, it bespoke secrets, layers, to the man. Avadhron's suspicions rose sharply.

After the meal, Zaidhron and Mariss whisked the food and dishes away while Tarnill and Jhendill folded the table and arranged the chairs for central discussion. Avadhron resisted the urge to scream at the idiotic expressions of adoration on everyone's faces as they seated themselves. Tarnill sat at Mattan's feet, staring up with eyes alight.

The alien met Avadhron's gaze with a smile, at least it was an ironic one, not the sweet amentia everyone else wore. "So you are still as displeased with me as ever." A statement, not a question.

"Just so."

"I hope I may satisfy you as to my intentions."

"Not likely."

Zaidhron waved a hand in Avadhron's direction. "Pay no attention to him. He's happiest when being skeptical and suspicious."

"It's kept you, the king, and many others alive."

The prince inclined his head. "I grant you that. In your occupation distrust is advantageous."

"Yet you never heed me."

"You never give me credit for having any sagacity," Zaidhron snapped. His lips thinned a moment, but his expression mellowed, and he smiled in hesitant apology.

Mattan cleared his throat, and Avadhron returned his gaze to the object of his displeasure.

"I'm sorry my presence causes you such vexation."

"What would you know of my vexations?"

"It is easy to see. You don't trust me, and you don't want me here."

Avadhron grinned, teeth clenched. "Quite straight!"

"Why? Why do you dislike me so intensely?"

"It isn't dislike. It's distrust. What have you done to earn my confidence? Come through your portal and smile and dote on us Teldheri like long-lost friends? Tell me about your people. What makes you different than us, other than skin color? How can you have learned our language so proficiently in only a few days?"

"We have a...talent for languages."

"What a dome heist!"

"No, it's true. Your language and ours have a common root. That makes it easier—"

"All of our clans' languages have the same common root. However, the complexities of say, Keladar, not to mention the various idioms and idiosyncratic syntax of some of the dialects, make full proficiency difficult." Avadhron turned to the prince. "Yet this alien"—he waved at hand toward Mattan—"has mastered our tongue with barely an accent and makes no grammatical errors whatsoever. I want to know how."

Zaidhron lifted his shoulders. "This is not your concern, *Security Chief*."

"Suck sand, *Your Highness*," Avadhron shot back. "You know it is."

"It isn't if I say so. I know the reasons why, and I am satisfied. Therefore, so are you."

Avadhron exhaled through his teeth and dropped his head for a moment to regain his composure, then bored into Mattan's eyes. "Answer this, then. Who are we to you? And why won't you tell us about our history? Why are we here? Why did your ancestors just leave us?"

"I don't know! I have no answers for you." Mattan looked down, his hands splayed on his knees. "I wish I did. I am merely an explorer. If I was aware of your past, I would tell you."

He caught the inference of the verb tense the alien used: *if I was*, not *if I were*—simple past, not subjunctive. His first grammatical mistake of the evening? Not on a wager. And Mattan averted his gaze as well. *Liar.* He could not use those details as proof to anyone but himself, but he held his smug victory deep inside.

Mattan frowned at him, uncertainty in his eyes, as if he knew he had been caught in a lie. Yet Avadhron knew he kept his own demeanor impassive. But if the alien felt defensive, now was the time to push. "Are you saying it wasn't your people who left us here?"

Crossing his arms, the intruder said, "No. But I don't know the history." He hesitated and brushed a hand over his straight black hair. "You have to understand, our world is very different from yours. We have various groups that govern themselves, not one central government. And factions as well. Who knows what some of them might have done in the past?"

Who knew indeed? But in this case, Mattan did know. Could he get the alien to admit it? Probably not, but being of a perverse nature, he had to try. He said nothing, just eyed the man. A sense of a predator stalking prey grew, and he let it fill him, relishing the mental sparring between them. The others fidgeted but remained silent. If only the two of them were alone, he could see how taut he could stretch the alien's nerve.

Mattan seemed to fight a smile, then cleared his throat again. "I understand you have a passion for living things and spend your spare time in the agri-domes. They are beautiful. One almost gets a sense of being in nature when in them."

So much for that challenge. He expected the man to last longer. "You can't feel the sun on your face, or the wind, or smell the freshness of open air." Avadhron pulled himself up a little straighter in the chair and shook his head. "And the humidity is too high. There aren't the sounds one would hear. It's not at all like being in a natural environment."

Mattan's eyebrows rose. "You speak as though you've experienced those things, yet Zaidhron tells me your people have had to live in domes for generations."

Stuffing his recurring dream deep inside, he gave a casual shrug. "I have a good imagination."

"So what precipitated your interest in nature?"

He glowered at the overly inquisitive alien. "Perhaps not having it."

Mattan inclined his head. "I'm sorry." His eyes glinted as he looked back up. "I understand you are in charge of all security."

Avadhron's fists clenched. "Why all the questions?"

"My apologies. I am merely curious."

Oh, certainly you are. Let me answer your question, you devious alien. "I am Chief of the Elites—specially trained guards. My men are the best."

"You say men, but you also have women as guards."

"The masculine is always used for collective pronouns."

"Ah, I see."

26

Did he? With his quickly learned fluency of their language, he didn't already know this? What was this intruder up to?

"As Chief of the Elites, you must have a very difficult job."

He leaned back with a glare.

Mattan seemed unbothered by Avadhron's posture or silence. After a pause, he said, "Zaidhron has tried to explain the causes of the violence. It is due to crowding and fear? Of the future?"

Why was this alien asking? Looking for weakness in their people, in their culture? What did he want? "If the prince talked at length with you, why are you concerned with my views?"

"You deal with those who break your laws, yet from what I'm told, you are held in esteem by many as fair, having sympathy. A rarity, I understand. What do you see when you look at your race and the dilemma confronting them?"

Avadhron's reserve boiled away. "'The dilemma confronting *them*'? *Our* planet is dying, and it confronts every one of *us* daily. Despite our best technological efforts, we have succeeded only in maintaining our existence in these domes and contiguous underground facilities."

"I did not mean to minimize your—"

"Have you ever dealt with the sense of being trapped, being helpless, having no hope? It can destroy a person. Some try to escape reality—with drink or mind-altering chemicals, for example, or through the Grid games, or distractions in media, but others lash out. Sometimes at each other, sometimes blindly at anyone in their paths, sometimes at their rulers."

In the quiet after Avadhron's outburst, Mattan stared down at his clasped hands. "So...if they were given hope, it might ease the unrest?"

He narrowed his eyes. "What are you plotting?"

"What if...what if I said I wanted to help? To bring other scientists here from my world to assist in trying to restore yours?"

He glared at the dark-skinned man, anger and a sense of frustrated inevitability rising in him. More aliens. More invaders. And what motives did they really have? Avadhron didn't believe in altruism. He glowered at Zaidhron. "Is that what this dinner was about, to cadge my blessing for bringing more of his kind here?"

"Not at all. We just wanted to give you the chance to see that Mattan is not some criminal."

"Do you expect me to merely accept that?" With his approval, no Sec-guards would be overseeing the alien or his accomplices, making whatever they were scheming easier.

Jhendill put a hand on his arm, her eyes pleading. "Their scientists could advance our efforts by years, even generations! Please, Avadhron!"

"If you have men assigned to each of the Elders that comes here, your patrol force will be reduced," Zaidhron said. "With the clan feuds and unrest, you can't afford that."

"This has already been decided, hasn't it? The king has sanctioned it. They're coming." Avadhron sank back in his seat, resigned at the guilty expression on Zaidhron's face. "Why did you bother with all this then? You don't need my approval."

"We would still like it."

"I would *like* this world to be a garden, but that won't happen." His lip curled. "Do what you wish. You will anyway. However, I demand all the intruders' names, where they will be housed, and with which teams they will work."

The prince smiled. "That is acceptable."

He glared at his cousin. "You know that if there is one security breach, my head will be forfeit."

"There won't be, you have my word." Zaidhron placed a hand over his heart.

"Your word cannot bind *him*." He nodded at Mattan. "And his word is unproven."

Calm, dark eyes bored into his. "I will prove my word, Security Chief Avadhron. In time."

Avadhron barked a laugh. "Am I to take your *word* for that?"

"I have pledged for him and his people." Zaidhron's tone took on a formality rarely heard. "That should be sufficient for you."

Grudgingly, he forced himself to give a formal reply: "Yes, Your Highness." He gave a seated bow and then sat back and rubbed his eyes.

Chapter Six

"Oh, the Elders are wonderful!"

Avadhron suppressed a growl at his wife's ecstatic reaction toward the aliens. He hunched over the viewer, reviewing the information provided on these Enaisi. At least he had a race name for them, and not the almost godlike moniker 'Elders' his people used.

"They have a version of an atmospheric scrubber with much more advanced capabilities than ours. Mattan has used it on another planet with superlative results. His colleagues Atesni and Dassel are adapting them into modules to fit in our processing units."

Avadhron gave a non-committal grunt as he highlighted Atesni and Dassel's files.

"Did you want some tea?" She called from the kitchenette.

"That would be nice, thank you."

Atesni, female, geo-engineer; Dassel, male, atmospheric chemistry. The details of their scientific backgrounds meant little to him and told him nothing of what he wanted to know. He'd met these first two aliens upon their arrival. Atesni, a striking beauty with a curvy figure, an observation which Avadhron was careful not to comment on to his wife, came across as determined and too serious. He suspected she could have a resentful temper. Dassel, taller and darker than Mattan, had a deep voice and slow, deliberate manner. Five more were scheduled to come to their world, eight aliens in all, infiltrating. And Avadhron still had no idea as to why they were really here.

He heard her footsteps approaching and thumbed the viewer to bring up routine security reports.

Her hands massaged his shoulders, then her arms slid around his neck. She kissed the top of his head. "Troubles at work?"

"Always."

"Is the unrest getting worse?"

Avadhron sighed. "In some domes it's eased due to the aliens 'help' in the Restoration Project. A sense of hope that will be short-lived since they'll see no change in their daily lives. However, the factions opposed to the project are incensed that more time, money, and effort are being directed toward it, rather than toward immediate concerns."

"I can understand their point, I suppose. It's hard to embrace the plans for a future you won't see, and live in crowded conditions, feeling despair..."

Avadhron put his own hands over his commoner wife's. "You would know."

"Yes. But I chose to look ahead."

She did. To rise to the top of a highly specialized profession was unheard of from a low-born, especially one from a clan with such a lawless reputation.

"You are a remarkable woman."

"I know." She leaned closer, and whispered, "See how I managed to snag such a powerful husband, of the king's own clan, no less?"

Avadhron smiled at her jesting misdirection of his praise, but it faded. "And it's not even just that. The king ordered East Valley Dome Six sealed after this last riot. West Ridge Dome Five will face the same sanction if they don't curtail their feud. And the three from Jonasel clan were found guilty yesterday, and executed. Thane Andhalan of Jonasel and his first table all condemned the action. They are howling for a thanes' conclave against Janadhan."

"So I heard," she murmured. "Have the other thanes concurred?"

"A few. Most agree with the sentence. If the bombers had succeeded, how many thousands might have died? Not that most would necessarily care if Ch'shalna clan was largely eliminated, but leniency could give rise to similar plots—and not just against us or other noble clans they might hate, but also against them from clans they are feuding."

Jhendill was silent for a moment, then said, "Things truly are escalating."

"They are."

"What will we do if war starts?" she whispered.

Avadhron twisted in the chair and pulled her into his lap, gazing into her eyes. "It already has. The increase in revolts is merely undeclared war. At this stage, open war would be easier, security-wise, although more deadly for many of the clans, if their domes were also sealed. The king just might declare martial law, slam down more firmly. Do you want me to give you the contingency plans we have in place if war is declared, such as restricting or even banning travel between domes as well as shutting down media access?"

"I don't want to hear the details. It scares me. Not for me, but for you." Her brown eyes searched his, filled with concern. "I worry about you. You would be in such danger."

Avadhron tightened his arms around her. "With my job, I'm always in danger." He pushed her back a little to meet her gaze again. "But at the first whisper of martial law or open war, you keep a breather and protective suit with you at all times." He paused, then said, "In fact, do it anyway."

<<>>

"Three riots in the last two days." Avadhron paced the room, clenching and unclenching his fists as he vented to his Second. "It's intensified since the North Plain earthquake."

"They're angry and scared. Between the power grid for the north-eastern sector being damaged and the near-breach of North Agri-dome Three—"

"Dome above, you think I don't know that?" Avadhron stopped and lifted a hand in apology.

Galadhan rubbed his eyes, which sported dark bags. He put in as many hours as Avadhron. "Chief, I think martial law is our only choice."

He hated to admit it, but Galadhan was right; this couldn't go on. Paldhran had been pushing for martial law, and only the prince's insistence had restrained the king. Martial law meant murder, giving their monarch an excuse to commit genocide against certain clans, yet was there any other choice? "I'm going to see Zaidhron."

Perhaps if the prince interceded with Janadhan, dissuaded him from personal involvement—ha! Foolish thought. The king would love to have the freedom to destroy for his own amusement.

Didn't the clans realize they were dancing to their monarch's sadistic tune?

He walked the hallways, trying in desperation to think of a resolution to no avail. He arrived in front of Zaidhron's office and took a deep breath before opening the door.

Zaidhron and Mattan sat, heads together, reading a data-paper and mumbling to each other, his cousin's pale skin and hair contrasting the alien's dark complexion.

The two men looked up, their faces both worried.

Avadhron's own concerns melted as he sensed a larger danger. "What's wrong?"

They exchanged glances, then Zaidhron said, "I don't understand all the details, but Mattan's people have discovered some disturbing facts." Tears welled in his eyes. "I never believed that our generation would see much improvement in our world, but I had a sense of hope for the future. That's fading."

Avadhron froze, his blood chilled. "So all that has been touted, saying their technology has advanced our efforts in many areas in a short period of time, is a lie?"

Mattan tapped the data-paper. "Things are more complicated than we first realized."

"And is this truth, or have your people conspired against mine?"

"Dome above us, must you always be suspicious?" Zaidhron slumped in his chair. "Our top scientists have scoured the data provided by the Elders and concur with their assessment. Our planet is beyond reclamation. Dead."

Avadhron clenched his teeth against a punched-gut feeling. He'd had no hope for so long, but clung to the desperate faith for the future held by his wife and kin. This sounded like a death pronouncement; his worst nightmares realized. "How did we not know this until now? Our scientists have studied our situation for years. Some have stated it's hopeless, but the majority have said we could reclaim the planet."

"Their technology has allowed a more detailed analysis. We can show you the results."

"Jhendill would understand, I wouldn't." Zaidhron's worried, furrowed brow made him back down a bit. More quietly, he asked, "Then what do we do?"

Mattan hesitated, glancing at Zaidhron. "I have been discussing it with my team, and we've prepared a proposal to present to our leaders. If they give us an immediate audience, I may have an answer, an...alternative. I do not wish to say more until I know for certain."

"I can't see any solution to this. Even your people cannot have the ability to stabilize an entire planet." Zaidhron swallowed and looked up at Avadhron, his blue eyes piercing. "I'm glad you have no children, cousin. I fear for my daughter."

In the ensuing silence, Avadhron stared blankly ahead. Finally, he remembered why he had come. "I bear ill news as well. Despite our efforts, violence is rising. I begin to believe we have no alternative but request martial law."

Zaidhron lifted his hands with a weary shake of his head. "No. It's not the answer."

"I don't like it either, but what other choice do we have?"

"We must try to reason—"

"Reason?" Avadhron's snorted at his cousin's naïve reply. "You cannot 'reason' with men who have none! Have you ever tried 'reason' when confronted with a mob bent on killing each other and anyone else in their way? They are afraid, and have no hope! They dare all, and who knows, perhaps they are looking for a quick death." *Our planet is beyond reclamation. Dead*—the words echoed as a final defeat in his heart. His shoulders slumped. "And I cannot say I blame them."

Zaidhron was silent, his face grim. When he finally did reply, his voice was low, subdued. "We all must struggle on...in whatever manner we purpose is best. Go back to your duties, Security Chief. I will...take your suggestion under advisement." His cousin inhaled raggedly. "I trust I need not advise you to keep this news quiet until we have a plan of action?"

What plan of action can one take against a planet which is unable to support life? Avadhron hesitated then bowed and left.

Chapter Seven

"What could they possibly want?" Avadhron grumbled to himself, staring the door of the conclave chamber. The burden of duties could not take his mind off Zaidhron's news last week. He'd found it harder to concentrate, and his sharp attitude had caused everyone, even Jhendill, to avoid him. Now the king wanted a meeting of the first table? For what purpose? What did any of it matter?

The door slid open, and he entered with a sigh. Janadhan sat at the head of the long table as clan thane. All the chiefs glanced over and stopped chatting as they saw Avadhron.

"About time," Cosdhral muttered.

He ignored his cousin's comment. Halfway around the table, he halted, glaring at Mattan, standing behind Zaidhron. Why was that alien even here if this was clan business? "I'll not sit with *him* at my back."

Zaidhron twisted in his seat, first with a frown at Avadhron, then nodding at the alien. "Please, my friend, take your place."

With a hint of a smile, Mattan moved to the end of the table, and stood, waiting.

Avadhron slowly sank into his chair next to his father, eyes still fixed on the intruder as the prince handed out data-papers while speaking.

"As you are aware, Mattan and his colleagues have been trying to help us to restore our planet to a livable condition. But you may not know that they, and our own scientists and researchers, are now convinced this is not possible. This is a detailed report for any of you wishing to peruse the facts."

The chiefs all talked at once, the overall cry one of dismay and a demand for explanation.

"It's all in the report," Zaidhron repeated several times in answer to the many questions.

"We have no time to read such a long, boring document." Janadhan waved a hand. "Explain to them. And don't cloud the matter with technical details."

Zaidhron bowed, his gaze flitting from one chief to the next. "Our planet is experiencing unchecked volcanism."

"What does that mean?" Dandhral, Avadhron's uncle, asked.

"Well, for example, the earthquakes which are happening more and more often, the increase of ash, steam, and poisonous gases from the proliferation of fumaroles, all these things are becoming more frequent, and that won't change. Our planet is self-destructing."

The chiefs again responded with exclamations of alarm. Zaidhron didn't appear despondent, but almost joyful, riveting Avadhron's attention. What was going on?

Zaidhron lifted his hands, his eyes alight. "Mattan has a solution for us."

The table quieted. Avadhron held his breath, peering at Mattan, who smiled. He had an answer from his people in a mere week's time? Bureaucracies didn't work that fast.

Zaidhron grinned. "His people are willing to allow us relocate to another planet. And his team will help with the venture."

Avadhron sat, stunned. A solution indeed, if one believed in their selfless assistance. His eyes narrowed. *What is this alien scheming?*

His kin exploded with interjections and questions:

"Another planet?"

"When? How?"

"What is it like?"

"How soon?"

Zaidhron nodded to Mattan. The Enaisi activated the holo-viewer on the table, and a blue-green planet hovered before them. The angle zoomed lower to one continent and lower still. Mountains, vast forests, rivers. Avadhron inhaled sharply.

Cosdhral leaned forward, his brown eyes riveted on the display. "No one lives on this world?"

"No." The alien set the view to a large, wide valley nestled in an immense mountain range. He pointed to the mouth of the vale, which widened to a plain swept with long green grasses. "This area would be perfect for training encampments. It has direct access to a portal complex similar to the one on your planet, and your people can deploy from there in various directions after they learn the skills to survive."

"Survive?" Dandhral spluttered.

"What would we need to learn?" Cosdhral asked.

Mattan locked eyes with Zaidhron for a moment, then raised his head and gazed around the table at them all. "Your people will have to study many new disciplines and learn a variety of skills. Smithing for example, to make rudimentary weapons and tools, and carpentry and masonry so that you may build sturdy homes and craft shops, and trades such as farming, herding, tanning, spinning, weaving, and innumerable others. You will have to rely on yourselves, not computers or your advanced technology, to do your work. But natural power sources are available so it will not be as primitive as it sounds."

"Why couldn't we have our technology?" Cosdhral asked.

Mattan hesitated a moment. "It's a condition of allowing settlement of this planet."

"Who does it belong to, then? Your people? Would we be tenants then?" Dandhral asked.

Zaidhron and Mattan exchanged glances. Dome above, what did the prince know? What had he agreed to?

"The planet will be gifted to us," Zaidhron said, "but with initial oversight by the Elders, to help us learn to live there. A previous man-made cataclysm had devastated that world, and Mattan is aware of our own past mistakes, which damaged our own, possibly increasing the instability here. We have agreed that technology should be limited to safeguard us and our new home."

Paldhran smacked a hand on the table. "Who gave *you* the right to agree for us?"

"I did." Janadhan said. "And you will speak with respect to my heir."

It took effort to keep stoic; the king participating, backing Zaidhron? Day of wonders! How much of this information did he already know?

His father's mouth dropped open, and he murmured an apology.

Avadhron returned his attention to the alien and the topic. "The notion that my people give up their ways, learn a different life...surely you know this endeavor is impossible."

"It is not. It's difficult, but not impossible."

"How can you say that? Our whole society, our mindset, is based on living with every convenience. You wish us to hunt for ourselves, kill the animal, and eat it? Plant crops and toil when most of my people have never been required to do any physical labor? Live in what? Caves? Crude huts? What am I supposed to learn to use as a weapon? A stone knife? A metal sword?" Avadhron stood and smacked the half-staff at his side. "This is my weapon and I'm blasted good with it. Your idea is mad. I don't know how you'll convince the clan thanes to go along with this insane scheme. It won't work!"

"It can be done."

"I don't think you realize how dependent on our computers and luxuries we are inside our domes. Or how ignorant of nature."

"My team wants to help. Can help."

"Your people know how to do all these things?" Avadhron sneered.

"We are explorers, and although our world has advanced technology, we often go adventuring and have to know survival skills." Mattan leaned forward, hands splayed on the table, his face earnest. "We truly only wish to help. We are not enemies."

With a snort, Avadhron sat back down. The room fell silent.

"If we wished your people harm," the alien said in a low voice, "all we would need to do is leave. Your planet is dying."

Dandhral rapped the table with his knuckles. "We should set committees to study—"

"And wait years, even a decade for any recommendations?" Cosdhral spat and tapped the data-paper in front of him. "Look at these figures. We don't have years. We might have already run out of time. We need to learn fast. Leave this place."

"You're rushing into this idea without thinking it through," Dandhral said. "As usual."

"I agree," Paldhran said. "How do we move a population through to a new planet and feed and clothe and shelter them all while they learn these skills?"

Cosdhral snorted. "You two have grown too cautious as your hair has started grey."

"Guard how you speak to me!"

"Will you read the data? We need to act now!"

"Your hysteria is not helping matters, Cosdhral," Dandhral said. "Calm down."

Leaning back, Avadhron mentally distanced himself as the bickering continued. Janadhan did not join in; he stared at the data-paper, his face pale. Avadhron would swear an almost palpable fear assaulted his liege. After a few moments, the king cleared his throat. "We have no choice."

The table quieted, and they all stared at Janadhan. Avadhron frowned. *What is this? Has something penetrated his self-absorbed myopia?*

Their monarch stood. "Do what is necessary. I leave all recommendations and plans to Zaidhron and Mattan. They are in charge of this project. It is your duty as chiefs to convince the clan thanes to go along with this and help in preparing their people."

Janadhan rose and strode out, leaving stunned silence in his wake.

"Well..." Cosdhral eyed Dandhral, who still wore a dazed expression. "That settles that."

Chapter Eight

Avadhron scowled as he entered Zaidhron's office. Mattan sat next to him, as usual. Those two were as twins these days, planning the Crossing, as it had come to be called. The alien pointed to the data-paper before them. "Treyor and Lennai have taken charge of the logistics of gathering supplies, food, materials for various crafts, tools, weapons—"

"Weapons!"

Mattan looked up at Avadhron's outburst. "You will have to learn to hunt, you know."

He dismissed the man and turned his gaze to his cousin. "You sent for me?"

"We need your support."

"Why?"

"Many of the commoner clans look to you, both because of your unprecedented marriage and your reputation for fairness. You could sway the thanes who are resisting the idea of relocating to another planet."

Avadhron had been surprised by how many clans had suspicions or even refused to agree to leave their world, including Fesdhel of Viltara, the king's top advisor. "What about the noble clans?"

"You have a following among them too. You don't realize your influence."

"Then you should be glad I haven't voiced my opinions."

"Haven't Mattan and his colleagues proven they're to be trusted?"

"Not until I know what lies behind their altruism. People don't help strangers for no reason." Avadhron glared at the alien. "What do you *want*?"

Slamming his hand on his desk, Zaidhron spat, "Just because you deal with clanless and low-born, and see people at their worst doesn't mean everyone is that way. There is good in most people."

Avadhron snorted. "I deal with *all* clans. And I have seen the lowest of acts performed by the high clans." His lip curled at thoughts of their king, but he forbore mentioning the crimes of the highest of the royal clan. Janadhan must have Ears in his half-brother's office. "Don't tell me of the good in people."

The prince closed his eyes with a shake of his head.

"Will you ever trust us?" Mattan asked in a soft voice.

Avadhron barked a short laugh. "Will you ever be honest with me?"

"What makes you so certain we have not been truthful?"

"You gave yourself away to me soon after you arrived. Tell me why your people exiled us here and why you came back, and perhaps I will change my mind."

"You truly are a skeptic." Mattan tapped the desk with his fingers, a sign he was nervous, and probably about to try to delve past Avadhron's defenses again.

Avadhron hid a smile; baiting and preying on the Enaisi had become a favorite pastime. "And you're a bad liar." He paused, remembering all the times he had known the man had lied to him. His body language always gave him away. "And you hate it. Why not just tell the truth?"

Mattan hesitated, his eyes flicking to Zaidhron. "Have you ever considered that others might be constrained to obey orders? That they might have no choice?"

A thrill surged through Avadhron. Finally, a glimmer!

"No," the alien murmured. "I've said too much."

"So you are under orders. To do what? Lie to us? Lead us all to another planet? For what reasons? We are already under a sentence of death on this planet. What awaits us on the new one?"

"Life!" Mattan yelled, then pressed his lips together and sighed. "What can I do to convince you—" He stared at Avadhron and slowly a smile grew. He leaned forward. "Come see this new planet! Let me show you its beauty, that we only mean to help."

"What do you mean by 'see'?"

"Visit it. With me."

Avadhron's eyes narrowed as he met Mattan's gaze. He looked over at Zaidhron. "What's this about?"

The prince shrugged. "Ask him, but I think it's a great idea. The planet's beauty will win you. It is breathtaking."

"You have been there?"

"Oh yes, cousin. And wept when we had to return. Go. See it yourself."

Avadhron fought the urge to choke his cousin. He went out-dome without notifying anyone? Left their *world* without word to anyone? But the king had given him oversight, so to whom then did Zaidhron answer? Certainly not the Sec chief in charge of keeping both his king and the heir to the throne safe. He swallowed a rebuke and through gritted teeth asked, "And would you be going with us, then?"

The prince's eyes sparkled, then he sighed and shook his head. "I am sorely tempted, but unfortunately, I have meetings with several clan thanes and some of Mattan's team over the next few days. We are taking the first of our people to the planet next week to view it and see its potential, and there's so much to do in preparation. If you go beforehand, you could add your voice to ours, help persuade those who are reluctant or opposed—"

Avadhron snorted. "You are assuming quite a bit, cousin."

"Prove me wrong then. Go see this new world." Zaidhron's eyes glinted again. "I dare you."

Willing to play on Avadhron's weakness, was he? The prince would not knowingly put his cousin and friend in danger. But that alien...What was he scheming? To take him there in advance and murder him to get him out of the way? Futile, without planning and help, as Mattan was no match for Avadhron's strength and training. Well, he wouldn't give him the chance to arrange anything. "Only if we go right now."

Mattan hesitated before nodding. "Then come."

Avadhron stepped through the frame and stood, fists clenched, trying to shake off the numbing sensation of the portal. The large control room was so similar to the one on his own world, save it was non-damaged and well-lit. Was he truly on another planet then? The assault of emotions at this reality rose up, and he ground his teeth to keep himself in check.

They shed their protective gear, laying them over a non-functioning console.

Wordlessly, he followed the alien down a corridor and into a lift, and they exited to a large, circular chamber with a domed ceiling, once again, almost identical to the one on his world.

Mattan swept an arm toward the wide doors of darkened glass across the room from them.

Oh no, he wasn't going to lead the way. Avadhron mimicked the gesture, and the Enaisi grinned. "Together then, my distrustful friend?"

"Don't call me your friend."

Mattan inclined his head and walked over to the doors, which slid apart with a *swoosh*. Air rushed in, and a shiver coursed through Avadhron from the chill of it, the hair on his arms standing up. He followed the alien out and—gasped, blinking. The brightness of everything blended into a haze of splashed color, and he squeezed his eyes shut. A variety of smells assaulted him. His lungs felt compressed, making it hard to breathe. Uncounted little sounds assembled into a cacophony of noise.

He blinked every so often until the light didn't hurt and then opened his eyes to see the sky. The blue went on forever! With spasms of helpless little gasps, he fell back against the rock wall next to the doors, one hand reaching for his face—but his breathing mask wasn't there. His heart thudded, and his stomach seized as if kicked full force. He couldn't move. After a lifetime of living in domes, the openness of this place seemed it would kill him. But why should it? He had been out-dome many times. Perhaps it was the sky—at home the sky was sullen, dark, a blanket covering the largeness that here went on into...forever.

Mattan held out a hand, offering help, but Avadhron shook his head. He closed his eyes once more and willed his body to obey as he listened the noises and felt the cool breeze against his face. Birds singing and chattering calmed and excited him, spoke to him of life and hope.

After his breathing finally slowed, he opened his eyes yet again and looked around.

This place—this was so like his dreams! The awe and incredible impossibility of that fact gave him strength. He took one step away from the building, then another, inhaling deep breaths of fresh air. A warmth on his head and back made him turn to look up, and he squinted. The sun. Clear in the sky.

They stood on a mountain, part of a range covered with trees. Brilliant green commingled with dark green as far as he could see. He walked to the edge of the platform and down stone steps to a nearby tree. His hand trembled as he touched the rough, grey bark. A sweet scent wafted to him on the cool breeze, a familiar aroma straight from his dream!

Tears came unbidden to his eyes. He walked over to a bush and stroked the spiky, needle-like leaves. They were unaccountably soft, at odds with their appearance. Leaning close, he inhaled the fragrant smell.

Avadhron squatted to brush the small blue flowers that grew in abundance, almost like a matted ground cover. His breath caught in his throat, and his sight blurred. He blinked the tears out of his eyes and stood to face Mattan. "I wish I could believe you. Trust you."

"You said I gave myself away to you. Are you so certain I'm not to be trusted?"

He snorted. "I'm a Sec Chief, and I'm the best. I can spot a liar."

"Then tell me."

"Besides the body language that gives you away? That night at Zaidhron's home. You said, 'if I was aware of your past, I would tell you.' Simple past. You did not use the subjunctive mood: 'if I were aware of your past.'"

Mattan chewed his lip while casting a contemplative look at Avadhron. "Perhaps it was because I had only recently acquired the knowledge of your language."

"Oh no," he said, laughing. "You learned our language too easily, and you speak it like a native. And I would know how you did that."

Mattan shook his head. "Not now. It's not the right time. You will understand...eventually."

Avadhron glared at him. "I thought you'd refuse to answer me."

The alien nodded toward the woods. "Let's walk."

With a shake of his head, he fell into step with his guide. His irritation with the Enaisi's evasions dissipated, replaced by the awe of this new world. Often he stooped to examine a plant, or paused to watch a small animal scurry away, and always Mattan waited, then they would continue on together in silence.

The wind picked up, and as a strong breeze swept his face, Avadhron inhaled, his wonderment not abating. Occasionally he gazed up at the sky, chiding himself that he needed no dome. The sense of largeness lurked ever at the edges of his mind, and he willed it away again and again.

After some time, Mattan cleared his throat. "I said before I was under orders."

Avadhron turned to stare at the alien's profile with a frown. "Yes, but not the purpose. What are you hiding?"

"Our shame."

A victory-rush of adrenaline shot through him. "So it was you!"

Chapter Nine

Mattan spun to face him with an anguished expression. "Not me! Some of my race, from ages back, yes. A few of us, my colleagues and I, wanted to do something for you, to help you. To..."

"Atone?"

"If you wish to look at it that way."

Avadhron scowled. "I don't believe in altruism."

"So I've seen."

"Your altruism cloaks your desire for expiation, is that it?"

"If that explanation will aid you in accepting our help, then yes."

"Your help will occur whether I approve or not. Why are you so determined to gain my approval?"

Mattan sighed and sat on a fallen log. "If I tried to explain, you would not believe me. Can you accept that it is important to me?"

"I can accept that it appears that way."

Mattan chuckled. "You are harder than a mountain and as tough to budge."

"And what will you do if I go back and tell my kin you have admitted your people were the ones who exiled mine to Teledhar?"

His face careworn, the alien shrugged. "I think we are friends enough now they would still accept our help. I hope so. I shouldn't have disobeyed and told you. If our leaders find out, they may withdraw their permission for us to assist you. You don't know how deeply we are shamed by our past."

"Then why did you tell me?"

"Your approval and help are vital."

"Why?" Avadhron yelled, throwing out his arms. He stopped; it seemed almost desecration to shout in such an idyllic setting. He lowered his voice. "Tell me why, Mattan. I have no great influence with my kin. They think I'm mad for not embracing your plan. I'm only a Sec. I don't carry enough weight to sway many, especially balanced against all the other chiefs and clan thanes."

"You have an important role to play. Many nobles of various clans will balk, and some want to stay behind, desiring the comfort of their old lives. The danger of your situation is not a reality to most of your people."

"What has all that to do with me?" He sat on a rock opposite the alien and asked facetiously, "Shall I use my men to force evacuation to this planet?"

Mattan sniffed. "You underestimate your influence. Not only that, you fail to see your importance when your people begin to move here."

"So explain it, then."

Gnawing his lip, Mattan stared at him with an inscrutable expression. "I cannot. It..." He stopped, rubbing his hands together between his knees. "You would not believe me."

Avadhron crossed his arms. "Back to that, are we? Sounds a bit too convenient."

Mattan lifted a hand. "You literally would not believe me. I'm not being humorous. You are...*meant* to come here. To help lead the people here."

"And how can *you* know what *I* am meant to do?"

"I...have a gift. Of being able to sense the purposes of people and understand their personalities and dynamics." Mattan paused, his dark eyes pleading. "Can't you just accept that you will be needed?"

"I accept nothing."

The alien threw up his hands. "Will you accept this planet? Would you like to live here?"

The sun shone through the leaves of the trees, dappling the flora and ground with light. Birds twittered above. And the air. Clean air. More beautiful than the dreams he had all his life. "Is this place truly the haven you claim?" Avadhron whispered. "What are the dangers here?"

"There are no hidden dangers, nothing devious," Mattan said. "Only the dangers inherent on any world. Some animals should be avoided. The ka'gua, for example, is a vicious reptile that can leap up on a man and rip his throat out in a matter of moments. The ballan, unlike most animals, will attack unprovoked, and despite its small size, can also be deadly. There are others, as well, of course. Look about at the mountains. They can be treacherous, even when one is surefooted. No place can guarantee safety, but this planet is stable, and can offer your people a future."

Avadhron did not answer. He stared at orange berries on a small bush with variegated, sharp-edged leaves. In the quiet that followed, the animal life displaying itself amazed him. A reptilian creature no longer than one of Avadhron's fingers, its body swirled with dark green and yellow, scampered across the log near Mattan. Tiny, black insects marched in a long line from under the rock where Avadhron sat to some distant destination. A grey and brown bird flitted down and settled on the twig of a bush, cocking its head sideways at the two men. It chirped happily, hopped to the ground, snatched an insect and gobbled it, then flew off.

During his entire career, Avadhron had prided himself that he was unable to be bribed. But this world had not only tempted him, but won him.

He desired it, coveted it. He would champion moving here to all his people. But he couldn't bring himself to admit that to Mattan.

He rose, letting his breath out slowly, and walked back the way they came. To his right, he saw stone steps leading downhill. He reached out to touch the bark of a tree and froze, gasping aloud. This tree, this exact tree—had been in his dreams! The pattern of the bark was identical; he was certain of it! His fingers brushed against the surface, then he examined the rough crevices in disbelief and awe. How could this be?

The stone path with trees lining the descent—he had seen this too! He pelted down the stone stairs. Mattan called him but he paid him no heed. The pounding of running feet drew close behind him, and he halted.

"Why didn't you answer?" Mattan asked, panting, as he caught up to Avadhron.

"This path. I know where it goes."

"What?"

Avadhron faced the alien full on, chin lifted. "You won't believe me. Likely, you will laugh or think me mad. But I have dreamed of this planet. I knew it earlier, but this, this is a special place of which I have dreamt. I can tell you what's ahead. It leads to a little stream that eddies into a pool before washing away further downhill. There are bushes there, like that sweet-scented one above. The area around the pool is filled with a type of yellow flower having dark, long leaves that shoot straight from the ground."

Mattan's face grew pale under his dark skin. "You...dream?"

Avadhron glared at Mattan, but he wasn't mocking. The Enaisi did believe him. And was frightened. No, more shocked.

"Do...many of your people dream?" Mattan whispered.

"We all dream. Don't your people? But I don't know of anyone else who has ever dreamed of something real they've never seen." *I don't half believe it myself, even though I'm standing* in *my dream!*

Mattan didn't answer, and Avadhron nodded at the path. "I'm going down to see it. Are you coming?" He descended without waiting for an answer.

The water and yellow flowers halted his steps. He spun to face Mattan with triumph, but the alien's sober expression stopped him.

"Avadhron..." Mattan licked his lips and seemed to start to speak twice before continuing. "This dreaming is more proof that you are important to your people and to the Crossing."

"If you want me to believe you, trust you, why must you be so cryptic?"

Mattan looked down for a long time, fists on his hips. When he finally raised his head, there were tears in his eyes. "I dream too," he whispered.

"Waking dreams—visions of you. Urging your people to Cross. And here. Rallying your people, encouraging them through the hardships. You are *needed* for this Crossing to be successful."

Avadhron stared at the Enaisi. This seemed too incredible to be true, yet standing within his own experience determined this dreaming, this foresight, was possible. Avadhron couldn't deny his senses. This *was* his dream. What all this meant, he didn't know, except...he knew, deep inside, this was where he—and his people—were meant to be.

He knelt on the ground and dipped one hand into the water. After a few moments, he gazed into Mattan's eyes, despising that he would be on the same side with the alien, but unable to see any alternative. "I will back the Crossing."

<<>>

Avadhron hung his half-staff on his hip while looking at the body at his feet and others nearby. Two domes had already recently been sealed. Would this be the third?

Even with that beckoning planet in his mind, bespeaking a glorious future, this present life, this present world drained his joy. How much worse for those who hadn't seen their hope?

One of the local Sec guards saluted, fist over her heart. "I notified medical. They're sending teams."

He nodded to her as another guard approached, limping, still holding his half-staff. "I thought things would calm down after the announcement that the Elders would help us Cross to a new planet."

"What did you expect?" Avadhron gazed around at the scene. "They all imagined we would merely line up and Cross, no training, no waiting. They have no idea what it's like. None of us would survive more than a few days without help."

"You've been there, haven't you, Chief? What is it like?" The first Sec asked, her eyes wide.

Avadhron exhaled in frustration. How could he put into mere words the glory of that world? "Yes, for a short visit, not a week ago. Have either of you applied for training?"

Both murmured they had.

"We're ready to start Basic with our families as soon as our turn comes. We applied as partners so we'll go through together." The Sec's face glowed with anticipation. "We'll begin Orientation when we're through."

The second guard nodded. "But in a way I feel guilty going. It diminishes our manpower here. And with uprisings becoming more frequent..."

"We need security over there as well. A new world won't mean new attitudes. And men are men anyway—they'll always be at each other's throats for one reason or another." A tickle on his cheek made Avadhron put his finger to his face. It came away bloody.

The second Sec gingerly put weight on his bad leg, wincing. "What is it like to be outside a dome, sir?"

Avadhron shook his head. "Indescribable." He smiled at the two Secs. "Study hard. You'll be there before long. We'll be taking the first contingent over soon. Once they've been oriented, we can begin bringing settlers over."

"Things are happening so fast."

"They have to."

"It's truly that bad, sir?"

Avadhron lifted his chin and stared at the shimmering, opaque shell of the dome far above, unable to answer. He didn't want to inadvertently cause hysteria.

"We understand, sir," the first whispered, her face grave. "We'll be ready. We'll be there to help."

Chapter Ten

His feet leaden, Avadhron walked toward his home. Even with more workouts—not only conditioning his body for the hardships of the new world, but learning how to use new weapons—that arrest-turned-riot still left him sore and exhausted. He glanced up at the tall structure, hoping Jhendill was at the lab so he could clean up before she saw him. She always fretted when he came home hurt.

His hopes were dashed as the door slid open and the aroma of a meal hit his nose, making his stomach rumble. His wife stood in the kitchenette picking leaves from plants on their garden wall, wearing her loose, knee-length night-trous and chemise—not her green lab jumpsuit. What? How long had she been home?

Jhendill turned and gasped, dropping the greens on the counter. "Oh no! Your face!" She rushed across the room to him.

"Just a flying shard. It's nothing. I'm fine."

"No, you sit here and let me take care of it." She pushed him at a chair.

He resisted, mumbling, "It's all right."

She shoved harder. "Sit!"

He sat—he had found it best to let her have her way. In a few moments she returned with their medkit. She leaned over to dab at his face, and he grinned at the view she afforded him. She straightened with a wry look. "You're right. You can't be that hurt. Now hold still."

His grin widened despite the sting as she cleaned the wound. "If you really want to tend to something—"

One eyebrow lifted in disapproval, but she didn't quite hide her smile. "Get clean and eat first."

His hands slid up over her hips, and he gently pulled her into his lap.

The eyebrow arched higher. "You stink of sweat, Ch'shalna."

He chuckled at their old game. "Royalty doesn't stink. We perspire. You low clans don't appreciate the difference."

"I know the difference the sonic will make." She jumped up, wrinkling her nose. "Get clean, Ch'shalna Chief. Then you can sample some low-clan cooking."

Avadhron rose and smoothly snagged her wrist before she could back away. He wrapped his arms around her and kissed her soundly, then whispered, "I shall have to see about putting you in your place, woman."

She brushed his cheek with her lips, murmuring, "Promises, promises."

<<>>

Jhendill had two chairs pulled up to the counter in front of their bowls and cups of hot tea by the time he returned from using the sonic. He liked it when she arrived home first; her cooking was better than his. He leaned over, kissed her, and sat with a smile. What would it be like when they were on the new world, able to sit and eat real food in the warm sun?

She glanced at his cheek but didn't comment. Subtle woman. She cared, but didn't hover over him; another quality that endeared her to him. He took a spoon of the stew, and after swallowing, commented, "I was surprised to see you home so early."

She gave a little shrug, staring at her stew as she ate. He waited, but she said nothing. Sometimes females wanted you to dig for information, and sometimes they didn't. And as good as he was at reading body language in suspects, he couldn't ever figure out which his wife wanted. He weighed his odds for survival in asking if, in fact, that wasn't the proper response. He cleared his throat. "What's wrong?"

She remained silent.

Should he wait, or ask again? He delayed his decision by taking a huge spoonful of stew, chewing slowly, and washing it down with the tea. Fortunately, he was spared having to decide. Jhendill took a deep breath and said, "My project has been canceled."

Avadhron leaned back. "Just like that?"

"The planet is dying. Why put time, effort, and mostly importantly, money into something that is futile." She dropped her face into her hands. He rose and wrapped his arms around her. She didn't sob or wail, just leaned into him, the only evidence of her weeping was an occasional hitch in her breath.

He had nothing to say. How could he console her when her life's work had just been tossed away like refuse? He couldn't bring himself to babble inane things like *it will be all right.* Her hurt was real, deep, and words couldn't make it better. He stroked her hair and continued to hold her until she sat up straight. Peering at her, worried, it was his turn to wonder if he should hover or back away.

She wiped her cheeks and sniffed, then smiled up at him, merely to reassure him, he was certain. Despite the red eyes and blotchy face, she was beautiful. He pushed strands of hair off her forehead and asked softly, "So what now?"

She shrugged, again with that endearing tilt of the head. "We inventory and pack the equipment. Some of it might be modified or utilized for other projects. I doubt any of it will be needed on that new planet."

"Your skills can certainly be used in other areas there. Our lifestyle will be simpler, but we won't be without science or technology altogether. We'll need your expertise."

She tossed her head. "Right now I'm just trying to adjust to the project's shutdown."

"Your life's work. I'm sorry."

She smiled up at him. "Thank you."

"For what?"

"For not telling me to cheer up because we have a bright future waiting."

"Your whole life, your goal has been helping to save our people. That was to be your contribution to our future instead of children. That is nothing inconsequential."

"See? You understand me."

He chuckled. "I'm glad you think so. But...what do I do now?"

She leaned her elbow on the counter, chin in hand. "Tell me again about the new world. Tell me it will be grand, and glorious."

"And convince you it will make up for your whole life being tossed out-dome?"

"Yes, please."

"I cannot promise that. But it is beautiful. A sun in the open, blue sky. Fresh air—Jhendill you have not lived until you have felt wind against your skin and smelled it! I...I cannot describe it."

"So you say, yet you talk of it until I think I can imagine." She sipped her drink. "But what waits for me on the new world? What will I do there?"

Avadhron hated his answer even as he said it: "We need to talk to the Enaisi. To Atesni and Dassel. Or Mattan."

Jhendill burst into laughter. "If you can even suggest we should give any heed to the Elders, then perhaps there is hope for me in the Crossing." She pointed to his bowl. "Eat, Ch'shalna, and after you can find something to cheer me up."

"I thought I just did."

"True. Something to distract me then."

He grinned. "Oh, I can think of something..."

Her eyes twinkled in response.

<<>>

Avadhron woke. Jhendill's side of the bed was empty and, from the kitchenette, he could hear the sounds from the dispenser and dishes clattering. He groaned. Not morning already. He sat up and flung the covers back. He raised his arms in a stretch as he stood. His muscles, surprisingly, did not ache despite his participation in suppressing the riot. He blinked as he walked into the lit room. Jhendill wore her lab jumpsuit.

"How can you be so awake in the mornings?" he said with a yawn as he rubbed his face.

She turned, her eyes flicking over his body with a slight smile. "You're out of uniform, Ch'shalna Chief." She handed him a steaming cup of tea.

He snorted. "Not for long. Unfortunately." He sipped the hot brew. "What will you be doing?"

"It will take quite some time to decommission all the scrubbers in use, and dismantle and catalogue them and the new ones we were modifying. I won't be lacking for work, but it won't be enjoyable."

"I'm sorry."

She shrugged and essayed a smile. "Get dressed, Ch'shalna. You'll be late."

Not knowing what else to say, or do, he obeyed his wife.

"I'm a Sec Chief, not a politician or a speech-maker." Avadhron continued reading the report in front of him as he listened to Zaidhron, although his mind was more on Jhendill than his work. The disheartenment in her eyes haunted him.

"If you state openly you support the Crossing, it will sway many."

"I have stated so openly."

His cousin snatched the data-paper from the desk. "Do so on the Grid. Make an appeal."

"Do you really think the clans will listen to a minion of the king who has recently ordered two domes sealed?" Avadhron retorted, grabbing the paper back.

"I've issued a statement from the king that although transportation in and out is still curtailed, food will be delivered to those domes. When the clan thanes surrender with a pledge their people will stop feuding and rioting, the domes will reopen."

Avadhron muttered a foul word. "Your idea or his?"

"A compromise."

Rubbing his thumb across the tips of his fingers, raw from the exercise of drawing back a bowstring, he snorted. What the clans needed wasn't just food, it was tangible hope. Not some promise of a new world, but something they could see, feel, truly believe in. They needed to feel useful, be able to have pride in themselves, to be able to build up, not tear down— his thoughts skidded to a halt as a cascade of ideas crashed over him. He smiled up at his cousin. "If you want that public statement, let me negotiate with those clan thanes—no! With *all* the clan thanes."

Zaidhron's blue eyes narrowed. "What are you up to now?"

"A radical idea. Get Mattan in here. This might be something we could use to our advantage."

"You...what—?" Not finishing the sentence, Zaidhron rushed out, likely not wishing to give Avadhron time to change his mind about actually having a discussion with that alien. He smiled as he returned to the report.

Chapter Eleven

"This is indeed radical." Mattan frowned, crossing his arms. "You truly have a wicked sense of humor, Avadhron."

"Humor? I have no sense of humor. Ask anyone. This is only reasonable. Keep them too busy to cause trouble."

"What if they try to cause trouble anyway? Refuse to cooperate with the training?"

"Start a camp on the other side. Surely your facility can be locked down to prevent sabotage or tampering. They can shelter inside until ready to live outside. If they wish to run away, if they wish to keep their feuds going, if they rebel, if they do anything besides train, let them try to survive on their own."

Mattan threw his head back and laughed. Zaidhron looked pensive but not displeased.

"It does put a burden on your team to be guards as well as teachers."

The alien lifted a hand. "As you said, they can obey or leave the training compound. I think they'll be fine with it."

"We already have a list of chosen people from various clans who are beginning to train and learn skills. What do we tell them? That they'll share those positions with the most lawless of our world?"

"*Those* are the guild leaders, the ones leading the craft training. These 'lawless' will be taken directly to the new planet. They'll begin as common laborers with the chance for a rise in position if they earn it." Avadhron leaned forward. "Look, this rids us of troublemakers, and gives them positive goals to aim for. The problem with many of the people is they have no hope, and no purpose. What do they live for? To be at the whim of a"—*king*—"government which tells them what to do, where to go, where to live, subsisting on a dying world which is literally collapsing around them. They are afraid, they are angry, living in desperation and despair. Take the most extreme of them and make of them our saviors. The pioneers to a new planet."

"What if they don't believe us? Think it's a trick to take them some place and do away with them?" Zaidhron asked, leaning forward. "Some clan thanes brought up that very question in the last meeting."

"I'll go with the first group and wear a cam. I can document going through the portal, walking outside, seeing where we will be living. You want something that will appeal to the people? Don't tell them of the new world, show them. Give them information, real, raw information, instead of the government-sanitized versions they are used to."

Both men stared at Avadhron, mouths agape. Finally Mattan muttered, "And you wonder why I said we need you?"

"The king will have to approve of this," the prince said.

"Then what are you sitting here for? Go talk to him. Just don't tell him it's my idea, or he'll never agree."

Zaidhron rolled his eyes as he rose. Mattan followed him out with a smug smile.

<<>>

Never had Avadhron known of meetings, plans, and events happening so quickly. The sense of urgency seemed to drive everyone, even the king. Had it really been a mere two days since he had broached this idea to Zaidhron and Mattan?

He glanced at his men standing watch in the assembly hall as the prince welcomed the thanes and named Avadhron as the one who called and ordered the meeting. He raised a hand, turning over control of the gathering and stepped back to stand beside Mattan. How extraordinary. He had thought his cousin would give one of his long, consoling speeches before letting Avadhron speak.

Without preamble, Avadhron began. "Controlling those who are discontent with life in the domes is increasingly impossible. We have a solution to present to you thanes." He pointed to the holographic map in the center of the dais. "This is a valley on the new world where I propose we send those who are...disaffected. We will begin with those held for crimes, and extend the program to include those you recommend due to their disruptive tendencies."

A man with curly dark hair stood. "Kaztar of Penadar Clan." Avadhron nodded permission and Kaztar continued. "I thought those in the first Crossings were all highly specialized and being trained in new skills."

"The training received by those leading the craft groups is much more intense."

"But they will be upstaged by criminals who will actually Cross before them?"

"By no means. Both groups will be part of the first Crossing. The leaders will go first, into camps prepared by the Enaisi. The worker group will merely receive survival and psychological training to help them adjust to living out-dome, and—"

"You would be putting us in a work prison then? In that little valley?" Camven of Rach'adar stood with his thick arms crossed. Avadhron sucked in his cheeks to check his smile. The rebellious thane had led riots even after his dome was sealed and, with many in his clan, was scheduled to be in the first group taken across.

"You will follow the prescripts of this assembly, Rach'adar." Avadhron indicated the map again, enlarging it. "This valley is not little. It takes four to five days to cross on foot, east to west, and twice that for its length."

"But it would be a prison?"

Avadhron locked gazes with the bald thane. "No one is being held prisoner, Thane Camven. It is a training area for workers with the long-term plan of becoming a tenant holding. Those who begin there may stay as crofters and have the protection and governance of Ch'shalna Clan. Or, once their skills are learned, they may choose to move from the valley to make their own way as lands and towns are settled."

Another thane rose, thin with fair hair. "Vervan of Toralna." After Avadhron nodded, Vervan asked, "These are people known for their involvement in uprisings and riots. You would send them to our new world without security to enforce proper behavior?"

"The Enaisi have offered to give oversight for those in the camps. Those who do not wish to obey the rules are free to leave. And to try to survive on their own."

"That doesn't sound very prohibitive."

Avadhron smiled. "You haven't been there. It is beautiful, but treacherous to us who have always lived in domes." He lifted his chin and let his gaze sweep over the thanes. "Our people have had their souls starved of hope, of purpose. Many of those involved in the unrest are those who merely seek a meaning, a usefulness for their lives. This proposal will give them what they crave."

"How do we know you will truly send us to the new world? That you won't just...dispose of us," Camven asked.

"You don't believe in following rules, do you, Camven? But I will address your question anyway. Your concern is understood, and the answer is simple. I will be leading the way."

"So you say."

"I shall be wearing a live cam as will others. The first Crossing will be seen by all our people."

"Cams can be broadcast through the portal?"

Mattan stepped forward. "As long as the portal is open, a data stream can be maintained." A process which wasn't as easy as the alien made it seem, but accurate.

A grey-haired thane stood. Avadhron didn't recognize him except by his clan colors, grey and dark green, Beshalt clan. "I will be heard."

He lifted an eyebrow at Galadhan, who whispered the thane's name into the comm.

"This isn't the proper forum for an Airing, Thane Hantor of Beshalt Clan," Avadhron said. "But if you have a statement or question, now is the time to speak."

"I don't trust your clan, and I certainly don't trust this Crossing."

"So noted. But that's why I'm going with this first group. And why we're using cams. So you can see we are telling the truth. And to give you glimpses of our new world."

"But it's said those who colonize will not be coming back. You are staying then?"

"I am not colonizing yet. I will be one of the few who will be allowed to return. Are there any who disagree that I am needed more on this side at the moment?"

A murmur rippled across the chamber with scattered laughter and jeers.

"The first Crossing will be in two weeks. Those already found guilty of sedition, feuding, or rioting will be going across. If there are any in your clans which you thanes feel would be good candidates for the first Crossing, submit their names."

Still standing, Hantor asked another question. "What if they don't wish to go?"

"Those convicted have no choice. Those suggested may go or find constructive use of their time here." Several voices protested, and Avadhron raised his own, letting it resound in the chamber. "The king has spoken. I am enforcing this law. Crossing to the new planet must take priority, and I cannot have my men stretched thin because of those who are not happy with this world. So we will send them to the new one."

"But what about the families of those going across?" Hantor asked.

"Their families will be given more complete training and join them later, unless they choose to go with the first Crossing."

"What about the dangers on this new world? What if people die over there?"

Avadhron didn't answer right away. He stared at Hantor for a moment, then around the room, waiting until the silence grew loud. Finally he said, in a low voice, "There are perils there, true, but *this* planet is self-destructing. Death is certain *here*."

Zaidhron stepped close, murmuring to tread softly. Avadhron shot a glare at him and lifted his arms toward the thanes. Perhaps it was time for a little hysteria. "Do I scare you? Do I make you afraid? I hope so. Our—world—is—dying. Most of you seem to not realize this. Help us take the disaffected across, so we may be protected and undistracted by their uprisings. Then we can concentrate on readying to Cross ourselves. On getting all our people to safety. To a new start."

Kaztar stood again and waited permission. "It seems you are giving these criminals an advantage over the rest of us. They're going over first, while we wait."

"Then why do you wait? Most of you haven't applied for Crossing. Why not? Afraid to lose the comforts you have here? Are comforts more important than your very lives and those of your families?"

Vervan stood. "Such plain talk from the royal clan. It clears the stench from my nostrils. I will back this idea, Security Chief Avadhron. Heartily."

"This action will take place whether you back it or not." Avadhron saw Zaidhron wince and added, "Your cooperation, of course, will make the process much easier, and I thank you for your endorsement."

"What's its name, this new world? What is it called?" Vervan asked.

Mattan stepped forward. "We call it Elyria. It means 'Second Chance.'"

For you or for us? But Avadhron didn't ask aloud.

Chapter Twelve

"Chief."

Avadhron glanced over at Galadhan. "Something wrong?"

"Have you seen today's *Beyond the Dome*?"

"Not yet. What now?"

"Did you know your brain is under the mind control of the Elders who seek to destroy us all?"

Avadhron threw his head back, laughing. Every person in the room stopped their work and stared at him. He curbed his hilarity and wiped his eyes. "Is that all?" He chuckled before continuing, "Wait until you see Elyria. If thoughts of its clear, blue skies don't control your mind, you are beyond hope."

"I can't wait to see it." Galadhan pulled a chair close and sat, leaning forward, his eyes shining. "You know I had refused Rulinn's necklet several times, yes?"

"Pretty woman. Can't figure what she sees in your ugly face, but yes."

"There's no future here. I didn't want to chance children who would be doomed."

Avadhron nodded. He'd had that same mindset before meeting Jhendill. Both agreed they would not have children despite Clan Law, which expected offspring from a marriage. Dome above, that would change now! He returned Galadhan's smile. "So you're going to accept the necklet, are you?"

"We're waiting until we're across. We want to marry under the sky, not a dome."

"Congratulations, man!"

Galadhan's grin widened. "Thank you."

"Now, will I get any work out of you since you are obviously preoccupied?"

"Chief. Have I ever let you down?"

Avadhron's smile faded, his reply serious. "No. Never. That's why you are my Second."

Galadhan rose, his lips pursed in lieu of an answer. "Better get back to work."

As Avadhron began to grin again, his Second pointed at him. "Watch it, Chief. Keep that up and I might think there's something to that mind-control stuff."

"Let me return to the daily reports. That will wipe any smile from my face."

A rueful nod was Galadhan's only reply.

Avadhron adjusted the cam attached to his ear comm. The trained craft teams had gone earlier, with Mattan and Zaidhron. And the Disaffected, as they were being called now, were finally poised to Cross.

Each group of the Disaffected would be accompanied by guards and one of the Enaisi as they were shuttled to, and through, the portal. Working out the details of moving so many prisoners hadn't been easy. And Avadhron didn't like that the aliens refused to wear weapons. Mattan's calm response that they wouldn't need them had raised his ire, but Zaidhron had intervened. As usual.

He turned to look at his people, crowding the large portal chamber in the Elders' mountain; the facility had been repaired so those inside would not need protective gear. Most of the faces, previously so hardened, so skeptical, were now openly curious, or afraid.

"Galadhan," he said into his comm. "Is the feed live?"

"Yes, Chief," came his Second's voice. "The media Grid is linked. Everyone can see and hear what's happening."

"The secondary cams, as well?"

"Yes. Both Camven's and Matsen's are active. People can choose which cam they wish to view, or they can split their views."

Thane Camven blinked, swallowing. The second cam-carrier, Matsen, a swaggering loudmouth, sneered at Avadhron.

"Then we're ready." Avadhron lifted his chin, his gaze sweeping the room. "I'm not one for speeches. So, let's go."

Camven had balked at Crossing, stating his position as thane should give him a reprieve, despite his crimes. Avadhron took the recalcitrant thane's arm. "You first, with me."

As before, entering the portal was a numbing experience. Senses seemed non-existent, yet one could feel taking the step through an empty blackness then—into the identical chamber on another world. Camven gasped, shaking. One of the Enaisi, Treyor, waited for them, and pulled the thane forward to make room for the rest.

As a wordless team, Avadhron and Treyor herded the Disaffected into the wide hallway.

"We're inside a building?" someone asked indignantly.

"Idiot," another voice said. "Didn't you pay any attention at the briefing?"

"You will be taken by lift to the Plains Exit," Treyor called, evidently not trusting everyone had listened to the earlier instructions. "A temporary structure has been erected, and those who need time to adjust to being out-dome may stay there." He gestured to Dassel, who led the way down a corridor and, turning away from the lift Avadhron had used before when he visited with Mattan, down a side passage. Avadhron brought up the rear.

They passed many closed doors along this long hallway; this place was much larger than the one on Teledhar. Not merely an outpost, a doorway to another world, but a base, or housing, or...what?

Mattan had announced that everything was nonfunctional or locked down, but still Avadhron tensed when some hands reached out for the control panels near doors. Dassel called over his shoulder, "Nothing works, and yes, you are all being monitored."

Arms whipped back to their sides, and Avadhron chuckled silently. Before long they all entered a gigantic room, crates piled high along the walls as well as with various pieces of equipment. Definitely more than an outpost.

Dassel turned as they reached a large door on the far side. "This is an entrance for a supply lift. We have to use this for such a sizeable group of people. When you leave this lift, you will be inside the temporary shelter, on the plain."

Avadhron had expected something small and tent-like, but the structure was enormous, the walls and roof constructed of a light-weight but sturdy alloy anchored into the ground. It also had moveable interior partitions, allowing privacy or sectioning for meals or meetings. Only the grass sprouting from between sheets of flooring indicated its being temporary. On the left, two crafters lay on cots with cloths on their heads. Long tables lined the center and several crafters sat, steaming drinks cupped in their shaking hands.

Three Enaisi—two women, Ismari and Ashani, and a man, Telkai—approached. "We shall take you to the entrance," Ismari said, her voice soft, her smile warm, as if these were honored guests, not malefactors. "How far outside you wish to explore is up to you."

Avadhron remembered his reaction all too well, and watched with amusement as several of the Disaffected, including Matsen, swaggered out the door. Every one of them fell to the ground, gasping. One curled up in a fetal position, crying. The Enaisi helped them to their feet and back inside. The weeping man was carried to a cot.

With a grin, Avadhron took Camven by the arm. "You railed against every convention, every rule of our society. You claim it was because there was no hope for us. Let me show you our hope."

Ismari stepped in front of them, and Avadhron brushed her out of the way with his arm. Camven resisted, his digging heels sliding on the flooring, but Avadhron merely switched to a force-hold tactic, used in subduing suspects, and dragged him forward.

Camven gasped as they exited the shelter. Clouds of various hues of grey covered the sky, and a misting rain fell. The tall, vibrant green grasses rippled and swayed, and copses and shrubs dotted the land in the distance. The smells of plants and wet earth rose like sweet perfume.

With Camven clinging to his arm, Avadhron stepped forward, away from the shelter, and turned to see the whole landscape. Mountains rose west, north, and east like huge walls enclosing the plain on three sides. To the northwest, a waterfall cascaded down a high, sheer cliff into a lake which trailed away south along the mountain wall.

"Is this the valley?" someone behind Avadhron asked.

"No, the entrance to the valley is northeast of us," Mattan answered. "See that break in the mountains to the north?"

"It's so big! It's...beautiful! This is...rain?" Camven gasped, holding onto Avadhron as if his life depended on it. He began weeping and sank to the ground, dragging Avadhron down to kneel next to him. "You weren't...lying! It's real!" He clutched Avadhron's jerkin. "Help...me inside. I can't...breathe."

With a wry smile, Avadhron hooked Camven's one arm over his shoulder and, his other arm around the thane's waist, helped him stand and walk back inside the shelter.

He lowered Camven into a chair at one of the long tables, then stood, watching him.

Ismari rushed over and set a steaming cup in front of the trembling man. She glared up at Avadhron. "You may help yourself from the urn, Sec Chief." She turned her back on him and sat next to Camven, asking him if he was all right.

"I'm fine. I will need a little time to adjust, but I'm fine." The thane raised his head and met Avadhron's gaze. "Thank you. I will order my clan to desist in any insurrection and to work swiftly to Cross."

Avadhron bowed. "I knew you would quickly see the wisdom of this, Thane of Rach'adar clan. You have a strong will, and your backing is most appreciated."

Camven laughed. "I thought you were the straight-spoken one, not given to flowery words."

"I only say what I mean. I proposed this idea because I could see the hopelessness that led to the riots, the rebellion. You were one of the leaders. Now, you see our hope. Now, you will be one of the leaders in building up instead of tearing down. This world was aptly named. It's truly a second chance for us all."

Chapter Thirteen

The day drew long, bringing over group after group, and darkness fell before the last arrived. The rain stopped, and the clouds tore into shreds dissipated by the evening breeze, revealing the night sky. Uncounted twinkling stars dominated the heavens, and almost directly overhead spread a mass of bright colors: a nebula. Those who had overcome their panic at being domeless stood outside in awe, exclaiming their delight.

"The nebula is fairly new," Ismari said. "It is still expanding."

"So over time it will grow? Cover more of the sky?" somebody asked. "Yes."

"There are dark spots, see them?" came a voice.

"They're shaped almost like little bells," another person murmured.

"Oh, they are!"

"Dome above," someone whispered reverently.

Several others chuckled, and one said, "Not anymore. 'Bells above' now."

More laughter.

"Or 'stars above.' Just look at them!"

While his people stayed outdoors, gazing upward, Avadhron withdrew to the shelter, feeling more drained than if he had fought rioters for three shifts. He murmured, "Day is over. Night's rest," and switched off the cam. Technically, day was beginning on Teledhar, but he wasn't going to belabor the fact.

He filled a cup from the spigot at the bottom of the huge urn, and sat at a table, sipping the hot liquid. It tasted nothing like the tea on his planet, even the rare real tea from plants in the agri-domes. Earlier, Ashani had explained the process to several of the crafters, from leaf to urn. But whatever plant it was from, it was delicious. And relaxing.

Mattan came over, grinning, and sat across from him. "Good work, Sec Chief. I think this will sway many of your people."

"I hope so, for their sakes."

Ashani brought over a steaming bowl and spoon. "Those preparing to Cross have been slowly introduced to real foods so their systems can adjust. Try this soup, and drink more tea with it. The herbs of the tea will help with any digestive distress."

Mattan tilted his head, smiling. "None for me?"

"You haven't eaten yet?"

"Too busy."

Ashani rolled her eyes. "Be right back."

Avadhron stirred the soup. "Is there meat in this?"

His smile broadening, the alien leaned back, a challenge in his eyes. "Afraid to eat the flesh of an animal?"

"No." Avadhron glared at him. "But my people might be."

Mattan chuckled. "You're right. It's only vegetables, but the broth is from a torchou, a plains herdbeast."

Ashani returned with another bowl and placed it in front of her team leader. She set a plate of something round and brown next to the bowl. The smell wafting from it was delightful. She stared at Avadhron, her dark eyes piercing. "I do not recommend eating the bread, or at least only eat a little. Your body isn't used to whole grains. And do drink the tea."

Dome above, females of all races must be peremptory. With exaggerated motions, he picked up the cup and took a large gulp. Ashani straightened with a frown and stalked away.

Mattan snickered. "That's two women you've managed to irritate in one day."

"Two?"

"Ismari is rather put out with you. Says you were cruel to Camven."

"Ask him if he thinks I was cruel."

"I'll wait until he's been moved to the valley. Once he's had to work the soil, he'll likely have many complaints."

Avadhron snorted in agreement and picked up the spoon. *Real food.* He ladled a vegetable and held it up. "How do you know we can eat all the vegetables here?" He paused then decided to hint at his suspicions. "Perhaps our bodies cannot eat all the same foods yours can."

The hesitant expression on Mattan's face was all too familiar. Avadhron put his spoon down and stared at the alien expectantly.

After several hesitations, the Enaisi finally said in a faint voice, "This planet...hasn't always been unpopulated."

"I assumed that from the size of the Portal Complex. Your people once lived here, didn't they?"

Mattan huffed a soft laugh. "I wonder how much you could work out if I did tell you nothing more."

"I won't let you make a game of this."

"I'm not trying to. That was meant as a compliment."

Avadhron refused to answer, just bored into Mattan's eyes, waiting. The alien smiled, shaking his head, but it faded. He ran his tongue over his lips, slowly, then leaned forward and whispered, "This is the planet from which *your* people originated."

Questions cascaded over Avadhron. Which to ask first? His quandary fed the silence. No. This was Mattan's responsibility; he opened the door, he would lead the way. "Explain please."

"I can't say more at this time."

"You would just drop that little bit of data and walk away?"

"This is not the place. Zaidhron knows a brief history, and I will share it with you, but not here." Mattan nodded at the bowl. "The soup is edible. And tasty."

He hadn't really doubted the food sources, merely wished to bait Mattan. The result had been unexpected, and pleasing. Little nibbles. Tiny dust specks of knowledge. But slowly, slowly Avadhron was gaining information. One day, he would have answers.

With satisfaction, Avadhron ate the soup.

While reading the data-paper, Avadhron rubbed his stomach, trying to ease the rumbling. He wished he had taken Ismari's advice and brought back some of their tea.

"Chief!"

Avadhron looked up at Galadhan's urgent tone.

"An earthquake has endangered Central Plain Domes One and Two. The local guards are requesting the travel restrictions be lifted to evacuate the inhabitants more quickly."

"That's standard procedure. Why are they wasting time?"

"The closest safe dome is ours—Palace Dome."

"Not Dome Three?"

Galadhan hesitated, frowning. "Dome Three was at epicenter, and a gaseous pocket was cracked. We have lost all communication from there, and I really don't think anyone's alive. The connected rail-tubes were destroyed, so Chief Paldhran is ordering guards from other domes to search for survivors."

They had to get Dome Two evacuated fast; that was the training center for those preparing to Cross. "Request granted for Domes One and Two but send some of our Elites with scanners to the entrances." Avadhron stood. "You're in charge here."

"Where are you going, Chief?"

"Dome Three."

"But—"

"I've had more out-dome experience than any of the local guards. I'm taking a shuttle in to transport survivors." Avadhron met Galadhan's worried gaze. "My orders, Second."

"No, sir. It's too dangerous, and you are needed to direct the Crossing."

Avadhron halted, eyeing Galadhan. "Where did you hear that?"

"It's known all over. The Elders hold you in a very special regard. They feel you are necessary for the Crossing to succeed." His Second stood, his lined face more careworn than usual. "You must not put yourself in unnecessary danger. I will go to the prince if I have to."

Avadhron clenched his teeth, debating whether Galadhan would truly make good on his threat, and finally ordered, "Send Thuldhan. He's had extensive out-dome and evac training."

Galadhan visibly relaxed. "Yes, Chief."

<<>>

Leaning back in a chair across from Mattan in Zaidhron's office, Avadhron watched his cousin pace.

"We lost so many people in Dome Three. And with the aftershocks, Dome Two now is uninhabitable. Where will we train those for the Crossing?"

Avadhron shrugged his shoulders. "On Elyria."

"Let them Cross before they've trained?"

"Why not? The facility itself is huge. Surely those not ready to live out-dome can be housed there. And the faster we get people off this planet, the more assurance we have that our race won't die."

Zaidhron whirled to face Mattan. "What do you think?"

"A sound idea. I think you should step up the screening process for those wishing to train as well."

Avadhron shifted in his seat and nodded at the alien. "What is your timetable for moving across the disabled and ill?"

"As soon as we have staff trained to care for them. They will have access to more advanced technology inside the Complex if needed."

"When do families begin Crossing?"

"We began last week. We estimate before this year is out, we will have five percent of your population on Elyria."

Avadhron sat up. "Five percent? Dome above, man, that's not enough! You've seen the reports, the timetable"—*not to mention my own gut warning that we're running out of time*—"we're all sitting on destruction that could happen any moment. We need to move faster."

"We need to train those Crossing, you know that. They'll not survive otherwise. And Mattan's people are already overworked."

"I thought the plan was for our people to act as trainers for those Crossing later."

"They're still learning themselves."

"That's an endless process. Let them continue learning by teaching. We need to get off this planet!"

Mattan nodded, eyebrows raised. "He has a point."

"All right." Zaidhron sighed. "We'll rework the schedule."

"I have another recommendation."

Both men looked at him with expectation.

"I think you should Cross, Zaidhron. I mean permanently. With your family." Avadhron hesitated then added, "And I think the king should go too."

"Now you're being paranoid."

"Each day, each hour is a time of grace. Central Plain's Dome Three is now gone, Two irreparably damaged. We felt the aftershocks here. Our clan, our leaders should be safe."

"Who would be in charge here then?"

"Dandhral and Cosdhral have been managing when you are away."

Zaidhron let his breath out slowly. "I will have to think about this."

"Don't think too long. I'm going directly to the king and advising him to Cross."

His cousin's mouth dropped open. "You think he'll listen to you?"

"I'm Sec Chief. It's my duty. Meanwhile, you think about yours. Safeguard our clan. Cross now."

"I will consider it."

<<>>

Avadhron approached the guards flanking the king's audience chamber. "The king is expecting me."

"Yes, milord. You may enter."

"This is a rare treat," Janadhan drawled from where he lounged on his throne. "And why would the Chief of the Elites want to speak with me?"

With a bow, Avadhron replied, "Your Majesty. I come with concerns for your safety."

The king threw his head back and laughed loudly. "You? Concerned for my safety?" He leaned forward, baring his teeth. "You despise me, *cousin*."

Avadhron stood, unmoving, not allowing any expression. His royal cousin regarded him, silently, through narrowed eyes. Slowly, he straightened, then settled back in the throne, his gaze still locked on Avadhron. Finally, he said, "Leave us."

The guards lining the room filed out. Janadhan rose and came to stand in front of Avadhron, so close their faces almost touched. "Answer me. You despise me."

He met his liege's challenge. "Quite straight. Sire."

Janadhan smiled. "Then," he whispered, "why would you be concerned about my safety."

"It is inbred as part of this clan. And as part of my training as a Sec. My first duty is to protect my king."

"Unnerving, is it? Your first spinal reflex is to protect that which you despise." Janadhan backed up a step, his expression and stance still taunting. "What would you wish to save me from?"

"The planet is unstable. You surely felt the aftershocks in this dome from that last quake. You should Cross, Your Majesty."

"And live in the dirt? I saw the vids of the groups you took over. There's nothing there. I would live in one of those flimsy shelters? I think not!"

"Sire, you declared we would Cross. You would defy your own edict?"

"Let a suitable place be built for me, then I shall Cross."

"This isn't about comfort, Sire, but about your very life. As Chief of the Elites, I have the right to—"

"I will not Cross, Sec Chief."

"You force me to convene a conclave. Call Question."

"If you call Question, I will have to voice my doubts about the Crossing."

Avadhron's thoughts slammed to a stop. "Doubts?"

The king frowned at Avadhron. "One thing I know about you, that I can count on, is that you are blunt with the truth." He hesitated. "I think I can tell *you* the truth." His hands clenched into fists, Janadhan walked slowly back to the throne and dropped into it. "I saw something. When we had the conclave, and I gave the order, it was because I was terrified. I saw...I saw the domes shattering, fire and ash shooting into the sky, I could see *me* trapped under rumble, gasping for air..."

He peered at Avadhron. "I think the aliens can read thoughts. I think they put that vision in my mind. Do you think I'm mad?"

Avadhron inhaled—and decided to be honest with his king. "No, Your Majesty, I don't think you're mad for having visions. I...I have had them since a child. I honestly do not think we can blame them for that."

"You–you have had visions?"

"Dreams. Since I was little. And when I went across, I saw the places of my dreams. The same trees, flowers..."

Janadhan sat back, staring at the floor. "So. I am not mad," he murmured. Finally, he looked up. "But...you think we can trust these aliens?"

Avadhron couldn't bring himself to say it directly; he fell back on Mattan's words. "If they wished us to die, they could just leave. We need to Cross, and we need *them* in order to Cross."

Janadhan waved his fingers in weary acknowledgement.

"But Sire, this is more proof you should Cross now. We must prevent your vision from happening. Your life is in danger."

"Prepare proper quarters for me, and I will Cross." He raised his hand to stop Avadhron's protestations. "Those are my orders, Sec Chief. And, you will tell no one of that vision."

"As I tell no one of my dreams." Avadhron lips twitched in an ironic smile. "We hold each other's secrets, Your Majesty. It is a day of wonders."

"It is that. Now get out."

Avadhron bowed and obeyed.

<<>>

As Zaidhron pushed the ordered piles of data-papers into a jumbled mess on Avadhron's desk so he could sit on the edge, the latter scowled up at his cousin. "You enjoy that."

The prince shrugged, smiling. "Getting even."

"For what?"

"The king has ordered me to Cross, and to begin construction on 'suitable quarters' for him. As if I didn't have enough on my shoulders."

"He took me seriously then."

"I don't know what you said, but yes, he did actually listen to you."

"I've been thinking..." Avadhron began.

"Again? Trouble is brewing."

With a glare, Avadhron continued. "I want to send Thuldhan as Sec leader on Elyria."

"Why not Galadhan?"

"I need him. I can't send all of my top people over. I wish I could. Guarantee their safety." Avadhron shook his head. "But Galadhan agrees with me. He's needed here for the moment."

"Have you talked to Thuldhan?"

"He, Galadhan, and I have discussed this. He's willing to accept the responsibility. He's got a keen mind and, more importantly, is even-tempered, which are both necessary over there."

"I won't deny that. How long until he's ready to Cross?"

"He and his family are doing the prelims now. Depends on the psych tests, but probably a week or two. You?"

"The same. Tarnill and Mariss both need to prepare."

"I'm glad you're going. It sets my heart at ease."

Zaidhron's blue eyes pierced Avadhron's. "It must be difficult for you. I know how you long to live there."

"The sooner we get our people to safety, the sooner I can go. I wanted Jhendill to Cross now, but she refuses. Her expertise is coming in handy. I don't understand all the technical details, but she went on-site after Dome Two was breached and helped with the oxygen generation systems to try to keep as much breathable air available as possible while the people were evacuated. They use an adaptation of her scrubbers, so it's the perfect place for her to work."

"You let her do that?"

"Let her? I wasn't happy at the danger she was in, but I couldn't stop her. Wouldn't." He let himself smile. "She would have gouged my eyes and ripped out my throat."

Zaidhron laughed.

Chapter Fourteen

Summer waned on Elyria. Early crops had been harvested, late crops planted, and settlements had spread over the plain, and in the valley as well. Zaidhron asked Avadhron to visit and see the progress they'd made. It was the perfect opportunity to corner the alien and get answers. He would not be put off longer. Mattan had promised; he was going to fulfill it.

He exited the portal to find the prince wearing a beautiful robe, blue with silver trim, the colors of their clan. A leather thong pulled his blond hair back from his tanned face. "It's so good to see you! I can't wait to show you what we've done."

As they entered the lift, Zaidhron asked how Cosdhral and Dandhral were managing administration.

"Dandhral muddles through reasonably well. Cosdhral dances too much for Janadhan, but we knew that would happen. How's Thuldhan fairing?" Without thinking, he raised his hand to his ear comm to call his Elite, but the comms didn't work here. He made a fist and lowered it to his side, pressing his lips together in irritation with himself.

Zaidhron noticed the gesture with a wry smile. "He's doing well, but he's not here at the moment. He's handling a problem northeast of here concerning some young men who decided they knew better than the encampment leaders."

"Some things never change."

"True."

"I do wish to talk with him, get an update, before I leave."

"I will see to it."

The lift opened, and Avadhron strode forward into the entrance shelter but halted with a gasp as the heat struck him. "Dome above, it's so hot! How do you breathe?"

Zaidhron laughed. "You will adjust. It's better outside. Come."

Avadhron followed quickly to the door—and stopped, but not for the cool breeze or the joy of seeing so many of his people spread across the plain. The encampments marred the beauty of the land. His disappointment must have shown in his face.

"These encampments aren't permanent, you know. Once the city is built, they will eventually be removed, and the verdure restored," Zaidhron said.

"City?"

"I'll show you the plans later. For now, let us give you a tour."

Us? Avadhron twisted to see Mattan standing nearby, smiling. He glared at the dark-skinned man. "Lead on."

"The people here are the newest arrivals. Some of our most experienced crafters have stayed to teach, of course. You should see the weavers. Look at this robe. Isn't it exquisite? Let's visit them first."

The weavers proudly showed their work, and Avadhron didn't have to pretend to admire their accomplishments. He was equally impressed with the potters.

"We have real dishes now, of our own making," Zaidhron said as they moved on from the pottery tents. "And the smiths have forged many items for us, from knives, to cooking pots—"

"Where do they get the ore?" Avadhron wiped sweat from his face.

"At first, the Elders brought us all the materials, but we actually have a settlement on the far side of the pass south of here to the west. We have begun to mine for ourselves. And there's a farming community there as well. Conditions aren't as nice as here, but they are managing. You jested once about living in caves, but they have found a large system of them, and claim they're happier in them than living domeless in the shelters. And we have established drayage routes to deliver goods back and forth. We use a barter system. No one goes without."

"All this already?" Avadhron asked, unfastening his jerkin.

Zaidhron's reply was drowned out by shouts of "Open it! Open it!" followed by a quiet *fwoohm.* Avadhron turned to see black smoke billowing from the windows and door of a temporary craft building. Men and women ran out, choking, covered with soot. Ash and flames shot from the top of the pipe in the roof.

"I told you not to close the damper!" yelled one.

"But the flue was on fire!"

"Is on fire, you mean! Didn't you check for creosote?"

The spluttered reply went unheard as Avadhron shook his head and continued the tour with Mattan and Zaidhron, his jerkin now slung over one arm. That was better. Beads of sweat formed again on his face, but the wind kicked up enough to keep him from being too uncomfortable in the unaccustomed heat. He occasionally lifted his hair and wiped his neck.

"Despite setbacks"—the prince waved a hand back toward the smoky commotion behind them—"our people are learning and adjusting fairly well, I think. We've had some spectacular failures, but spectacular triumphs as well."

"I've heard some had trouble adapting to living outside a dome." Avadhron gazed up at the white clouds drifting across the blue expanse; he felt his heart would burst with wonder and joy. Would he ever tire of the sky?

"A few took a little time, but overall they've all managed well." Zaidhron grinned. "You've missed some of the excitement."

Avadhron met his cousin's eyes with caution. "Oh?"

"Although you tend to see the darker side of man, you are one who appreciates and studies his nature. We have had some...interesting events. You would have enjoyed being here."

Avadhron lifted his eyebrows but Zaidhron continued walking, as did Mattan.

How well did his cousin and the alien handle the rebellious and the Disaffected? For that matter, how did Thuldhan?

"Are you going to say no more about these interesting events?"

"We'll get to that. For now, let me show off the rest of the settlement."

A mouth-watering smell filled the air, and Avadhron looked for the source. Off to the left, past several shelters, three herdbeasts turned on spits. At each spit, two striplings brushed a thick liquid from large pots on the beasts.

He nodded at the youngsters. "What is it they're doing?"

"They're basting. It keeps the meat from drying out and adds flavor. Or something." Zaidhron chuckled. "I'm not sure of all the reasons. I just like to eat them."

Nearby, several huge kettles simmered over open fires. And an enticing aroma drifted from a craft building. The prince pointed at it. "That is our bakery. We have found that cooking is a skill to be learned as well as all the other trades. Thus those that are learning to cook prepare food for the rest of the camp."

"Your people are adjusting to the differences in time, too," Mattan said.

"Yes." Zaidhron turned with a grimace. "The twenty-six hour day was difficult until we changed our schedules. We've switched to a four meal day, which helps. We have breakfast, luncheon, a late afternoon repast, and then our last in the evening."

Avadhron nodded. The sun, when not hidden by the clouds, shone down from a high angle. Had he missed luncheon? The roasting herdbeasts made his stomach growl loudly. Zaidhron glanced over at him with a chuckle, and he scowled at the prince.

"Luncheon will be served soon, although the herdbeasts likely won't be ready until evening meal."

Avadhron didn't answer, but he did look forward to sampling this planet's victuals. He would, however, take back some tea to ease his digestive woes this time.

His cousin turned east toward a distant grouping of shelters, and

Avadhron followed. At least the grasses between these far buildings and the main encampment still grew tall, save on the path they trod. The grass rustled in the breeze; the scent sweet a balm to his soul. As they drew near, a malodor hung in the air. Wrinkling his nose and trying not to gag, he asked, "What is that?"

"Your tanners," Mattan said with a smile.

Several boys knelt on the ground, scraping hair off the skin of animals stretched on frames. One, having maybe fifteen years, looked up as the two Chiefs and the alien approached. "Your Highness!" He stood, whipping his hair out of his eyes with a quick toss of his head, and bowed. "I'm ready to go back to helping my parents. I won't cause trouble any more."

"Your punishment was one full rotation of the greater moon. When that is done, your master will release you to your parents. If you have not caused him any grief in the meantime."

"But—"

Zaidhron raised a hand. "No more! Go back to work."

The boy's shoulders slumped, and he plopped back down onto his knees in front of the skin.

Avadhron allowed himself a small smile as they walked past. "His crime?"

"Rebellion. He refused to take part in chores and disrupted the camp. But he was only a follower. A man, Kolrik of Jessel clan, incited others. He was disgruntled that the new world didn't follow his romantic illusions." Zaidhron whirled to face Avadhron, eyes wide in affected surprise. "It is dirty here, with no air filters, Security Chief, did you know that? One must work and sweat and deal with aching muscles and blistered hands and bath in cold water. The days are too hot and the nights are chilly and getting worse as autumn approaches."

Avadhron threw back his head and laughed until his stomach hurt. Finally he managed to say, "He is the only one who has had such feelings? I expected all our pampered people—even our low clans have it easy compared to what is required here—to rebel against what needs to be done."

"Oh, we have had quite a few." Zaidhron shrugged with a sad smile. "The tanners have helped somewhat with the milder cases. A few became violent and were exiled, although my heart ached to do so. I'm not sure if any survived. The rest have been sent to work a farm settlement about a day's walk to the south. Kolrik was one of them." He walked on silently for a few steps. "I hope he mends his ways. He has great leadership potential."

Avadhron nodded at Zaidhron and Mattan. "I warned you both. I take it Kolrik's incitement was part of the interesting events?"

"Yes, it was. But despite everything, see what we've accomplished!"

His cousin swept his arm out to indicate the settlements across the green expanse. "We have a large, thriving community here and more within two days' walk. Men proud of their accomplishments, especially considering the hardships of living here in such new and primitive conditions." He slapped a hand on Avadhron's shoulder, his blue eyes alight. "Come to my home. Let me show you what we're about to start."

Chapter Fifteen

Avadhron followed them northwest and soon came to a shelter marked by Ch'shalna clan banners waving in the breeze. Guards flanking the entrance snapped to attention and saluted, fists over their hearts. He eyed the new living quarters of the Second at Table for their clan—one man away from being king. Behind an interior partition, he saw a wide cot with a thin mat and sleeping furs. A large table dominated the room, with papers—pulp not data-paper—strewn over it. Candles set in carved wooden holders held down some of the larger sheets.

He picked up one of the tapers. "You've already learned to make candles and paper?"

"Crudely, but yes. Mattan's people have been a great help."

With a nod, he cut his eyes to the alien. Mattan had said almost nothing since the tour started. Was it because he knew Avadhron didn't like him? No. That had never stopped him before. What did his silence signify?

Zaidhron pointed to a large paper. "Look at this. We are designing a city to be built here, with 'suitable quarters' for the king."

Leaning on the table, he studied the plans. He frowned and straightened with jerk, suppressing a shudder. "You are planning to enclose people in narrow, tightly planned streets similar to the ones we live in now? Dome above, why?"

The prince blinked. "You don't like it?"

"I think I just said that."

"What do you suggest, cousin?" Zaidhron asked.

"Open spaces. Set the city in sections."

"How?"

"I'm not a designer. But we have lived closed in for too long. Give people a sense of, of bigness. I would not be able to live in a place where the buildings were crammed together and all I could see were walls. I want to see sky and trees, and flowers, and the birds flying—" Avadhron's voice cracked. He turned away, detesting that he had displayed his feelings so openly. He cleared his throat. "Do what you will, but when do you start? And what will you use for materials?"

"This is the one time we break our rule and use our technology." Zaidhron spoke quietly, and at the low, serious tone, Avadhron spun around to stare at his cousin.

"The city will be built here," the prince said, "and part of what it will do is guard the lifts of the Portal Complex which exit here on the plain. So we are going to use SDC-12. We can build a portion of the city before winter hits so the people won't be in flimsy, hard-to-heat shelters."

"SDC-12? Are you mad? We vowed to leave all our technology behind! If you breach that agreement once then a second and third time become easier and—"

His cousin put up his hands in a conciliatory gesture, but Avadhron sneered and backed up a step. "Don't try to placate me in this! We made an agreement—"

"Only in this matter!" Zaidhron said. "Only where it concerns places of the Elders."

"What do you mean 'places of the Elders'?"

"There are three other spots besides here that your people could access—to their detriment," Mattan said. "We are going to build facilities on each one of them, as a protection. Your synthetic stone is stronger than anything we have, so we have asked that it be used in the construction."

Avadhron had the urge to pull out his hair, or better, grab Mattan by the throat. He clenched his fists, then slowly unclenched them as his mind took hold. Yes, it was best that his people be kept from any access to the Enaisi's technology. It could tempt them, or worse—from what he had gleaned from Mattan's attitude and that of his colleagues. Would they withdraw their permission to use the portal if they felt the settlers trespassed?

"Your Highness! Your Highness!"

A boy hopped up and down outside the entrance of the shelter.

The prince turned. "Yes?"

"Hatriss is asking for Thuldhan, but the guards say he's not here. I don't know what to do. Palitt is causing trouble again. The matron wants her out."

Zaidhron nodded. "Tell Hatriss I'll be there shortly."

The boy ran off, and the prince rubbed his forehead with a sigh. Then he met Avadhron's eyes and smiled. "I think I'll let you handle this."

"Is this the same Palitt that is our distant cousin?"

Zaidhron's smiled widened. "Your former betrothed. Yes, it is."

"I thought this was a day away from work for me."

"You're Ch'shalna. You are honored to serve."

"Suck sand."

Zaidhron laughed as they exited the shelter.

"So, who is Hatriss?"

"The head cook. Palitt has been a trial."

"I can only imagine." Palitt had been his arranged marriage when they were babes and both families had fumed when he broke it off when he came of Age. He had not wanted to marry and beget children who had no future. Besides, she had always been difficult, believing her kin status gave her great privilege. "Why did she even volunteer to Cross? With her attitude, I would think she'd wait for 'suitable quarters.'"

"She was tagging after a noble she was trying to hook. He escaped cleanly however." Zaidhron leaned close. "He married a commoner. She was livid."

"Ho! Doubly, I imagine." Palitt had taken Avadhron's marriage as a personal slap in her face, even though it took place years after he broke commitment with her.

"She is not easy to be around, that is certain."

"She never was anyway."

They shared a laugh, then Avadhron asked, "Have there been many cross marriages?"

"No, Torach'al's is the first and only, actually. His thane called down curses upon you for starting such a despicable trend, you know. And quite a few nobles erupted like fumaroles over it."

"I can imagine." Avadhron remembered eruptions from his own family when he had announced he was marrying Jhendill—including Zaidhron, although his cousin now puffed with pride over the cross-marriage and doted on Jhendill like a sister.

"Yes, and we used you to advantage. I was certain you wouldn't mind."

As they approached the cooking area, they could hear a woman ranting. "—realize how important they both are? What were you thinking to just dump that fat into the compost? You've worked here long enough to know what needs to be done. You just wait till Thuldhan gets here. He'll see to you!"

"You have no right to talk me in that fashion. I'm Ch'shalna clan!"

"You certainly are," Zaidhron said.

Palitt spun and simpered at the prince. "Cousin!" she cooed.

Zaidhron stepped sideways and gestured for Avadhron to take charge. Palitt's smug expression gelled into hard lines. Now, Avadhron smiled.

Several workers, hunched over basins and tubs scrubbing or peeling, paused to listen.

"What is the problem, Matron Hatriss?"

"She dumped all the day's fat into the compost cart. All of it! And now the compost is just...rubbish!"

Years of training kept Avadhron's expression bland, but by the blasted wastes, what was Hatriss talking about? From the looks on the other workers' faces and on Zaidhron's, whatever Palitt had done wasn't trivial. "Is this her first offense of this kind?"

"She never does her share, Sec Chief. Or does the work badly."

"What needs to be done with this ruined compost? No way to...salvage it?"

Hatriss shook her head, arms crossed. "No, nor the fat. It must simply be tossed in the midden now. All wasted!" Her voice was filled with regret.

"And where is the...midden?" *Whatever that is.*

"South of here. We have midden carts, rubbish is carried there as often as is needed, then sorted and what cannot be salvaged for reuse is burned."

Ah. So that's what a midden is. "Then I suggest hauling midden be Palitt's new chore, since she is fit for no better work."

Palitt arched her back and shook her balled her fists at Avadhron. "What? How dare—"

Avadhron bared his teeth, leaning over her. "I have spoken."

Her face paled, and she stepped back, eyes wide. "But cousin, surely you cannot mean it."

"If you wish to eat, you will do your assigned task, and do it properly. Hatriss, who oversees midden...removal?"

"A man named Calsov."

"Calsov will report to you each day on Palitt's work. If it is satisfactory, she shall have earned her food for the next day. If not, she will go without."

"But–but you cannot do that!"

"I am second highest in rank on this planet. Did you hear Prince Zaidhron stay my order?"

Palitt glanced from Avadhron to their cousin.

Zaidhron's expression was somber. "Attend your duties, Palitt."

She backed up, frowning, shaking her head. "But you *can't!*"

"Go." Zaidhron waved a hand in dismissal.

She stood frozen, then finally turned and walked away. Avadhron watched her with narrowed eyes for a moment, then said, "I would send word to whoever serves food to not allow her to eat without express permission from you, Hatriss."

"A sound idea. She's a sneak, that one." Hatriss expression became wary. "Begging your pardon to speak ill of Ch'shalna."

Avadhron barked a laugh. "We cannot reward individuals for merely being born in a particular clan. Hard work is the benchmark for approval and advancement here."

Zaidhron snorted quietly, and Avadhron glanced at his cousin. "Do you gainsay that?"

"No. That is what we've been trying to instill in all the settlers."

Hatriss bowed. "Thank you for your assistance, Security Chief Avadhron."

"I hope this solves your problem, Matron."

"She's Calsov's problem now."

The men smiled and moved on.

"What else is there to see?"

"So much. You haven't seen the basket weavers, their work is amazing. And we have herders now who are being taught how to properly care for the herdbeasts. There are various types, some are good for their hair and some for meat. Some are climbers and others graze on the plain. I told you of the miners and farmers. And we have men training as foresters who are providing us with wood with direction from the Elders."

Avadhron stopped. "You're cutting down the forests?"

"We need wood for many purposes. But we're not just indiscriminately destroying forests. It's selective cutting with the Elders providing guidelines and showing us how to avoid negative impacts. They've had much previous experience and learned some lessons the hard way, from what Mattan has said."

Avadhron frowned at the alien, who shook his head. "Believe me, the forests are vitally important. Part of what we are teaching your people is how to maintain the integrity of this world."

"I hope so." Avadhron gazed at the trees to the south, on the ridge bordering the plain, thinking of his dream. And the questions he wished answered by Mattan. He turned to the two men. "I want to see the mountain again."

Chapter Sixteen

The doors slid open, and Avadhron stepped through, inhaling deeply. Ah, cooler atop the mountain, and so many different smells than on the plain because of the trees and plants, like that one aromatic bush he now knew was called verga. And the sounds! Leaves rustling, birds singing, and noises from unseen animals as well. Yes, given a choice, this is where he wanted to live.

Without waiting for his companions, he raced down the path to the little pool of his dreams. He stopped short upon seeing it; the yellow flowers were gone.

Of course. They bloomed earlier in the season then died back into the ground. However, another type of plant, thansas, had sprouted, growing in clumps with dusty-green, rounded leaves; he remembered them from reading about Elyria's flora. He squatted to examine them more closely.

"They will grow bigger and bloom in about a month."

Avadhron rose, lifting his chin as he faced Ismari. "Yes, I know. They're called thansas."

"Very good." She smiled. "I'm not surprised you've been studying the plant life. You've always had a passion for botany, haven't you?"

He didn't answer.

"I hope you get to see them bloom. The flowers are beautiful."

"Ismari, where did you go?" a youthful voice called.

"Here," she replied.

Several Teldheri came stumping down the stone steps to join her. Avadhron's lips thinned. This was *his* place. "What are all of you doing up here on the mountain?"

Most of the group stopped, mouths agape, staring at him. One boy, however, held out a large basket filled with green leaves. "We gather, Security Chief."

"Yes, mostly herbs for medicines and cooking." A stripling girl scooped a handful of something out of her lined basket. "These are sweetfronds, sir. They're used for tea, to aid digestion."

The boy nodded. "We gather those, featherfronds, avalare, hadra, ch'illeya, gossa—"

Another girl shushed the lad. "The Security Chief doesn't need a lesson in herbs."

"If you do, Ismari is the one to teach you," the boy said, his eyes shining. "She's a botanist."

Was the boy's excitement truly about plants or was he infatuated with the alien woman? Avadhron nodded and waved an arm toward the uphill path. "Don't let me stop your gathering. I wouldn't want to be the reason you were behind in chores and got in trouble."

"We can't be in trouble if Ismari is with us." The boy grinned up at her, and she smiled back like an indulgent parent. "She keeps us safe, too."

Avadhron glared at her, hoping she would take the hint and leave with her pupils, apprentices, or whatever they were.

Mattan and Zaidhron ambled down the steps, talking softly to each other. Ismari turned, arms spread, and gestured for her gatherers to continue. The striplings bobbed their heads in quick bows in passing the prince as they hurried back the way they came.

The two men joined Avadhron at the pool.

"This is the place of your dreams?" Zaidhron asked.

Avadhron's face prickled with heat, and he clenched his jaw. "You told him?"

"Yes, as he also knows of my foresight."

Zaidhron nodded. "How he saw you were the prophet to lead our people in this endeavor."

"Prophet?"

"Now, wait, I—"

"*Prophet?*" Avadhron spun to Mattan. "Did you truly call me that?"

Zaidhron pulled on his arm. "He did. You dreamed of us moving here, and have seen things that needed to be done for the Crossing to be a success."

"I may have dreamed of this place, but I never dreamed of anything else. And what I suggested was only common sense. Does the whole encampment know of this nonsense? And of my dreams?"

"Only us, cousin. But Mattan and I have no secrets. We're as brothers."

Avadhron snorted. "Are you truly? So you know the complete history of our people, and his?" He jabbed a finger at the alien. "You tell me why your people exiled mine to Teledhar. Why we were taken from this planet, which you claim was our original home."

"It was...prejudice. My race felt yours were inferior. Some factions practiced genocide, but some few felt pity and wished to offer your people a safe haven. The ones left on Teledhar weren't exiled, they were rescued. The rescuers didn't know the planet was unstable. And in their naïveté, they didn't realize that giving a new society advanced technology without adequate instruction would lead to...damaging mistakes, further accelerating the problems which led to your people eventually being forced to live inside domes."

"Why mostly children? Our spotty history indicates children were dumped there with only a few advisors, which we called Elders, who then left us."

Mattan looked up into the trees. "They were the ones easiest to rescue from...those practicing genocide. Show an innocent child and you can gain sympathy. Many who were in hiding gave their children to the rescuers in fear of the alternative."

Avadhron clenched his teeth against rising bile. "What sort of monsters were your people?"

"Not all of them," Mattan hissed. He took a slow breath, then another before continuing. "Eventually a war waged due to the treatment of your people, with catastrophic consequences. This planet was abandoned, shunned, and we called it 'Our Shame.' But slowly, the planet recovered from the devastation wrought on it. It had some help, atmospheric scrubbers, for instance."

"The ones you gave to Jhendill, to further her work." Avadhron grimaced, remembering his wife's tears. "Until it was shut down."

"Yes."

Avadhron squatted by the pool and let his fingers play in the cool water, trying to assimilate what he had been told. "Does anyone else know about this?"

"No, but signs of our past habitation on this planet, and of the war, are evident. We cannot hide from it, but I will not elaborate. The shame is too fresh to us."

"You say that as if you remember it."

The alien shrugged. "It is what you might call a racial memory."

"And what differences in our peoples caused yours to consider ours inferior? I see no great deviation other than variations in skin and hair color."

Mattan hesitated and locked eyes with Zaidhron.

"Go on. Tell him," the prince murmured.

"My race have abilities yours have not. We can sense emotions, for example. And some of us have foresight."

Avadhron leaned back on his heels, frowning up at the alien. "Like my dreams?"

Mattan paused a moment then replied, "Yes."

"But...if I have foresight, then..." He stood. "What is the link between your race and mine?"

"We..." Mattan stopped, staring at the ground.

"We have a common root," Zaidhron finished. "But his people began genetic experimentation. As they 'improved' themselves, they looked upon those unaltered as inferior. Some even considered us no more than livestock."

"The best of my people looked upon yours as pets to be protected. Which is how the Teledhar project began. They wished to save as many as they could."

"And you? Why did you really come to Teledhar?"

"To see how your people fared."

Avadhron's lips twisted in disbelief.

Mattan threw his hands up. "Truly. And once there, I determined to help save you. My team backs me, and I have enough influence that we have no hindrances in bringing your people back to their home world."

Avadhron rubbed his forehead in silence. Neither of the other two spoke. Finally, he said, "Upon what did your people base their genetic improvements? Was foresight something that existed and upon which you ameliorated?"

"Actually, foresight is the one ability we have never been able to tie to *any* gene or combination of genes. We cannot predict who will have it, or how strongly."

"Some of us feel it isn't genetic at all, but is spiritual," came a female voice from behind.

Avadhron spun to see Ismari, standing by a tree.

"The young ones have taken their gatherings down to the plain," she said with a smile to Mattan. "We're alone."

"You're intruding," Avadhron spat.

"I think not. My brother and I are co-leaders of this undertaking, although I let him think he's in charge."

Brother? Avadhron glanced between Mattan and Ismari. "No mention was made to me of a sibling relationship between you two when I was given reports on all the Enaisi who came to Teledhar."

She tipped her head. "Was it important to your security?"

Avadhron scowled at Ismari's flippant tone. "How much more about yourselves did you neglect to tell us?"

"Your security knows what it needs to. I think my brother finally realizes he must confide in you as he did in Zaidhron. Although he's still reluctant to say all."

"Oh?"

Mattan held up his hands. "I have no wish to hide anything from you. But your suspicious nature made me hesitant, wondering how much to reveal at a time."

"How much more is there?"

"You know a concise history now, I believe." Mattan glared at his sister. "Except theories which a few hold to, despite no science to back them up."

"The Laws of the Maker back me up. Foresight was a gift."

"That's all superstitious nonsense."

"So you say, but you don't really believe that."

Despite himself, Avadhron smiled at the bickering siblings. Ismari twisted to look at him. "What do you find so amusing?"

Startled, he found himself without words. Zaidhron laughed. "Did you forget he told us they could sense emotions, cousin?"

"I did."

With a flounce of her head, Ismari said, "I'm not staying to provide entertainment for this churl." She strode up the path, back stiff.

All three men watched her for a moment, then Mattan shrugged with a grin. He gestured at the stone steps. "Shall we go? It's time for the afternoon meal."

Avadhron gazed about with a sigh, wishing he could spend time here alone, but they would never allow it, and it with good reason. He'd not survive long if any of the dangerous animals he'd been warned about came hunting. Reluctantly, he nodded.

Chapter Seventeen

Avadhron strolled about the settlement, the heat of the day dissipating as the dusk deepened. The sweat on his skin long ago dried, and the wind blew more strongly raising chill bumps on his arms. Lit torches dotted the landscape, giving a warm glow but allowing for eerie shadows between the shelters, and people gathered at the fires through the camp, comparing their days, complaining and bragging and laughing.

A straight-backed, tall man jogged over and bowed. As he lifted his head and put a fist over his heart, Avadhron spied the shadow of a dark, trimmed beard on Thuldhan's square jaw. Avadhron pointed at his own jaw, eyebrows raised. "What's this?"

His Third grinned, a bit sheepishly. "Some of us are experimenting since hair-growth inhibitor is not allowed. Shaving with a bare blade has a few drawbacks, sir."

Avadhron snorted. "I can imagine." He had seen many of the settlers with beards, but to see one of his own men with facial hair was jarring.

"You do not disapprove, then, Chief?"

"Why should I?"

"Some have said we should have a cleaner, neater appearance."

"Some? Noble clans, no doubt, or ours at the least, feeling we should be above the commoners in looks, enh?"

"Prince Zaidhron does keep clean-shaven."

"So he does. It's his choice. I will leave it to my Secs if they wish to forego risking a blade at their throat." Avadhron peered closely at his Third's face. "How easy is it to trim?"

"Compared to shaving? No challenge." Thuldhan's grin faded. He lifted his chin, a sign he was in full Sec mode. "Did you get my report, sir?"

"I've downloaded it from one of the Portal consoles, yes, but I haven't read it yet. I wanted to speak to you in person. Has anything noteworthy happened?"

Thuldhan hesitated, grimacing. "In negative aspects, only two major events. A worker became incensed that he was set to a task with a man from another clan, one his had been feuding. Before his workmates could intervene, he'd attacked the poor fellow with an axe."

Avadhron clenched his teeth with a hiss. "Fatal?"

"Yes, sir. Following the rules you and the First Table set down, we banished the attacker from the settlements with only the clothes he was wearing."

"Has anyone seen him since?"

"We found him eight days later, dead. He'd been mauled and half-eaten. His body was brought back to display. It has deterred feuding and violence."

Avadhron rubbed his face. "A pity two deaths had to occur to bring that about. It won't be the last incident though."

"I agree, sir."

"So many of our people have been consumed by clan pride and hatred for those not kin. Any outbreaks of fighting from either side of that feud?"

Thuldhan slowly shook his head with a tiny smile. "No, sir. A few began mouthings, but the rest of the settlers kept any disorder from occurring. It was quite...inspiring, actually. You would have been proud."

"There is that." Avadhron inhaled deeply, imagining the sight: the people themselves quelling a disturbance, preventing a possible riot. "What was the second?"

"A worker decided he wasn't going to take orders and walked away from a valley camp. It was Matsen, if you remember him."

Avadhron did. He was in the first group of Disaffected to cross, one who had worn a cam. He had no doubt of the outcome. "And his body?"

"What little the ka'gua left almost wasn't worth bringing back, but we did. Just to show those in the valley Matsen's bragging was foolish and deadly."

"I'm sure it quelled others."

"Yes, sir."

"Anything else to report?"

"Much. The prince has probably given you a briefing though. Overall, the people are working hard and, as you proclaimed, giving *comparatively* little trouble now that they have busy hands and a sense of purpose."

He clapped a hand on Thuldhan's shoulder. "Good! Let's discuss the implementation of policy changes in open sky here compared to what we projected we would need while back in the domes."

His Third gestured Avadhron toward the security quarters with a bow.

The meal that evening was delicious. Avadhron sat on a bench made from a log, a hot mug of tea cupped in his hands, listening to everyone talk of their day's accomplishments.

Sparks flew from the fire, dancing high into the air. The Bells, as his people had already come to call the nebula, and the stars shone brightly. Both moons were visible, the larger trailing the smaller across the sky. A slight breeze made him smile. This was life. The only thing missing was his wife sitting next to him.

What would it be like when he and Jhendill lived here? It wouldn't be long. He wished she'd Cross now. He'd have to talk to Atesni or Dassel and see if either of them could convince her.

"When are you returning, sir?" asked one of the settlers.

Avadhron inhaled deeply, loving all the smells, even the acrid smoke. "I must return soon. I should have already gone back, but it's very hard to leave."

There was murmured agreement.

"Although I do miss some things," another settler said. "I had high rankings in some of the Grid-games."

"I miss sweets," someone complained. A burst of laughter and groans erupted from almost everyone, followed by a chorus of which ones they had liked best.

"I miss a lot," said a man with shaggy dark hair. "But not enough to want to go back."

"I'd go back if I could," a stripling grumbled with a glower at a nearby couple, likely his parents.

"To do what, boy? Die?" asked Avadhron. "The quakes have increased. We lost Central Plain Domes Two and Three recently, and the scientists have warned it's going to get worse."

The youngster shrugged.

Avadhron contained his rage, merely snorting as a reply. He rose and strode toward the entrance shelter and, following what he'd seen others do, tossed the dregs of his tea into an arc on the grass. He heard the prince call his name but didn't stop. A hand grabbed his arm. "Stay a few minutes more."

He whirled to face Zaidhron. "If I do, I cannot guarantee I would be able to stay my tongue. How do you deal with such idiocy?"

"I let it slide, unless it becomes rebellion. You hold things too tightly, cousin."

Avadhron barked a laugh. "I think you hold things not tightly enough."

"Oh, believe me, letting go is an effort. When will you return then?"

"When 'suitable quarters' are ready. It hurts too much to go back through the portal. When do you think you'll have something ready for the king?"

"We're going to start on the foundation for the first section this week. It will be some time. Months. We can't build as fast here with SDC-12 since the raw materials aren't on hand, we have to wait as they're delivered. Once we get established, the process will be easier and faster."

Avadhron nodded. "You don't need to give me an explanation, although I will let the king know the likely timetable, and the reasons if he asks." He paused, frowning. "I don't think he's really looking forward to leaving."

"No." Zaidhron smiled sadly. "Like many of our people, he doesn't see the reality of the situation."

"Or his current comforts are more important than the spectre of the future."

"True." The prince set a hand on Avadhron's shoulder. "Be well, cousin."

"And you likewise." Stifling a regretful sigh, he entered the lift.

Avadhron tapped his fingers on his desk, his gaze unfocused, his mind literally a world away.

"Chief?"

Galadhan stood before him, a wry smile on his face. "Thinking about Elyria?"

He sat back with a snort. "I need chastising."

"Consider it done."

They shared a smile, then his Second asked, "What's the latest word?"

"The first building is finished, and they've started foundations for nearby structures in that range of the city. The king will be Crossing soon. He's doing the prelims now. My father will be going too, as his personal guard."

Galadhan's eyebrows rose. "That leaves you in charge of all security, not just the Elites."

"I'm thinking of giving you charge of the Elites since I must take his job."

"Are you—"

The room shook, and a sickening dread coursed through Avadhron. Galadhan dove for his locker—as did every other person in the office; his men knew the protocol should an earthquake threaten their dome. And their first task was to don their body armor. Locker doors banged, and his Elites began to suit up.

He stood, snatching his own armor and pulling it on. "Paldhran," he said into his comm, prompting it to call his father.

"Yes?"

"Where is the king?"

"That's my concern. You secure the dome."

"He should be evacuated."

"I'm with him. I'm taking care of it. Just do your job."

Avadhron ground his teeth. As the Chief of the Elites, the king's safety *was* his job. "What about the First Table?" he added, thinking of their close kin, the clan's advisors.

"*Your* job, Sec Chief."

"Chief." Galadhan, already in his armor, had one hand to his helmet. The lines on his face seemed more hardened than usual. "Central reports this isn't a mere earthquake. A volcano has just appeared out of nowhere in the Northwest. It has destroyed Agri-dome One and Two, and the entirety of West Ridge is out of communication. The last message was that the ridge was collapsing. Earthquakes have hit the all over the plain and East Valley. It seems almost every dome has been breached. The rail-tube system is down. All of it."

The blood drained from Avadhron's face. *This is it. Our time of grace has ended.*

Chapter Eighteen

"Emergency evacuation," Avadhron ordered. "Get all shuttle teams launched. Fadhalan's Team is in charge of getting the First Table out. Paldhran is already evacuating the king."

"No place is safe. Where shall we take them?"

"The portal. Elyria."

"Right, Chief." His Second barked orders into his comm as he ran out. Avadhron followed, synching his ear comm to his armor's system, as they both rushed toward the administrative headquarters. People darted in both directions, screaming.

"Jhendill?"

Galadhan shouted at those in the corridor to get to the shuttle docks.

"Yes, I'm here."

Relief flooded him. He pressed a hand to the side of helmet in a futile effort to hear her voice more clearly amid the chaos. "Board the first craft that presents itself. Go to the portal."

"Are you trying to order me, Ch'shalna?"

"Please. Cross to Elyria!"

"Are *you* going?"

"I can't. My duty is to see to the safety of our people."

"So is mine. I'm with Evac Group Three, and we're on our way to Centrals Plains Dome Five. I'll be in charge of the in-dome scrubbers. Don't worry about me, Ch'shalna. I'm in an enviro-suit and am as safe as can be."

A suit wouldn't protect her from all the various dangers of the volcano or earthquakes. He took a deep breath. "You be careful. Stay close to that team."

"I will. You be careful too."

Avadhron paused then added, "I love you."

"I love you too, Ch'shalna."

Avadhron closed his eyes for a moment. *Duty. Concentrate on my duty.* Another rumble and sickening heave threw everyone sideways into the wall. Screams echoed down the corridor. He pushed up and continued to run, Galadhan at his side.

"Up. To the surface," Avadhron ordered. Their ancestors had felt the most important offices and chambers should be below ground in case of a dome breach. They hadn't foreseen a future this bleak.

His father's voice, sounding weak, repeated his name in the ear comm several times.

"Yes, sir?"

"Help...us."

He stopped, feeling the blood drain from his face. "Where are you?"

"Near the north docks. The king..."

"Father?"

No answer.

Avadhron grabbed Galadhan's shoulder. "The docks. Janadhan and Paldhran have—" He couldn't say it, even think it. "They need assistance."

"Right."

The two men bolted for the nearest stairs, passing many who were running the opposite way, some screaming or crying, others silent, faces white, probably in shock. Quite a few hadn't donned their enviro-suits. Several grabbed them, begging for help.

"Get into your suits. Get above ground," Avadhron ordered as he and Galadhan kept moving forward. They reached the stairwell and raced up. Another rumble and dust and small bits of rock fell on them as they caught the handrail, their footing lost. He gazed upward. Fallen stone blocked the passage above.

Wordlessly, they half slid down the debris-covered steps, hanging on to the rails. The nearest stairs were northward; both men pelted down the corridor and around a corner—and stopped. A collapsed wall barred their route.

"Blast! SDC-12. Best we have," Galadhan muttered, as they turned and ran back the way they came.

"Ten. When this was built, our best was SDC-10. Or maybe nine."

"Picky," his Second retorted.

"Northeast?" Avadhron asked as they approached a corridor junction.

"Why not?"

"Paldhran. We're trying to get to you. Do you hear me?" Silence. He tried the king. "Janadhan. Are you all right, Sire?" No answer. He shook his head at Galadhan. "We have to find a way to them."

"We will, Chief."

Walls bulged ominously as they rushed to the next stairwell. He paused to look up as they entered it. "Seems clear." They wound their way upward, Avadhron eyeing the widening cracks, waiting for another rumble to topple the column and bury them under tons of synthetic stone.

He didn't feel any safer when they reached the top; they still had to escape this building. Not that being directly under-dome was less dangerous, but hopefully they could get to the shuttle docks without detours.

The stairs were near an exit, but the doors hung askew. They tried to force them apart but gave up.

"All the effort to keep us safe in case of a dome breach. Didn't they think of earthquakes?" Galadhan asked.

"Dome breach was a real fear, earthquakes didn't happen then like they do now." Avadhron peered around them. "We'll not get out this way. Come on."

"I'm wondering if we'll get out at all," his Second grumbled as they ran east along a passage toward the next exit.

"Such an optimist," Avadhron muttered, refusing to give in to his own doubts. "We're only one door away from being free."

Galadhan snorted.

Past the curve, a buckled wall blocked their way forward, however through a breach atop the rubble, they could see the dome glittering high above.

"There!"

Both men clambered up the broken stone and stood for a moment, getting their bearings. Tiny cracks radiated like webbing in the shimmering canopy overhead with jagged, dark streaks marking where pieces were missing. Avadhron had known this was the end, but the reality of seeing the breached Palace Dome made him pause and take a deep breath to clear his emotions and mind.

Galadhan pointed down to their left. "Looks like we can climb down over here."

They carefully picked their way back down the wreckage of the wall until the distance was barely more than their own heights. They dropped, and Avadhron gritted his teeth against the jarring through his legs. *Not as young as I was.* They raced north to the shuttle docks. The ground was riven in places and they had to jump across cracks and around steaming fissures.

The docks were a ruins, the surface ruptured into heaving piles, the locks destroyed; this whole section of dome had been obliterated. Avadhron again tried to raise his father or the king through the comm. A cursory look at the devastation showed nothing. But if the bodies were underneath...

Avadhron attempted to connect to the Grid to triangulate Paldhran's comm tracker and Janadhan's. Unsurprisingly, it was down. He did have an alternative though. If he was close enough, he could trace using his own comm. He tried his father's tracker, but received nothing; he was either too far away or it was broken. The king's returned a faint blip. He turned to see where his Second was, but he was out of sight.

"Galadhan."

"Yes, Chief."

"Use your comm to trace the king's signal. I'm getting a weak reading, if you can pick it up as well, we can narrow the search."

"On it, Chief." After a short silence, his Second replied, "I have it. Not very strong. I'm heading west."

"I'll go east then."

A few moments later, Galadhan said, "It's growing stronger, Chief."

"On my way."

Avadhron turned around and ran, past the shuttle locks. What had they been doing *here?* He could see Janadhan panicking and just bolting, but not Paldhran. The blip grew louder, and a short distance ahead, Galadhan waved.

As he approached, the likely scenario seemed to be what he suspected. The king's body was farther away than his father's as if he had been running and Paldhran chasing. Both bodies had been slashed and skewered by giant shards of the dome's shell. Blood covered the surrounding ground.

He knelt by his father, oblivious to the blood on his boots and knees. It was futile; he was obviously dead, eyes open and fixed behind the cracked visor, but Avadhron checked his suit's vitals anyway. Slowly, he rose and gazed over at Galadhan, squatting next to the king. His Second shook his head.

I hope you have suitable quarters now, Janadhan.

Straightening his shoulders and lifting his chin, he said, "Let's sweep the dome for survivors."

<\<\>\>

Avadhron and Galadhan, joined by Elite One after the team had evacuated their clan's chiefs and families, had almost finished a patrol of Palace Dome. He finally gave in to his worry and contacted his wife. Although the Grid itself was down, at least basic communication between domes were active through their satellites. One small advantage.

"Jhendill. Are you all right?"

"I'm fine, Ch'shalna. I'm fine." Humming machinery could be heard in the background along with hysterical yelling.

"Are you still in Central Plains Dome Five?"

"Yes. I can see a shuttle loading people nearby, where a rail-tube twisted and breached the dome. The craft is floating awfully low. I think they're trying to fit too many in."

"Those vehicles do look like they're lumbering when filled to capacity. The shuttle teams know their jobs."

"I hope so. It's such chaos, and everyone is so scared. I've seen parents beg for us to take their children while they stay behind. My heart is breaking. And some are nearly rioting, not caring who is in the way as long as they get to a shuttle. Guards are having a hard time controlling the crowds."

"I don't blame them for being frightened." Avadhron glanced about the commons. The lawn, once dotted with miniature trees and flowers, now lay waste, covered in ash, the ground buckled, steam and noxious gasses belching into the air.

"Where are you, Ch'shalna?"

"Palace Dome."

"But I heard the dome shattered!"

"Sections of it are gone, yes. We're sweeping for survivors." He lowered his voice. "There haven't been many."

"I know. It's the same everywhere. It's horrifying."

His comm vibrated. "I have to go. Be careful."

"You as well. I love you."

"Love you too." He hit the comm switch on the helmet. "Yes?"

"It's Mattan. I came over to help with the evacuation. Is it that bad?"

"Worse. Every dome has been breached. We're running every shuttle and skiff to ferry people to the Portal."

"We're clearing space and preparing areas within the Complex for the survivors. It's already crowded, and that's not going to improve, but we'll make do. What's the logistics of this? How long to get everyone off planet?"

"Days. Perhaps even weeks." Avadhron stopped as the realization hit him; with the whole north and west gone, and all the remaining domes breached, the number of people had been significantly reduced. "Or...I–I don't know. We've lost entire domes. Maybe not as much time as that." *How many have died? Tens of thousands? More?*

"I'm sorry. Treyor and I are going to stay here to coordinate those Crossing. Ismari, Ashani, and Dassel are organizing things on the other side. We're getting them through as quickly as possible."

"Understood." He hesitated then added, "Thank you."

"You're welcome, my fr—Avadhron. Be safe."

He snorted and thumbed off the comm.

<><>

They found no evidence of life in East Valley One. His team finished their sweep and headed back to the skiff. Despite his armor's built-in enviro-controls, Avadhron felt sweaty. And his incessantly itching back wasn't a welcome distraction from his exhaustion. How many hours had they been searching for survivors and helping load people onto shuttles? They dare not stop, yet he knew his body couldn't continue indefinitely without rest. He downed another stim, provided in his armor, and ground his teeth in guilt for having limitations.

"How are you, love?" Jhendill's voice in his helmet was the best catharsis he could ask for, at least under these circumstances.

"Still working. You? Have you been able to take any breaks? Or eaten?"

"I try to doze while traveling between domes, but it isn't easy. We've had rations several times from the shuttle's kit. You? Oh, you're in armor. Sorry."

"Yes. Sucking nutrition through a straw isn't quite the same as a meal, but it helps." He didn't mention the stims. "Where are you?"

"We've moved to East Valley Four. Can you have another evac team sent here? Survivors say there's a pocket of people alive and trapped underground. We have our hands full."

"We're on our way." At least he'd get to see her, perhaps persuade her to Cross.

"Elite One," he prompted into his comm. "We're heading for East Valley Four. Report of trapped survivors. Double-time it."

A vibration ran through the skiff, evidence of yet another earthquake underneath the craft. A fumarole erupted slightly to their right, and Avadhron veered around it. To their left, a fissure ripped open, lava pouring out like a sauce bubbling too long on an induction hob.

"Avadhron. Avadhron?" Mattan's voice sounded worried.

"I'm here."

"Send out word to your teams. It's worse. The Portal Complex has had energy disruptions and some structural damage. I think we need to go through now."

"I'm heading for a group in East Valley Four."

"You're taking a risk of your life, man!"

"My wife is there."

A pause, then: "Well, hurry!"

Avadhron snorted assent, then keyed a frequency to warn his all teams to report to the Elders' mountain and Cross.

As they approached East Valley, they could see Dome Four no longer had a dome, save shards along the outside. *How can Jhendill maintain the integrity of air in-dome when there's no dome?*

"Jhendill."

No answer. He repeated her name, still nothing. His chest tightened, and he stared at the remains of Dome Four with an increasing weight and fear settling on him. Forcing himself to keep a calm façade, he opened the comm to all local Sec channels. "This is Security Chief Avadhron requesting report from anyone in East Valley Dome Four. Report."

"Sec Guard Tontinn reporting, sir," came a woman's voice. "Another earthquake just hit, we need help."

"On our way. I'll use your comm for direction."

"Yes, sir."

Next to him, Galadhan set the skiff's nav to use the guard's tracker as a beacon. They weren't far away. Avadhron soon landed, the craft almost dancing as it slid to a stop. He jumped out and ran toward a shuttle, prompting Tontinn's name into his comm.

"Here, sir."

A suit of black armor stood and limped forward from a nearby structure. A wall had collapsed, leaving the insides open, girders twisted, floors askew, cables hanging. Ash hung in the air like a fog.

Avadhron raced to the guard, his worry flooding out in one word: "Jhendill?"

"I'm sorry, sir. The earthquake hit with the team inside the building. I had come out to get a pallet for an injur—"

"*Where is Jhendill?*"

"Inside, sir."

Avadhron bolted for the ruins, ignoring the voices that called to him. He climbed over the rubble, and into what had been a hallway. He looked left and right into doorways, calling her name. He found a jumble of bodies in one area, crushed under fallen stone; several evac members and those they had been trying to rescue. Jhendill wasn't with them.

He continued on and discovered more corpses in a heavily damaged room. He picked through the rubble, checking each one. Beyond a demolished wall, legs stuck out. Someone appeared almost sitting, propped against a column, but as he sidled past fallen debris, he could see the body had been skewered by a girder. Jhendill's mouth hung open as if in a silent scream, her eyes blank. A cry ripped from his soul, and he fell to his knees, fists clenched on his thighs.

Chapter Nineteen

"Chief?" Galadhan's voice was soft. "I'm sorry, Chief."

"Don't tell me I have to leave her!"

"There are more people to rescue. It's your duty, sir."

"Suck sand. I set you as Chief of Elites. Do *your* duty."

"My first duty is to you. And I repeat what you have said in times past: duty now, grief later."

"I was wrong."

"You? Never!" Galadhan grabbed Avadhron's shoulder. "Chief. You must keep on."

He jerked his shoulders forward out of his Second's grasp. Galadhan caught him in a force-hold, impelling Avadhron to his feet, then loosened his grip. *A mistake.* With a snarl, he spun, ready to fight. Two Elites seized him by the arms. His Second smacked a hand to each side of Avadhron's helmet. "Duty, sir!"

"Duty!" Avadhron spat, then sobs overtook him. Hands freed him as he bowed over. He tried to turn back to Jhendill's body, but Galadhan slung an arm around him, guiding him toward the door. "Let's go, Chief."

The ground rumbled again, and with shouts of "Out! Out!" his Elites dragged him from of the room and away from the building.

They turned to see the whole structure collapse. Avadhron's life collapsed with it. His life buried beneath its ruin. He stood, immobilized, unable to think.

"Chief?" Galadhan's face blurred in front of him.

He grabbed his Second's shoulders and snarled, "If you say duty one more time—"

"There are survivors nearby. A little south of here. They're calling for help on the medical channel."

Avadhron inhaled. Unfair. He should not still be breathing when she did not. He took a second breath.

A third. He couldn't make himself move. He just breathed. Cursing himself for each one.

"Chief?"

He gulped, and finally he nodded. "Let's head there."

"We may need both the skiff and shuttle, and Tontinn's not a pilot."

"You pilot the shuttle. Lead the way. I'll follow in the skiff." Avadhron gestured for his team to go with his Second.

Galadhan held up a hand, his eyes boring into Avadhron's. "Our Elites will ride with you, Chief."

He glared at his brash subordinate, but the man didn't look away. *He knows me too well.* Finally, Avadhron said to the team, "All right. You're with me."

His Elites hopped into the skiff, exchanging glances. Galadhan's pursed lips as he climbed into the shuttle were his only comment.

Avadhron followed the shuttle to the coordinates of one of the comm's trackers. It was underneath a medical complex. The Elites spread out, looking for some method of gaining entrance into the facility. The remains of a lift finally provided a way down, and they descended using rappel spools. The survivors were a mix of patients and medical personnel, all in enviro-suits. His team began a practiced evacuation. Several needed to be carried, including a small figure laying on a mat in the corner, away from the others.

As two of the Elites approached her, one of the medics spat, "Leave her to last. She's clanless. They only brought her here to die. Should have left her in the street."

Avadhron spun, his spine stiffened. With a barely audible growl, he strode over, pushing both guards out of the way. He took a few moments to check that her suit was properly sealed. Considering the medic's attitude he was surprised it was; perhaps some other medic, or a patient, had done the job. He then lifted the woman gently, and carried her toward the lift, gazing into the frail face. She weighed almost nothing. The medic opened his mouth, but as Avadhron glared at him, he shut it.

He set the old woman in a sling attached to the bottom of the tensile wire, and the spool hauled her up. One after another, the patients went up followed by the medics. Galadhan narrowed his eyes at Avadhron. "You next, Chief."

"Not taking any chances, are you?"

"No, sir, I'm not."

Avadhron clipped the spool's wire to his armor's harness. "Suck sand," he spat as he rose.

The biased medic gestured frantically by the door of the shuttle. Avadhron crossed to see what he was complaining about now. "What's the problem?"

"He doesn't want to ride with the old woman, sir," Fadhalan, leader of Elite One, said, nodding at the pitiful creature lying in the ash. The others, again, gave her wide berth.

"Then he doesn't have to. We'll take both vehicles instead of just the shuttle." Avadhron stooped and lifted her, looking down into her wrinkled face. She wouldn't meet his gaze. "What's your name, old gran?"

"I'm nobody, sir," she mumbled. "Leave me to die."

He let his tone become authoritative. "I asked you your name, woman."

Startled, she met his eyes for a moment, then looked away. "Asila."

"You are now Asila of Ch'shalna Clan. I have spoken." He glared around, daring anyone to say one word. The medic's mouth was agape. Galadhan's eyes sparkled, his lips pursed in their usual denial of a smile.

He carried his new kin to the skiff. "Make her comfortable," he told Tontinn.

The ground shook again, and they all clambered into the vehicles, his Second and the survivors in the shuttle, and his Elites, Tontinn, and the old woman with him. "Galadhan," Avadhron said into his comm. "I'll see you at the portal."

"Yes, sir."

"Mattan," he prompted. "We're on our way. One shuttle and one skiff."

"We're ready. The seismic activity is increasing exponentially. Hurry."

"Understood. Galadhan?"

"Chief?"

"Keep the channel open. Mattan says things are getting worse. Be careful."

"You too, sir."

Mattan had the right of it. The skiff shook and tilted several times as the ground broke, belching ash and fire into the air. He wove the vehicle to avoid the destruction underneath him. To his left, Galadhan was doing the same with the shuttle.

"Watch it, Chief," his Second said as lava spewed high before them. He veered and glanced over. Galadhan had avoided it too.

The portal was close now. The heaving ground blurred by as they closed the distance. Another vent erupted right in their path, and again, Avadhron steered the skiff around it. A flash burst to his left—the shuttle tumbled and crashed. And exploded.

No! Galadhan!

His Elites cried out as Avadhron gripped the controls, ignoring his shaking, his anger, his loss; he had to get the rest of his people to safety.

Finally, he saw the portal ahead, and aimed for the enormous platform at the entrance. The skiff slid in the worst landing he'd ever made, almost colliding with the door, recently repaired—and now newly destroyed in this cataclysm. Other shuttles and skiffs sat abandoned nearby.

Mattan and Treyor stood inside, wearing their own versions of an enviro-suit.

"Where's the shuttle?" Treyor asked.

"Gone." Avadhron couldn't trust himself to say more. He carried Asila into the structure. The lights were dim; were they saving power for the portal or had the place taken damage? "How many shuttles are still out there?" he asked.

"None, we think. We lost contact. This complex isn't safe. We must go through now."

"What if they're still alive? You'd cut them off?"

"We can maintain power to the portal from the other side. As long as the earthquakes don't wreck the structural integrity too badly, people could still come through." Treyor nodded at the stairs. "Let's go!"

The circular staircase wasn't easy to navigate, especially without adequate light, but he descended as quickly as he could with Asila in his arms. Someone's hand steadied his shoulder the whole way.

Once in front of the portal, Avadhron handed the old woman to Treyor. "Get her across. And my people. I'll stay to the end, in case others are still out there."

Treyor glanced at Mattan but did as he was bid, and Tontinn followed.

"Go," Mattan said, but the Elites didn't move.

"We won't leave until the Chief does." Fadhalan's blue eyes glinted in defiance.

"I see." Mattan crossed his arms, his head tipped, staring at Avadhron.

"You will go," Avadhron snarled at his people. "That's an order."

"No, sir," Fadhalan said, as the Elites all stood shoulder to shoulder. "We are directly disobeying you. Sir. If you Cross now, you can charge us."

"And if I don't, you stay here and die with me."

"Yes, sir."

He glared at Fadhalan's team, Elite One. They all knew him well, and he, them: Petill, slender but deadly, her chin set, showing her determination. Merdhil, his brown eyes challenging. Emadhrel, Dach'alan, Jhuliss—all unmoving.

Don't they understand? How do I Cross without her? How do I live without her?

Rumbling shook the structure, rocking everyone almost off their feet. Along one wall, a crack appeared, spreading upward.

"Go!" Avadhron yelled, pulling on Merdhil's and Emadhrel's shoulders. "Get out of here!"

His Elites all regained their footing and stood, unmoving. Their eyes hard, lips set into thin lines.

Idiots!

"Would she want you to die here?" Mattan asked, his voice soft.

"Would Galadhan?"

Avadhron clenched his jaw, anger rising like bile in his gut. He looked around the dim chamber, on his world, not of it, but still being destroyed by it. *I wish I could have at least said goodbye to her!* Swallowing a sob, he whirled and stepped through the portal.

Chapter Twenty

Avadhron struggled up from blackness. The acrid tang of smoke assaulted his senses along with the crackling sound of fire. His lids were crusted shut; he tried to blink, rubbing his eyes—and remembered. The shock, the loss, cascaded over him. Jhendill's face, pale and lifeless, Galadhan's shuttle tumbling and exploding, his father's body, his Elites daring him, willing to die with him if he would not Cross.

What happened then—after passing through? Rage had taken him over, and many arms held him as he tried to lunge back through the portal. Beyond that, he had no recollection until this moment.

He didn't want memories. Or life. Why wouldn't they let him go back? What did he have here without Jhendill? He rolled onto his side, squeezing his eyes shut. The grief hurt too much to even allow tears. Jhendill's face, the curve of her eyebrows, her intelligent brown eyes filled with humor or sarcasm, the angle of her cheekbones, the feel of her hands at the nape of his neck, threading through his hair—he would never again see her, touch her, hear her voice...

How was he to go on living without her?

A warm weight settled on his shoulder. "Avadhron?" Zaidhron whispered. "I'm so sorry."

Part of him wanted to give in to the grief and cry; part wanted to flip over and slam his fist into—*king!* Zaidhron was now king. Duty won control. He twisted and sat up to find he rested on the floor, on a thick mat of sorts. He came forward onto one knee and took his cousin's hand, setting his forehead against it. "I swear fealty, my liege." It wasn't formal, but would do until an official ceremony. He gazed up at his new liege's face. "I'm sorry. Your brother is dead."

"I...know. How did it happen?"

Avadhron related the scene, and his deductions. Zaidhron puffed a breath out, tears in his eyes. Finally he whispered, "He didn't want to Cross. He got his desire."

The affection Zaidhron had for his older half-brother and their complicated relationship mystified him. But now, at least, perhaps their people could be led forward into a new life by a good man.

Which launched another question: the First Table. Fadhalan had gotten them across, but he knew no details. Had any been injured in the cataclysm? "What about our close kin? Dandhral? Cosdhral? Their families? Are they well?"

"They're fine." Zaidhron smiled and gestured for him to rise. "Let's get you some food. We have much to do."

Avadhron peered about the dim chamber, noticing it for the first time. The shimmering white walls, obviously, were SDC-12. One end had a box-like structure built into the wall containing a softly crackling fire. Thick mats on a wooden frame sat opposite with a table covered with papers and two lit candles shoved against the window, probably to make room for Avadhron's sleeping mat.

"Do you like it? It's very basic. This is the only building finished so far."

From the window, which radiated chillness, a swirling whiteness beat against the glass, obscuring his sight, and beyond, all was dark. Nighttime then. He tentatively touched a finger to the clear, icy pane. "Not glass?"

"A thin extrusion of SDC-12. Our glass-blowers can't make anything this fine yet."

"And that...is snow?"

"It's a blizzard." He swung a small pot suspended on a metal rod away from the flame. "The snow is between hip- and shoulder-high outside, and even higher, with drifts. We're straining to find places for everyone, provide food...once we go out that door, there's nothing but total chaos." He picked up a large, earthen cup from the ledge atop the fire-box and dipped it in the pot. "We don't really cook in our chambers, but with the weather so bitterly cold, it's nice to have something to help take away the chill."

He handed the cup, still dripping, to Avadhron. "Enjoy. One of the few privileges accorded to the—to the king."

His cousin stumbled over the title. Avadhron ignored it. "Few privileges? I don't understand." He sipped the drink. It wasn't tea, it was broth. Very tasty. His stomach seemed to wake up and want food.

"This chamber. Privacy." Zaidhron shook his head. "How your evac teams did what you did until the very end..." He picked up a small round of bread, not as big as his hand, and ripped it in two, then offered half to Avadhron, staring expectantly.

Obediently, he took the food from his king's hand and bit into it, listening as his cousin continued.

"This building wasn't meant to house more than a few hundred. Your teams brought over thousands. We couldn't keep count, shuttle after shuttle plus the skiffs dropping off people. We just kept pulling them through. Some were brought here at first then we had to leave the rest in the Portal Complex. The Elders opened up dark, empty sections. They have heat, light, and water, but we haven't enough mats, blankets, food..."

Avadhron stopped chewing. "How many? How many did we save?"

"As I said, we couldn't count. Thousands. Between six and eight at least." Zaidhron bit into his half of the small loaf.

He did the math in his head. "Assuming all the shuttles and skiffs loaded and unloaded quickly, plus time to the portal and back—no..." He frowned, numbers forgotten, remembering his Second's shuttle exploding. "Some were lost." *Galadhan. You never saw this world. You were to be married here.* The ache in his heart spread deeper; Jhendill would never now see the stars, eat a meal with him, start a family...

He set the cup and bread on the ledge above the fire-box. "Let's get to work."

The king shook his head. "You finish that food. It will be long before we eat again. And this is the last of the yeast bread during the crisis."

Dutifully, he swallowed the bit of bread, and chased it with the broth.

Zaidhron opened the door.

Avadhron halted, shocked. The wide hallway was jammed with people, the air heavy with the smells of too many in too small a space. They huddled, some sharing blankets. Others had nothing. Most slept, but a few wept quietly or stared ahead with blank expressions. Some looked up at them, lost, as they picked their way across the passage to the landing of a broad stairway. Hands reached out, grasping at Zaidhron's robe, or Avadhron's trous.

"We're doing what we can. We'll bring food to you as fast as possible," Zaidhron murmured, then shook his head at Avadhron. "This breaks my heart. So many Refugees, so little provender. It was so sudden, and in this storm we can't even send for help from the other encampments."

People slept on the steps as well, curled into themselves, leaving little room to pass. The odors of too many bodies again pressed on him, but so did the more pleasant smells of food. His stomach rumbled.

On the lower flight of stairs, the wall to the right gave way to a railing, and a huge chamber came into view. Avadhron slowed, his hands sliding on the banister as he descended, taking in the sight. "This room is large enough to act as a bay to several shuttles!"

"We call it the Great Hall. The entire camp can have meals here. We also use it for meetings, assemblies, dances, almost all gatherings, especially in the winter."

Two enormous fire-boxes stood at each end of the chamber. Six huge square columns in three rows of two divided the place into four large sections. At the base of each was another fire-box, open on each side. All were ablaze, the only light in the place.

"It's so dark, though."

"It's night outside. We have about three hours before day's thirteen. Although that's a misnomer, really, as it is dark more than thirteen hours during the winter, but that's how people began referring—"

"These...fire-boxes," Avadhron interrupted, to keep his cousin from expounding on his digression, "do they heat the chamber well?"

"Fireplaces. The ones in the center are open hearths. The whole building has radiant heat, but in the cold weather, it doesn't do the job, especially in the Great Hall." Zaidhron flashed a smile. "Besides, it seems we Teldheri enjoy the comfort of a fire."

"Are we still Teldheri—now?"

Zaidhron shrugged. "Teledhar is all we know of our past, of who we are. 'Teldheri' is our identity."

He acceded this point with a slight bow of his head and returned his gaze to the Great Hall. Tables had been taken apart and stacked against the outside wall. People, it seemed, were stacked too, crowded together, sleeping, or just laying still. A baby squalled in a thin, piteous voice. Another joined in, then more, climbing into a chorus of wailing.

Avadhron turned to his cousin. "Parents passed children forward, to go before they did. How many orphans do we have?"

"Too many. We're giving quite a few of our people purpose by having them care for the babies and little ones. We can't even begin to reconnect families yet. We're merely trying to keep them alive."

Another thought hit him. "The old woman. Asila. Where is she?"

"Ah, our honored, newly adopted family member. Just the sort of stunt you'd pull. She's being tended. Your Elites told the story and personally took charge of their new 'cousin.'" Zaidhron tilted his head. "How would you know she wasn't clanless because she was a criminal outcast?"

"I didn't know. I didn't care."

The king gave Avadhron a sad smile. "You never have concerned yourself with clan differences."

Reminded of Jhendill, he clenched his jaw. After a moment, he cleared his throat. "There's work to be done, you said. Let's get to it."

Zaidhron inclined his head and, at the bottom of the stairs, turned left into a hallway, also filled with Refugees. "Our kitchens," he murmured over his shoulder. "The most important thing we can do now is try to provide food."

"If the encampment is normally only several hundred, how will you feed thousands?"

His cousin spun to face him with an anguished expression, grabbed Avadhron's sleeve, and leaned close. His eyes darted to the nearby Refugees. "I don't know," he whispered.

Chapter Twenty-One

Zaidhron straightened abruptly and spun around, continuing into the kitchen.

The heat in the large room was almost stifling. Men and women stood at tables in the center doing various tasks, chopping, peeling, mixing. Along the outside walls were...counters? No, workers stirred bubbling pots, and a man wielding a long metal rod opened a door beneath one of them and poked at the fire. This world's version of induction hobs.

"Shifts of people are cooking around the clock. I don't know how many meals we can get to the Refugees each day, perhaps only one. We've assigned section leaders to try to keep track of what's been distributed where. It's easier here than in the Portal Complex. Mattan's whole team is there, coordinating—"

"But the food. You said you didn't have enough."

"We're using our winter's store. We'll make do somehow. When the weather breaks, we can get help." Zaidhron peered at a smooth, black board hung by the right side the door with writing on it.

Avadhron touched the surface and asked, "Slate?"

"Yes. As we take meals to each section, we mark it off."

"We?" The king himself was doing menial tasks? Dome above, the man needed to concentrate on finding solutions! Altruism and servanthood could be taken too far.

"Yes." Zaidhron smiled slightly, tiredly. "But for now, I'm bringing you to a conference to discuss how we might bring in food and supplies."

His lips thinned, Avadhron regarded his cousin. He looked more careworn and drawn than usual, with dark circles under his eyes. "When is the last time you slept?"

"I...can't remember."

"You need to sleep."

"There's too much to do."

"Take me to this conference. Then you are going to rest. Where is Mariss?"

"Threatening me, are you?"

"She is the one person to whom the king answers. Where is she?"

"In the Complex, helping in the infirmary."

Of course, with her medical background, where else would she be? "Good. After the conference, you will sleep while I carry out your orders, or I'll talk to Mariss."

Zaidhron frowned, averting his eyes. "Come," he said, his voice choked.

Leaving the hot kitchen, they continued down the hallway away from the stairs and Great Hall, picking their way around bodies. A small room on the left side had a fireplace and many sleeping Refugees. From further down on the right came the clatter of dishes and banging of pots. A peek inside revealed people leaning over huge washtubs, industriously scrubbing.

At the end of the corridor to their left, along the left wall, was an embrasure enclosing a door, not wooden but made of SDC-12. The king placed his hand on the scanner and the door slid aside to reveal an antechamber housing a lift—a small one, not the large supply lift used when bringing the settlers over.

"Was this lift just built?"

"It was repaired recently, and this building erected over it intentionally, not only for protection to the entrance, but to allow direct access to the Complex."

Zaidhron set his hand against a second scanner, opening the door. "And as you can see, we do restrict entry. Your biometrics have been added, by the way."

They entered the small, circular chamber, and his cousin explained that the controls were in Enai and used a holographic display. The interface could be changed to show different sets of buttons for various areas of the complex.

How large was the blasted facility?

"This one"—Zaidhron indicated with a finger—"is for the main conference level." The lift descended, traveled sideways, then rose again. The door opened, and he followed his king again, threading through Refugees crowded in the corridors.

They came to a door whose frame was lit in a blue glow, similar to that emitting from the edges of the portal when active. After his cousin palmed the square space below a control panel, they passed into an antechamber. Strained voices could be heard from the inner room. As they entered, the Enaisi named Lennai was speaking.

"—do not have enough food supplies. We have saved all these people to watch them starve."

"That is not acceptable," Tarnill said.

"I agree," Zaidhron replied.

Everyone turned. Dandhral, Cosdhral, and Tarnill crowded around a six-sided table with Mattan, Treyor, Lennai, and Ismari. The Teldheri all bowed.

"You have started this meeting without the king?" Avadhron glared at his kin.

Her eyes flashed. "Do you question your king's daughter and heir to the throne?"

"You are not yet of Age to be Confirmed as heir. And yes, I do."

Zaidhron lifted a hand. "It is all right, cousin."

"Do leave off," Cosdhral moaned. "Mattan could sense you two approaching, so Tarnill called the meeting to order."

Avadhron turned to Mattan. "You sensed? You claim you can detect others' emotions, but you are also able to tell proximity?"

"Emotions are stronger when a person is close at hand. And your personality is extremely easy to sense, Security Chief."

"His title is now commander," Zaidhron said. "Or prince, since he has heirship until Tarnill is of Age and Confirmed. But I doubt he will allow that title used."

The reality of that fact sank through Avadhron, chilling him as he met his king's sad smile.

"My apologies." Mattan bowed. "Commander."

He searched the Enaisi's expression and posture for the least fleck of humor or sarcasm, but found none. One day he would find an excuse to drive his fist into that alien's face. He focused his attention on Cosdhral, inhaling deeply as he returned to the interrupted topic. "How long have *you* known about their empathy?"

"For some time," his cousin replied. "I couldn't say exactly. Why?"

Avadhron snorted, but didn't answer. Right now he needed concentrate on their problem. He straightened and stepped to the table. "How are we going to feed and clothe all these people?"

The Enaisi must stand to discuss matters as there were no chairs in the room. Meetings would probably be much shorter that way; he did approve of that. The table itself was curiously bare except for a blank indentation in each of the six sides that he would wager was a control board. A slight circular depression graced the center, for a holographic display, perhaps? He let his hand stray over the panel before him, but nothing happened.

"We cannot hunt in this storm," Lennai said, his brows drawn together, "and the snow will be too deep for travel afterwards. How do we feed thousands when we only have enough for a settlement of four or five hundred?"

Mattan placed a hand on Lennai's shoulder. "We have done this much, we will not let anyone starve."

"We also have to think of clothes, shelter. The facilities are beyond capacity for this many," Tarnill said.

"Could we not use the portal to bring food and clothing from your world?" asked Cosdhral.

The Enaisi all hesitated, exchanging glances.

Mattan shook his head. "I have already requested help, and my people are...not willing to do more." He grimaced at Zaidhron and Avadhron. "I have explained briefly to your chiefs that my people are prejudiced and do not wish to have any further contact with your race."

Cosdhral frowned. "Why would deed us this planet then?"

"It was deeded to Mattan by our council elders," Ismari said. "They owed him greatly, and he called in the debt."

"Ismari..." her brother muttered.

"I will say no more, but if you think you can go forward without some knowledge being passed to the Teldheri, then you are a bigger fool than I thought."

Avadhron found no humor at the moment in watching the siblings bicker, and before Mattan could retort, he asked, "What about other planets?"

Everyone turned to gaze at him.

"The portal is able to reach other planets, isn't it? Would there be a way to bring food and supplies here from other worlds?"

The Enaisi all shook their heads.

"Mattan's favor was the last they would allow," Lennai said. "Those of us who have allied with Mattan have had access to the portal restricted to this world only besides our own."

"It would seem your people's politics are as sand-blasted as ours," Avadhron said dryly.

Tarnill shot him a dark look. Did she see no faults in the system? Or did she take his remark as criticism of her father, or perhaps for herself, as future heir to the throne? He made his answering gaze a challenge. *How will you fare when your time comes?*

"We are all but outcasts." Ismari lifted her chin. "But we are proud of it."

Zaidhron smiled sadly. "For our sakes, we thank you for the sacrifice you've all made. We do not take it for granted."

"Our consciences led us, what else could we do?" Treyor asked, a defiant glint in his eyes.

"The question now is, what do *we* do?" Avadhron crossed his arms. "We need food, and clothes, for thousands."

Tarnill sighed. "That is the circular discussion we have been having."

"Once the snow abates, can't we send for help from the other settlements?" Avadhron asked.

"We will, but they cannot do much. They barely have what they need to survive the winter. Even if we strip them of their herds and food stores, it still wouldn't feed everyone."

"Can't we hunt?" Avadhron asked.

"Hunting takes time." Lennai shook his head. "And to hunt enough animals to provide food for all these people daily—"

"Soup," Ismari said. "There's nutrition in broth. It won't work long-term but will keep them from starving for now."

"It will still require an incredible amount of hunting and gathering," Lennai said. "And how do we accomplish that in the middle of a blizzard?"

Chapter Twenty-Two

Mattan inhaled, then let his breath out slowly, fists on hips. "We have no choice but to use the maglevs."

"Do any of them still work?" Treyor asked, his eyes wide.

"Some of the lines are undamaged, to a point. One stretches to Estan and the hub there is intact."

"If the blizzard hasn't hit that area hard, it should be mild enough to gather and hunt," Lennai said. "But we'd need hunting parties. How many do we have?"

"Hunting teams are no problem, but they aren't used to everything winter might throw at them," Treyor said. "Some of us at least should go too. And we can take those who know how to run a base camp. I'll begin a list with that in mind."

"We still have to resolve the question of how to get the food to each person." Mattan rubbed his eyes. "Our current method isn't working."

A picture of dome-disaster assistance crews burst into Avadhron's head. The homeless rescued and given temporary shelter and clothes, serving lines offering meals. He crossed his arms. "There is another problem. What do we do *with* all these people? Once the shock wears off, their grief, anger—all their pain—will issue forth, and for many, in destructive ways. We need to find something to occupy them, give them purpose."

"I take it you have a solution?" Lennai asked.

"I think we can combine both problems into a single solution, or a partial one at least. Do you have any huge rooms in this place, comparable to the Great Hall?"

"Not that big, no," Treyor said. "The biggest are some of the laboratories, but even they're not on that scale."

"What about the cavern chambers? Those are enormous," Ismari murmured. "And expanding into them would give us more room."

The other three Enaisi stopped as if struck. Mattan stared at the table, unmoving, and the others regarded him silently. Finally, in a soft voice, he said, "I think that would be most befitting."

Avadhron looked from brother to sister. "Is this one of those times when we will have to endure not knowing what has you so dismayed?"

"For now. Our concern must be for the living."

Not the dead. Part of the past of which they were ashamed, no doubt.

Another tidbit filed away for later. Mattan was right; they needed to concentrate on the living. His mind strayed to Jhendill—and he snatched his thoughts to *now*. His only reason for staying alive was to serve his people; that must be his only focus and intent. "One answer to two problems: create service lines."

"What do you mean?"

"A rotation system. People line up to receive a meal. Soup or broth, whatever we have to offer. After they eat, they go to given tasks. Cleaning dishes for the next group, caring for children, finding family members, helping clans to reunite, scrubbing the facilities—I would wager that right now the privs are well used and not well cleaned. We have a multitude of chores and duties which may be delegated."

"But—"

"And if we rotate schedules, there will be more room for those sleeping, and only so many to feed per shift."

"That's a staggering undertaking," Dandhral said doubtfully, speaking up for the first time. "To organize thousands..."

"The problem won't go away by ignoring it, or wait for a committee to study it," Avadhron countered. "We have to act now, give our people direction and hope. We must certainly have those here who served in the dome-disaster assistance crews, so we are not lacking in those with experience."

"I agree," Tarnill said. "What do you say, Father?"

Zaidhron leaned on the table, his whole body seemed to sag. "Yes."

"Have you slept yet?" she asked, putting an arm around his waist.

Avadhron used his best Elite Sec voice. "Your Majesty, you must sleep."

The king shook his head. "When we are finished."

"But Father—"

"No. Continue."

Crossing his arms, he glared at his stubborn cousin, but obeyed. "We need a way to correlate data, determine exactly how many people are here and in the Great Hall building, organize them into work groups."

Mattan lifted a hand. "I think we can provide that. Now, we don't know exactly how many survivors we have yet, but we can estimate that on the Great Hall side are between fifteen hundred and two thousand. This side has four to five thousand, at least. Probably more. We need to arrange a system of communication between both sides. Runners to carry messages, others to gather information from people, so we are able to help families reunite, and clans. The thanes can then organize their kin according to abilities, make certain children and babies are cared for.

"I know we have scribing rooms above the Great Hall, however if we do open up the lower levels"—Mattan glanced at his fellow Enaisi—"we will have the capacity for using more modern methods of tracking families, clans, duty rosters, assignments..."

"We need to get started on that immediately," Lennai said. "I'll inform Ashani and Telkai to begin recruiting those who can be runners. Some of the older children would be excellent for that task."

"Good, and I think Dassel and Atesni should head up a search for thanes and those with dome-disaster assistance experience." Mattan gazed about the room. "Am I forgetting anything?"

Everyone exchanged glances with shrugs or shakes of their heads.

Avadhron crossed his arms. "Yes, you are. The chiefs of my people should guide this endeavor."

Mattan's eyebrows lifted, and he smiled. "Putting us in our place?"

"No, putting us in ours. This is to be our world, for our people." He nodded at his cousins. "When Cosdhral and Dandhral are not bickering, they actually make a good team. Dandhral is exemplary at organizing, and Cosdhral at implementation. And they know our clans and ways."

Both men gaped at him. Were they surprised at their cousin's suggestion? Or at his affirmation of their abilities?

"What are your thoughts, Sire?" Avadhron asked.

"Continue, Commander," he murmured.

He inclined his head. "It is their right and duty. And I think having two members of the First Table in charge of this undertaking would benefit my people from a psychological angle."

Lennai frowned. "I thought your people despised their rulers."

"Many of them do," Avadhron said. "But that doesn't mean they don't have an inbred pathology for wanting those rulers to care for them."

Cosdhral barked a laugh, then quickly coughed. "I think you might be right."

Mattan rubbed his chin for a second, a smile spreading. "Dandhral and Cosdhral, would you be willing to coordinate this effort with Dassel and Atesni?"

Dandhral straightened, his eyes lighting up. "Yes. My biggest drawback is a facility with which to assemble and correlate all the data."

"That is no problem," Lennai said. "I'll take you to an office which has computer access. Dassel and Atesni will meet you there, and you can begin the task."

Mattan lifted a hand. "Let us adjourn. We have much to do."

As they all filed out, Zaidhron said, "Stay, Avadhron. I must speak to you."

Tarnill put an arm around her father. "You need to rest."

"This is important." The king stared into Avadhron's eyes. "Cousin, you know I give you my full trust. But I don't want you in the Hall right now."

Avadhron frowned. "My liege?"

"You are...abrasive. You have too little patience for foolishness. And we have literally thousands of people who have no concept of how to live here. They need compassion."

"You think I cannot be circumspect?"

Zaidhron quirked a smile in lieu of an answer. Avadhron clenched his jaw; yes, he was brusque at times, but—

"Also, you need to learn survival yourself. Thuldhan knows this place, how we address situations—"

"Then he needs to tutor me!"

His cousin shook his head. "Learn the wild, Commander, and the ways of this world. Thuldhan can instruct you on procedures once you gain footing in survival—"

"I should learn my office here!"

The king raised his voice, authority ringing as he had rarely heard before. "Learn—to—survive!" He pointed at Avadhron. "I have spoken."

Grinding his teeth, he inclined his head in obeisance. "I still need to talk to him. I am making him my new Second."

"So be it. Talk. Fill in your empty ranks. But when the hunting groups leave, you will be with them."

Avadhron forced himself to bow. "My king."

Chapter Twenty-Three

Thuldhan was the physical opposite of Galadhan. Tall, broad-shouldered, and charismatic where his best friend had been spare, spry, and dry. Zaidhron was correct; he was the right person to lead security at this time, both for his experience and personality. But the decision still rankled.

Avadhron and his Second ascended the stairs, his subordinate finishing a tour as he answered questions on changes in protocol on the new world. One of the chambers on the first floor above ground served as their security headquarters for now. Thuldhan opened the door and bowed his superior in. This room was much bigger than Zaidhron's. Several Secs sat at tables, writing diligently. Shelves along the walls held files and scrolls in crosscut, angular compartments and an archway opening into a larger space beyond lined with similar shelving and racks for storing reports and documents. The writers looked up and, realizing who had entered, stood.

Avadhron gestured for them to resume their work, gazing about in bewilderment. "I will have to defer to you in many things, Thuldhan."

His Second inclined his head. "The scribes are our new computers, Commander. They transcribe and order all documents. If you have questions, they can more than likely provide the answers."

The Secs nodded or murmured assent, then continued their work.

Avadhron gazed around the room. "In that case they are my witnesses. I state for the record that you are my new Second, Thuldhan. And set Fadhalan as the Chief of the Elites. Both will have to be confirmed later by a vote of the First Table, but we haven't time for formalities right now."

Thuldhan blinked, frowning. "But he's not First Table."

"That the Elite leader is of the First Table is tradition, not requirement. He has my trust, and with the decimation of our people, we must look to put the best in charge, even if not the closest kin. Remember that in any position you fill or assignment you designate during my absence."

Thuldhan inclined his head. "Any special orders, sir?"

"No. Carry on as you have been. You have things well in hand. You've had to deal with clashes between the mindset of Teledhar and that of Elyria. The trouble now is being inundated with literally thousands who have no preparation for this world, or the changes needed in both attitude and outlook.

"You do have all the Secs and Elites that came over during the Final

Crossing, which increases your manpower. But be certain they have at least a minimal briefing to understand the methods under which we conduct ourselves and our duties on Elyria. My Elites should, I hope, have a better grasp, due to the training Galadhan and I have—" Avadhron stopped and swallowed to regain his voice. "Tell Fadhalan I trust any rearrangement he feels should be made in the Elite teams because of losses."

Thuldhan bowed. Avadhron clenched his jaw against the emotions raging like a sandstorm. He must change the subject. "I am told because of this crisis, the Enaisi are opening up lower levels and allowing use of their computers. I don't know if that includes security or if it will only be used for clan-mapping and duty rosters."

"Let's go see." Thuldhan smiled. "And I can discover for myself about these newly opened areas."

Avadhron accompanied his Second to the ground floor. Thuldhan gave his commander a more thorough run-down of the control panel in the lift, then said, "Let's find out if this cavern area is already accessible." He pressed a button. "This was nonfunctional before." The lift shot downwards, and his Second smiled. "The Enaisi do work quickly."

"Who of our people has access to these lifts?"

"First Table, and me, as acting head of security." Thuldhan's mouth twisted in a wry smile. "That might have to change with this crisis, enh?"

The door slid open to reveal a wide hallway consisting of rounded walls of smooth, black stone with arches at given distances.

"Looks almost as if someone tunneled through solid rock," Thuldhan whispered.

"Perhaps they did," Avadhron returned quietly, walking over and placing his hand on the nearest impost. "Although these arches appear to be extrusions, like we build with SDC-12. Interesting."

His Second shrugged. "We can ask."

Avadhron snorted.

Light glowed from sconces all along the corridor. People hurried here and there, carrying things, calling orders, asking questions, directing others. A woman in a simple dress with a blanket over her shoulders and clutching a pile of scrolls saw them, walked over, and bowed. "Sirs. The Elders request we stay in lighted areas to reduce the chances of getting lost. If you wish to see the Hub, as they're referring to it, it's this way."

They followed her down the hall, glancing through doors as they passed.

"How big is this place?" Avadhron muttered.

"I have no idea, Commander," Thuldhan answered, "but considering it not only houses the portal but also had various laboratories and living accommodations for all its people, I would say vast."

The woman stopped, pointing to a door. "Here you are, sirs." She bowed again and moved off before they could thank her.

Avadhron and Thuldhan stepped through to see a large room filled with computers and work stations, a place where all the logistics of this undertaking could be coordinated. A hub, as their guide had said. The walls in here were not black but a light grey, but still they looked seamless, as if extruded, not stone set upon stone. Did his people's technology directly evolve from the Enaisi's? It seemed so.

Cosdhral and Dandhral sat at a computer, conferring quietly. Quite a few thanes occupied other computers, some with advisors gathered around them. Other groups huddled, discussing matters in earnest. Several young people stood at the walls, some talking with each other, others looking bored.

"They have wasted no time," Thuldhan murmured.

Treyor straightened from a computer, waving a data-paper, and called, "Runner!"

A stripling strode forward and took it.

"This is to be taken to the hunters. Do you know where they are?"

"Yes, sir. One level below, near the cooking cavern on the east side."

"Good lad. Go!"

The boy ran off. Treyor walked over to where Tarnill, Mattan, Lennai, and Ismari all gathered at a holographic map. Avadhron approached them, Thuldhan following. They turned to nod to the newcomers then returned their attention to the display.

Treyor glowered, crossing his arms. "The staff in charge of the base camps have already departed, along with supplies. The hunting teams have also been assigned. As soon as the hunters have all assembled, we shall be ready to leave."

Mattan nodded. "Excellent." He turned to his sister. "How much can we expect to find growing at this time of year?"

"Some few wild root vegetables and tubers might still be harvestable. Corbita used to grow in abundance in parts of Estan, so we may be fortunate there. But other than that, I am uncertain we will find much more than a few frostberries, which will do no good to the thousands in the Complex and Great Hall."

"I doubt we'll get enough of anything other than meat to feed them. If that." Treyor frowned around the table. Was his brooding because he realized the unlikelihood of providing food to all the Refugees? Avadhron could sympathize. It was a daunting burden.

"Not if we wish to give each person a dish of vegetables, but allowed to simmer in a soup, the nutrients will be beneficial. My biggest concern in gathering is herbs, and in that, even in winter, we'll have plenty." Ismari smiled, dimples flashing in her cheeks. "Trust me, Treyor, we'll succeed."

"You're always so optimistic."

"So are you. Don't disbelieve now. We must keep ourselves positive."

Treyor met her gaze, jaw muscles flexing. "How can you..." He paused then finished, "be so naïve?"

"I'm not. Your speciality is politics. This is mine. Let me worry about plants and cooking."

Mattan waited a moment, eyebrows raised, then said, "I think we have the food gathering sorted, but what about clothes?"

"The hides from the animals, can't they be turned into various garments?" asked Avadhron.

"Yes, boots, jerkins, gloves. Many items are made from hides," Tarnill said.

Lennai shook his head. "But that takes time, and will not be enough for the thousands—"

"It's a start," Ismari said. "And don't forget, hair and wool can be used. But we will need more people than just the ones currently knowledgeable in the craft of spinning thread and weaving."

"That will give some Refugees a trade to learn, keep them busy," Avadhron said. "But at this moment, we need to think of food. How soon do we leave?"

"Quite a few are trained to hunt and gather, even if it's not their primary occupation. There are two main camps. This is the one where you will be going." Treyor's hands flitted over the control console, and the holographic display over the table changed from the logistics lists to a landscape; a largely forested land with some meadows and the sea to the east. The image zoomed closer to a specific area. "That's the Estan rail hub. We'll have people transport the food back, instead of doing it ourselves."

"Are you going to allow the Teldheri access to the controls for the rails?" Lennai asked.

"It's already been done. Some of their rail-tube operators survived. Our system isn't so different, they're both maglevs, ours is just underground." Mattan turned to Avadhron. "I would suggest you go primarily as a hunter and gatherer rather than a campsite worker. You'll partner with some of us to begin with. Perhaps Telkai. He's a good huntsman, and Ismari, as our botanist, can direct you to the correct plants to gather from."

"Do you truly think this is wise?" Tarnill asked. "Another loss at the First Table would be a strong blow to my people."

"She's right," Avadhron said. "Regardless of their personal feelings toward our clan, they need a sense of continuity and security."

"Nothing is guaranteed, but if one of us is with you, you are as safe as possible on this world."

Avadhron huffed a mirthless, ironic laugh that these aliens had to ensure the safety of the Sec commander. "When do we leave?"

"As soon as we can join our hunting parties. Hunger will not wait." Mattan looked around. "Let's get busy."

Chapter Twenty-Four

As the group dispersed, Thuldhan saluted his commander, then bent close to Treyor, pointing to a display and murmuring something.

Mattan beckoned to Avadhron. "Let me show you where you'll be staying while here. We're arranging special accommodations for the hunting parties. Come."

He followed the alien into the hallway and to the lift. After a short drop, they exited to a similar-looking corridor and continued walking. He looked around, craning his neck to stare at the cross vault in an intersection. "It would seem the largest portion of the Complex is below the surface."

"Yes. Our power sources, access to the rails, many long-vacant laboratories." Mattan smiled, but it seemed more sad or nostalgic than happy. "Our peoples both tend to have an inclination for underground or covered places."

"You don't find that on other worlds you've visited?"

"Very few. However, I can't say if your people followed the customs of mine when you were first settled on Teledhar or if it was truly genetic."

"Trying to distance yourself from my race?"

"Not at all. Just stating that, scientifically, I cannot posit it is an inherited trait."

Avadhron sniffed and nodded at the walls. "This looks cut out of rock."

"It is and isn't. It was tunneled then reinforced with synthetic stone. As we come to side passages, stay on the lighted corridors." Mattan pointed to a hallway branching off. "They indicate the areas we are going to use. This place is a maze, and we don't want your people to get lost. And there are places down here that are potentially dangerous, which we have cordoned off."

I'm certain you have—for our 'safety' not your secrets, oh no. "So, what disconcerted you and your team when Ismari first mentioned the cavern chambers?"

Mattan sighed. "You will never stop, will you?"

"No."

The Enaisi stopped and turned to face Avadhron with an anguished expression. "You remember what we told you that day on the mountain?"

"About the prejudice and genocide of your people against mine? Yes."

Mattan bowed his head, fists on his hips. "The huge chambers down here...they were once used to...cage and experiment—" He inhaled and looked up, tears in his eyes. "It caused the war and this planet's being named Our Shame. The horrors—"

Despite his dislike of the man, he felt an aching sympathy with the pain Mattan displayed. He could be faking—Avadhron had seen skilled manipulators put on amazing acts—but somehow he knew the alien was genuinely distressed.

"Now...we have a chance to use those chambers to shelter and feed your people. It seems only appropriate."

Avadhron could find no answer, save a curt nod.

Light streamed out of one doorway, and they entered. The chamber was enormous, at least as large as the Great Hall, and again, pale grey not the black of the corridor. Everyone was busy: scrubbing the floor and walls, carrying in tables, hooking up huge wash basins to the existing plumbing system, and setting up a series of induction hobs and ovens.

"Where did your people get all these appliances and equipment?"

"I told you, this place is vast. We have many kitchens, but they're spread out and small. We're moving everything to these chambers."

"And there's more than one?"

"There are four. And plenty of rooms nearby them for the overflow."

"What about privs? And areas set aside for cleaning—do you have sonic showers or laundering stations?"

"The bathing tubs in your Great Hall won't be enough, of course, so we're opening the hot spring pools for the hunting parties—and perhaps to more of the workers as we draw up a schedule. Even with the pools we don't have adequate facilities for everyone. We have a few sonics in the laboratories, but are looking into setting up more to help with cleaning both people and clothes. The construction of those will take time."

"At least all this preparation and activity is giving my people purpose."

Mattan smiled. "That it is." He lifted a hand as if to clap Avadhron's shoulder, but stopped and instead gestured further down the corridor. "Let's continue on. We have rooms set aside for those who are on the hunting teams as quarters when here, so we will have a guaranteed place to rest uninterrupted."

"Will we be returning here frequently?"

"I'm actually not sure yet. But we want to have lodging available. We will be very uncomfortable in the freezing outdoor temperatures. However often we come back, we'll be cold and exhausted. You've never experienced winter, living in controlled-atmosphere domes. It's going to be...trying." The alien smiled. "But I doubt it will defeat *you*." He nodded toward a door. "There is a bed in here for you, and a place for personal items."

The room had six cots and accompanying small cabinets. Mattan waved his hand inside the doorframe and a light came on. "First choice is yours. We'll be bunking with several of your best hunters. Most are teams of two, but you and I will team with a man named Kental initially."

"You? Not Telkai."

"I thought it better if you were with me, at least at first."

Avadhron didn't care who his partner was, but to be arbitrarily assigned? Through gritted teeth, he asked, "I have no say in this then?"

"I suppose I should have consulted you. My apologies. But I felt that the best protection of the Second at Table was with me."

"You are the best at everything, aren't you?" Avadhron sneered.

Mattan stared upwards with a silent chuckle, but when he answered, his voice and expression seemed bitter. "The best at everything—except wisdom." He brought his gaze back to rest on Avadhron, the sadness in his dark eyes brightening to a challenging smile. "I know being my partner will be a sore trial for you, but I'm sure you'll be able to endure it."

"With or without comment?"

Mattan laughed. "With, of course. And very cutting, I'm certain."

Avadhron turned away from the Enaisi and gazed about the unembellished chamber. It reminded him of the quarters used by the unmarried security guards back home. His mind halted—would he ever be able to call this planet home without Jhendill? Galadhan would have stood at his shoulder, goading him into rallying, or at least into trying. Without his wife and best friend, he merely existed. He took a deep breath.

"Choose a bunk rearward, milord," came a voice from behind him. "Not that it makes much difference, but it's a bit farther from the door if noisy—and nosy—neighbors are filing past."

Avadhron turned to see a small, wiry man with thick, reddish hair and beard and intense blue eyes. He carried a bundle of clothes and wore a long, curved bow on his back, as well as a quiver of arrows.

Despite his burdens, he managed a low bow. "Kental, milord. Of Delangar clan."

Ah, so this man did not know of his new title. Good. He certainly would not share that information. Milord was bad enough. He smiled at the hunter. "'Commander,' please. Although if a wild animal were about to attack, I am certain I would much prefer my name be used—loudly." Avadhron inclined his head. "I am honored to meet one of our best hunters, Kental. I hope you will be able to instruct me."

The redhead blinked, a wry smile spreading over his face. "It seems strange to think the commander of security would look to me for instruction. I will try to do right by you, sir." He bowed again.

Avadhron glanced about the room, and following the hunter's advice, pointed at the back, left corner. "I'll claim that one."

His fellow Teldheri whisked by him and dumped his belongings opposite on the right-side bed.

"Don't get comfortable, Kental," the alien said. "We're leaving soon."

The hunter straightened with a grin. "It will be good to be under the sky again, and in a new place, I'm given to understand. What's it called, Mattan?"

"Estan. Or it was in times past. I'm sure your people will rename it, as is their right and privilege."

"You are as bad as the nobles, with your genteel talk." Kental's smile belied his complaint.

"Plain talk and talent are more important here," Avadhron said. "But don't expect the nobility to give up 'genteel talk.' It just may be the only thing that separates them from those they consider beneath them in a world when all must wear the same woven cloth or leather garments."

"Your talk is at the same time genteel and plain. You are a bridge, sir. And for my part, not that I am anyone in particular, I salute you." Kental came to attention, fist over his heart.

Before Avadhron could reply, Telkai strode in carrying a pile of clothes. He dumped them onto Avadhron's cot. "Here. Donated by your guards. Fortunately, several of them have shoulders broad enough and similar height. The cloak on top is thick and will help keep you warm and dry once we arrive in Estan. Tie the hood tight or you'll freeze off your ears." The alien unslung the pack from his back. "This is yours too."

Avadhron stared at the pile. "Am I discommoding too many of my people with all this borrowing?"

"They are all spares, I assure you. No one is walking about half dressed," Telkai responded sardonically.

Avadhron shot a dark look at the perpetually ill-tempered alien as he began shoving all the welcome donations into his pack.

The dour man smiled at him, but with a contemptible edge. "Your own clothes, especially your jerkin, gloves, and boots might be an advantage. Although I think the cold will convince you otherwise."

Avadhron narrowed his eyes at the sneering Enaisi, but before he could say anything, Kental replied, "Leave him be, Telkai. He'll be fine. He's as tough as SDC-12, this one."

The alien chuckled darkly. "And how do you know? By his vaunted reputation? We'll see if you feel the same way when you have to teach him how to hold a knife or pull back a bowstring."

"Those I have already learned. Do you think I didn't study to prepare for the day I would Cross?"

"Well, you're Mattan's problem, not mine."

Avadhron ignored Telkai as he pulled the cloak over his jerkin. He hoisted the pack and nodded to Mattan. "I'm ready."

"Then let's go."

Chapter Twenty-Five

They walked down several corridors until they came to wide opaque doors. Once through, the air became chilly. They continued on down one corridor then another until the walls gave way, ending at a platform allowing access to the maglevs by means of ramps rising to meet the rails. Lights illuminated the entire boarding area. He peered uncertainly at the guideways disappearing into the darkness ahead. Being underground, and on an unstable world at that, was not a new experience, so why should riding a vehicle through a tunnel cause him consternation?

A railcar waited on the nearest track. The design differed from the ones on Teledhar, in some ways more sleek, yet it had an older, less sophisticated look. Or perhaps merely 'older' was the proper word. This one had been sitting for how many years unused?

"Does it work? And safely?"

Mattan nodded, picking up a pack lying on the floor and the cloak next to it. "We have several in operation. I've ridden them to the few destinations still intact. A small service stop exists in one spot, but there's no way above ground anymore. A few moments farther is the nearest hub, Tinshal, which has access to the surface. After that, just a bit south, is Estan, our destination."

"Why Estan and not Tinshal?"

Mattan shrugged. "I can't say. Treyor made the team assignments. I don't think anyone was given a choice. The base teams have already deployed. I'm not sure of the schedule but some hunting parties might also have left."

"How long will it take to travel there?"

"Less than half an hour, by this world's count. We'll have to get you a new timepiece, although for the most part we figure times of day through the sun. Another thing you must learn." Mattan walked to the entrance of the first railcar. "Let's board. The others should be here shortly."

Avadhron stepped inside. The car smelled of...something very old. Beyond musty, but mixed with a tangy, unpleasant smell that reminded him of cleansing agents. The seats were scraped bare, no cushions or cloth covered the hard surface on which they were to sit. They faced inward, and by their curved shape, had at one time been comfortable. So very different from the utilitarian ones in Teledhar's tube-rails, which crammed in as many people as possible.

He walked farther in, peering closely at the structure. The body shell and windows all seemed intact, but micro-fractures wouldn't be visible to the eye.

"The cloth rotted ages ago, so we removed all the padding." Mattan tossed his pack on the seat nearest the front, then pulled on the cloak. "We have piled blankets up here so we can sit on them, if we wish to cushion our backsides. The rest of the supplies are loaded in the back section. The car has been cleaned, somewhat, although I fear the smell of...ancient days will linger for some time."

"Ancient? How long has it been since these maglevs have been used?"

Mattan hesitated then, with raised eyebrows, replied, "Hours."

Avadhron frowned, and the Enaisi smiled. "Didn't I say the first teams had already left to set up camp?"

"You checked the tracks and the cars for safety?"

"Yes, when I knew your people would be coming here. Just in case they had to be used, we made certain they were in working condition."

"How long before that had they been in operation?"

"Oh, ages ago."

"That's conveniently vague. How long ago?"

Mattan grabbed a blanket and spread it across his seat, taking care to smooth it with his hands. "I can't remember exactly." He sat and peered out the door. "Ah, here come our fellow travelers. Welcome!"

Avadhron glared at the alien as set his pack on the floor. He followed the dark-skinned man's example to create some padding before sitting, filing away the avoidance of eye contact, evasive reply, and rapid change of topic for a future time.

Kental stepped inside and looked around with open fascination. "Hmm, well, I think our railcars were much nicer, don't you, Commander? At least they had sparse cushions, but I dare say these will do the job."

"Less talk and more moving," a loud, deep voice rumbled.

The redhead chuckled and walked past Avadhron and Mattan. Without another word, the hunter grabbed a blanket and folded it as a cushion, as the deep-voiced person strode onto the railcar. He was tall, solidly built, with a large nose, beard, and shaggy hair loosely pulled to the back of his neck with a leather thong.

"A bit bare, isn't it?" he boomed. "But then, we're hunters, aren't we, not pampered nobles."

"Not all nobles are pampered, Gilder. Look at our Security Commander here. Can't call him pampered."

"Yore pardon, milord." Gilder bowed, then scowled at the redhead. "Not sayin' all nobles are pampered, you scrawny reject of a hunter."

"Least I don't thump through the woods scaring away what we're supposed to be hunting."

"You track, I aim. It works."

"I can aim just fine—"

"Please, both of you." Mattan held up both hands. "We have more teams waiting to board."

The redhead settled back against the window with a grin. His large partner passed him, chuckling. He either didn't notice the others were using blankets to pad the seats, or he didn't care. He plopped down unconcernedly with a loud sigh next to Kental.

More people boarded, nodding at each other, and inclining their heads or bowing outright at the noble in their midst. Ismari walked in dimpling at her brother, then her eyes strayed to Avadhron and the smile faded. He gave his best supercilious expression and enjoyed the ensuing frown and toss of the head. Nice to know he could antagonize at least one alien.

"Are we on manual, or is one of your people in charge of operating the tubes, Mattan?" a hunter asked.

"Neither. One of *your* operators is always in the control center, even though we have basically one line in use, and there's little to it." The alien glanced about with a smile. "Since we are all here, shall we?"

"By all means, Elder. Let's not waste time!" Gilder slapped a knee.

Chortling a bit, Mattan leaned forward to touch a panel. "We're ready, Laninn. Everyone's here, and the supplies are loaded."

"Yes, sir. Off you go, sir," a woman's voice filtered over the comm system.

A front lamp came on, and the railcar lifted with the same telltale feel as the ones back on Teledhar. It began to move and picked up speed, racing underground into barely illuminated darkness. Not that one could see out the windows anyway with internal lights.

The similar sensations—the vibrations, the sounds of both the creaking of the body shell and the wind rushing past—were slightly soothing.

"Almost like back home," someone murmured.

"This is home now," Gilder replied.

Gradually, Avadhron felt the car banking, slowly changing direction. He tried to picture where they might be in relation to the holo-map he'd seen. "You said Estan was southeast?"

"Yes. This curve you feel takes us east to the Tinshal hub. We'll then wait for the guideway to realign so we can go south."

"Didn' think we'd have anything like this here. Been used to walking everywhere," Gilder muttered with a chuckle.

"Our old systems weren't supposed to be used," Ismari said. "But we can't let thousands of people starve. Even so, you hunters will have to work ceaselessly until this crisis is past."

"How long do you think that will be?" Kental asked.

"At best estimates, we have between six and eight thousand Refugees to feed, clothe, and teach to survive. If the weather were pleasant, the task would still be incredibly difficult."

"This might be a boon, in a way," Avadhron said. "Imagine, once the Refugees became accustomed to being out-dome, how many could wander off, not realizing or believing the dangers. We may save more because of the winter cold than we would have otherwise."

"Might be something to that, sir," Gilder said. "Even those with training don't always understand why we have the rules we do, or take 'em seriously." He rolled up his left sleeve to show still-red scars. "Got my arm mauled by a ballan. Would have been killed if this stunted whelp"—he dug his elbow at Kental—"hadna been there."

"It was a mess. I couldn't believe they saved his arm. Surprising, it was."

"A bit of good fortune, and good nursing." The large hunter beamed at Ismari.

She smiled at him, but flicked her gaze to her brother. Mattan's expression revealed little, but Avadhron would swear he was not pleased. What was this undercurrent between the siblings? Blast, but he was going to wring all the secrets out of that alien. And soon!

The car slowed, and Mattan said, "Ah! We're at the hub. The guideway will pivot and realign to head south. From here it's only a few minutes."

An increasing vibration brought a frown to Mattan's face. "The turntables for the guideways are one of the weaknesses of this system. Moving parts give out more readily. When this crisis is past, we must see to their maintenance."

"Shouldn't you have done that already?"

"To guarantee they work, yes. To get them in prime condition, no."

"What if they quit working while we still need them?" a woman asked, leaning forward.

"And are you going to ensure these tubes continue to function indefinitely, past this crisis?" Avadhron asked.

"Between your people and mine, we could repair the turntables if needed, Adara." Mattan turned his attention to Avadhron. "And I think it's wise to maintain these rails in case of future emergencies. Your king thinks so as well."

The vibration ceased, and again the railcar lifted and hurtled forward.

"Gather your gear, we shall disembark as soon as we have stopped."

The car lowered upon arrival, and Avadhron stood along with

everyone else, slinging on his pack. The door slid open and the cold hit him, making his shoulders hunch involuntarily. His breath burst out in a shocked exhalation that was almost a whistle, and a mist puffed from his mouth. He blinked. More vapor blew out in a mirthless laugh as he considered Telkai's suggestion that he might not be tough enough for this climate.

Chapter Twenty-Six

Everyone crowded out onto the platform. He didn't think the cloak he wore would help much against this freezing weather. Never mind. He would have to make do. These people all were, so it was possible.

Avadhron frowned at the polished, black stone, which ended abruptly where the ramp stretched upward toward the light, changing to pale grey walls up the sides of the incline. Were the different colors indicating levels, usage, varying times of construction, or did they signify something else?

"Everyone grab something to take up," Ismari called, pointing to the back of the vehicle. The rear door was already open, and folks swarmed around it to help get the rest of the supplies to the surface.

Avadhron flexed his fingers in his gloves as he waited for a turn, then chose a wooden crate. He hefted it and walked up the ramp—or tried to. He slipped several times but finally made it to the top and into the ruins of a building. The roof was gone, and the walls, once a pale grey, were now streaked and stained. Vines grew over crumbled stone. The ground and dead grass were partially hidden by frosty clumps, and a white powder generously dusted everything, but a path had been cleared and, as evidenced by swaths of striations, raked smooth.

All around, trees reached bare arms up toward a drear, overcast sky, and soft, white flakes fell.

Campsite workers shouted directions to the newcomers as to where to deposit the supplies. Avadhron followed the gesture of a worker pointing left. Crates of various sizes had been stored along a broken wall. He set his offering with the others and straightened, eyeing the snow. He removed a glove and scooped up a handful, marveling at its icy beauty and at the speed in which the cold stung his skin. The shimmering quality of it reminded him of SDC-12. He shook off the melting particles and gazed at his now red, throbbing fingers. He wiped his hand on his trous and pulled the glove back on.

He helped finish bringing up the supplies, then stood, watching workers bustle about. Everyone had a purpose and knew what to do. Except him. How could he help when he had no idea where to begin? He wandered past more bits of wall and fallen stone, taking in the site. A large shelter had been erected, similar to the one at the original Plains Encampment. Smoke rose from several cylindrical pipes standing tall above it. Smaller shelters fanned out symmetrically from the central one, each with its own smoking pipe. Many fires dotted the camp, some with a pot hung over them, and atop a fire pit, a beast turned on a spit, as he had seen the summer before.

Two men hurried along, poles across their shoulders, buckets hanging from each end. Another worker rushed in the other direction also carrying the same strange contraption. As he passed, he panted, "One more trip should do for now. See if Darbel needs help."

He stared up at the beautiful, endless sky, loss, helplessness, and anger warring in him. Why had they insisted he come? At least at the Great Hall he could be of some use, helping his people and diverting his mind from Jhendill and Galadhan.

"Avadhron."

He didn't turn at Mattan's voice. Boots crunched behind him, then the alien said softly, "I, along with Kental, am going to personally teach you survival and the basics of hunting. I'm certain it won't take you long."

"Why did you want me here? I know it was you who suggested it to Zaidhron. Had to be." Avadhron turned, staring into the Enaisi's dark brown eyes intently, wishing he could see the man's soul. "Why? You'll be taking time away from real hunting to teach me. I'm useless here."

"You need to learn. Fast. And...I am ready to tell you a few more things."

Avadhron inhaled sharply. Mattan held a hand up and continued, "Let's get your gear stowed in our shelter then eat. We'll have several hours to hunt.."

The alien pointed across the camp. "That's ours, the one just to the right of the Gathering Tent."

"'Gathering *Tent*?'"

Mattan chuckled. "After complaints that the shelters were no better than tents during some bad summer thunderstorms, it's what we've ended up calling them. The main tent is, of course, where we all gather."

The entrance of their shelter had a flap overlaying it. As additional protection and insulation from the cold? The alien lifted the flap aside and slid the door open. The walls seemed solid enough to keep out the winter wind and snow, but he doubted they would stop the chill. The answer to that problem sat in the middle of the room: a small black box with a pipe leading through the roof radiated heat.

A thick matting covered the ground, and bundles of heavy fabric were rolled up along each side by the outer wall. Packs and sundry had already been deposited.

"It looks like our hunting companions have been here. We'll be three teams per tent, similar to our rooms in the Portal Complex. Although as I said, at first you and I will be with Kental. Ismari wants to keep Gilder around the camp for the one day at least, just to see how well he's healed. Then she'll decide if he's ready for a full day's work." Mattan dropped his belongings near the rolls to the left, and Avadhron did likewise. "Now, let's eat."

Feeling like a lost child, he continued to follow the alien. They ladled soup into bowls from a pot simmering over a fire, took them to the Gathering Tent, and sat at a long table with the other hunters.

After one scalding sip off his spoon, he blew on the soup to cool it while listening to the banter. Various accents indicated a wide variety of clan affiliations; these men had forged strong bonds across lines of clan and status. Jhendill would have loved to see it.

Sorrow and anger threatened his stoic façade. He clenched a fist in his lap and stared at nothing, willing away his emotions. He wasn't alone in grief; not one person could have escaped having friends or family die in that final catastrophe. He must continue on.

A cup was set in front of him. He glanced up to see Ismari's golden eyes as she leaned across the table. "It's tea, and it's hot. Be careful."

Soft words? A kind look? Had she sensed his feelings? Ire rose afresh; he needed no sympathy. Pressing his lips together, he offered a curt nod of thanks and turned slightly to his right as if paying attention to Gilder and Kental interrupting each other while trying to tell a story.

Kental squatted down just outside the camp, pointing at small marks in the snow. Avadhron joined him, pushing back on the bow set over his shoulder; it would take time to become accustomed to the feel of this new weapon, and the quiver as well. The knife at his thigh was a bit more comfortable as it took the place of his half-staff. He didn't think he'd ever get used to being cold though. His nose felt numb, and his fingers despite the gloves.

Mattan stood behind them, adjusting the straps over his shoulders attached to a wooden frame called a sledge. This contrivance had no wheels, but dragged on the ground. Their game would be lashed to it to make hauling back to camp less of a burden.

"See those, Commander? Bird tracks. There are several kinds here. Those little'uns, those are some type or other of bird family we started calling dustbirds, there's dozens of varieties and we haven't learnt 'em all. The tracks are in pairs. These birds hop. And see how three toes are forward and one is back? That backward one is the hallux. Now, with the other two, they're almost the same, but this here has—"

"Kental, I know you are our most learned tracker," Mattan said, sliding his fingers under the straps again, "but I fear you'll overwhelm the commander with your knowledge. We need to track what we can eat. We have thousands to feed."

The redhead stood, his knees cracking loudly. "Right you are, sir! Sorry. I get"—he grinned—"sidetracked."

The Enaisi groaned, and Kental winked. "Let's find some meat, Commander."

With a nod to their left, the alien said, "I think there are some pindouru this way."

"More of your Elder tellings?" the hunter asked.

Hesitating, Mattan's gaze flicked to Avadhron. "No."

"Tellings?"

"They can sense not only where people are, but animals too," Kental said with a hint of pride.

Avadhron's eyebrows raised.

Mattan assayed a crooked smile. "One of the things I was going to explain."

"One of many?" he asked, flatly, locking eyes with the alien.

In the silence, the hunter cleared his throat. "I can't do tellings," he said softly, "but I think I shouldn't be here."

The Enaisi lifted a hand. "No. Avadhron and I will have a long talk later. Now we need to hunt."

The mix of humor and horror in Kental's expression spoke volumes. He seemed to be able to track not only animals but undercurrents of conversation. He whistled through his teeth, then asked, "So how far are the pindouru?"

"You tell me, Tracker. I didn't have to sense to know where to find them. Let's see how you do."

The hunter's eyes narrowed, but a slow smile spread. "All right, Elder. I'll take the wager." He scrunched his nose, peering about, and wandered between trees.

With a jerk of his head, Mattan signed they should follow their tracker. "This region is heavily wooded, and has some wildlife Kental is unfamiliar with. I wasn't jesting when I said I wish to see how he does."

The hunter studied the area, at times squatting down to peer at the ground, or leaning over to look at the bare branches of bushes, or the boles of trees. Avadhron watched, trying to ignore the ice needling through his skin, settling into his bones. He fought the urge to sniff from his seemingly frozen nose.

At length, Kental turned back to them, cocking his head. "The bark of many trees looks nibbled off, and the twigs off the scrub. What caused this?"

Mattan grimaced. "The natural predators of these unprovocative animals died out. The ka'gua only abide in rocky areas, and the ballan and other aggressive creatures aren't enough to keep up with the rapid breeding and subsequent overpopulation of the pindouru. And, unfortunately, they eat only a certain vegetation, which is found specifically in this region, so they haven't migrated as some others have done."

"So in the winter they get so hungry they gnaw the bark off trees?"

"Yes, off the busai trees, anyway. And worse, it's often not enough."

The hunter rubbed under his nose with a gloved finger, squinting. "Starving they are, you mean? And I thought our 'worse' was it being the wrong time of year to hunt."

Mattan hesitated. "Try to aim for the males. The females are near to dropping their young, or just have."

"That I know. With so little food, how many mothers and babies will die?" Kental asked.

"Too many."

Scratching his cheek, the redhead stared off into the woods. "Poor critters. Seems to me...this planet needed people, just like we needed a planet." He turned to stare at Avadhron. "Caretakers, Commander. That's what we need be for this world."

He just nodded, trying not to shiver too overtly. But he filed away the suggestion; the hunter was right.

Kental's introspection ended as he flashed a grin. "And as far as tracking goes, I know where we can find a large group of those pindouru." He pointed at the trampled ground, packed snow mixed with scat. "Tracks as could be seen by a blind man." He leaned close to Avadhron and whispered loudly, "Didn't have to look a moment to see that. Was the t'other thing that had me puzzled."

An edge of a smile touched Mattan's lips as they followed the path to their quarry. In an undertone he said, "A group of pindouru is called a pounce, by the way."

"Is it? Hm." Kental's nose scrunched up. "A pounce. So...do they?"

"What?"

"Pounce."

"They leap a bit when they run. I don't know how that name came about. If anyone knows, Lennai might."

"Huh." The hunter nodded and said over his shoulder in a hushed voice, "This way, Commander. We must come 'round so as to be downwind, or they'll smell us. And we try to go softly. Easier on packed snow than in autumn leaves, for sure."

Their boots did crunch, and Avadhron tried to set his feet down as carefully as possible to avoid noise. Before long, their tracker threw up a hand, stopping their progress, then pointed. Some distance away, beyond a thick sentinel of trees, he could see brown motion amid grey trunks.

Kental took off his bow, with a nod to Avadhron to follow suit. "Ever killed before, Commander?"

"Only men."

The hunter stopped, then with a hesitant smile, said, "Then perhaps this won't be so hard on you, the first time."

"Not necessarily."

Kental's eyebrows lifted, but he made no comment.

Mattan gestured toward the pindouru. "The taller ones with wider shoulders? Those are the males. The females are less likely to sit upright while carrying their young, which also gives an indication of which ones to aim for."

"And where do I aim? I would think the head, to kill quickly and leave the hide undamaged."

"If you're accurate enough, yes." the hunter eyed Avadhron. "Your pardon, but you're not used to the cold, and the way you're shaking, you'd best aim for the widest part of the body."

"Then point out a large target."

Kental tipped his head, grinning. "Lots of spice in you, isn't there? All right, then, Commander. Bow ready. We'll take two down together. There's not much breeze to account for."

Avadhron removed the heavy glove and flexed his hand in the fingerless hunter glove. He drew an arrow from his quiver. Despite all his practice, he felt fumbled fingered, but then, his hands were chilled and partly numb. He took aim, pushing aside the thought of the death of this animal, only the need of his people.

"Now!" Kental hissed.

Avadhron sighted the animal over his fist, let the string slide off the tips of his fingers as he had done in many practices. The arrow flew—but merely grazed the animal's back. The creature stood, frozen, not running as it should, as all its pounce were. In a swift, practiced motion, Kental drew a second arrow, nocked, and loosed it, hitting the pindouru squarely. It fell.

"You held it, didn't you, Elder?" the hunter asked softly.

"Yes." Mattan's voice was a whisper, and he was pale under his dark skin. The alien managed a wan smile and nodded that they should continue. Now didn't seem the time to ask questions though. They quickly loaded the animal on the sledge and returned to the task of tracking, following the blood spoors, since Kental's first target had run off wounded.

The creature hadn't gone far. They found it on its side, eyes wide and staring, short puffs of mist blowing from its nostrils, its sides heaving. The hunter squatted and, with a practiced motion, slit the throat neatly.

Once the second pindouru was lashed to the sledge, Avadhron stooped and picked up the straps. Neither man said a word as he followed them, dragging their food back to camp.

Chapter Twenty-Seven

Before Avadhron could even drop the straps of the sledge, workers swarmed to remove the carcasses. Kental called to one, "How many is this for the day so far?"

The man scowled. "Not sure. Ask Darbel." He grunted as he helped hoist the animal and carry it to the hanging area to bleed out.

"We should go out again," Kental said. "This is your first day here, and in the cold. Do you wish to stay and rest, Commander?"

"I wish to help feed my people. Lead the way." He shrugged on the straps before Mattan could grab them and followed the tracker back into the woods.

It was dusk as they returned from their third foray, so the trio remained in camp. Kental helped peel hides. Since keeping the animal skins intact was of high importance, it was determined Avadhron should learn that task after the Refugee emergency was over.

A stripling led him to a log by one of the fires. He welcomed the heat and felt somewhat thawed, although his backside remained icy from the cold wood. The lad sat next to him to teach him how to split bone to extract the marrow, which he was informed was highly nutritious. He was then shown how to rough-shape the split bone into an awl by holding it against a rock and using a small stone as a hammer. After splintering and snapping a few, he learned how to support the bone on the rock as he carefully crushed the edge little by little. A pile of rough awls grew to his left until the youngster returned and began polishing them into a finished product.

The boy didn't talk, leaving Avadhron to his own thoughts. Despite his efforts to keep his focus on the activity around him, his mind wandered to Jhendill, her expression when he found her, then shaking that off, wondering what it would have been like to hunt and sit by the fire with Galadhan. Rulinn! He had forgotten about his Second's fiancée. Had she gotten across? Was she here, had she been told? He mentally shook himself, but the circle repeated again and again: his wife's face, Galadhan's shuttle exploding. He blinked at the piece of bone in his hand, feeling suddenly bereft of energy and purpose.

A grunt as someone sat down on his right.

"So Commander," Kental clasped a handful of bones. "You learn quick."

"My duty is to my people. I must learn quickly in order to preserve them."

"You talk as if it is all on your shoulders, sir."

"I feel it is."

Kental didn't comment, just began working on his own project. His bones were larger and had been broken at an angle. The tracker used a small, sharp-edged stone as a file to create serrations on the open end of the bone. "These are called fleshers. They strip the fatty tissue from the hide. We need lots more of 'em now. We're not trying to dry the hides here though. Too many and we've not got the salt. We send 'em back by the railcars. The Elders say they can dry 'em more quickly by a method in the Portal Complex." He glanced up with a quick smile. "They'll make nice warm sleeping furs for our people."

Others gathered around the fires, still doing chores, fashioning tools of various bones, using a shaped stone tool to grind something in bowls, and other tasks foreign to Avadhron's knowledge. Cooking smells wafted through the air, and his empty stomach reminded him he was alive. The guilt he felt for surviving wasn't meet, but his mind and emotions waged war.

"Evening meal soon," a cheery voice caroled. Laughter and scattered cheering followed. Quiet conversations grew into more inclusive ones as people asked how other groups fared in their work of the day.

"How about you, Kental?" someone called. "How did Lord Avadhron do in the wild?"

"The commander is as tough as SDC-12. He stayed with us the whole time, despite this being his first day and unused to the cold."

"Did he actually make any kills?" another voice asked, with a slight sneer.

Avadhron opened his mouth, but the hunter answered first. "He has good use of a bow. And yes, he slit the throat of several pindouru. He's not—"

With a quick chopping motion, Avadhron stopped Kental's reply and glared at questioner. "I'm right here. Ask *me* how I did."

Before the person could redirect his question, Telkai swaggered up with a sardonic smile. "How did you do?"

"Today I helped to feed my people. Tomorrow I will do the same."

"And no doubt it is your honor and privilege to do so."

Avadhron stood to face the sour Enaisi. "It is. Do you know aught of that, alien?"

In the ensuing silence, the only sounds were from the crackling of the fire. He refused to back down or look away from the sneering man, whose eyes seemed black in the flickering firelight.

"Enough," Mattan ordered.

Telkai dropped his gaze, his jaw clenched, then spun and stomped off.

"It's been a long day, let's not let differences flare, shall we?" Mattan smiled and nodded toward the Gathering Tent. "The evening meal is ready."

Everyone rose, but Avadhron didn't follow the crowd. The Enaisi stayed behind too. "After we eat, I'll explain a few matters."

"I notice you don't say you'll explain 'everything.'"

"I will answer any and all questions you have. You have my word."

"We've never established what that's worth."

"Perhaps tonight we shall."

Avadhron sniffed and strode to Gathering Tent.

Mattan brought two cups over to Avadhron's table. He smiled at the few still sitting nearby. "I need to speak with the commander about a few concerns. Would you mind?"

With almost worshipful looks, the lot of them rose with murmured assent and scattered.

"They will make gods of you 'Elders' yet."

Shaking his head dolefully, the alien sat and pushed a cup across the table. "I honestly wish more of them were like you."

Avadhron snorted. "I doubt that." He straightened, stretching his spine, then wrapped his chilled hands around the warmth of the mug. "So, begin."

Mattan smiled, a bit smugly to Avadhron's mind, and said, "Not only can we sense emotions, but also physical sensations such as hunger and cold and pain."

Physical sensations? Avadhron didn't answer right away. His tangents of thought flew wild, and he blinked. Many questions unfolded. He cleared his throat and asked, "So...you sense what we physically feel? And how often do you trespass on our privacy?"

"We don't, except in emergencies."

"And I'm to take your word on that?"

Mattan leaned forward, his brown eyes intense. "The Rescue is over. We saved as many of your people as we could. You are still vitally necessary, but I will not be conciliatory any longer to gain your cooperation. I have done with it. So take my word or not. We are not voyeurs."

Seething anger warred with a smoldering ember of respect. So this alien did indeed have a backbone? "So then how do you avoid being *voyeurs*?"

"We block. It's like putting up a wall. We cannot selectively choose what to feel. Do you think it enjoyable to be privy to someone else's life—from the inside, so to speak?"

"Is it?"

"If I stopped blocking right now, I'd feel how you are chilled to the bone, your aches and exhaustion, and your grief. Is any of that enjoyable?"

"And how do you know what I feel?"

"How long did you tirelessly strive without rest, getting as many of your people to safety? You only slept a few hours after arriving. You've strained and toiled all day, lifting and dragging carcasses as well as other chores in camp. And your grief, need I sense to understand how deep that is?"

Avadhron didn't answer, couldn't. He stared at the cup cradled between his hands. If he moved, spoke, he would break. He dared not even blink. He hated the pounding of his heart and his ragged breathing, hated that his body gave away his turmoil.

Mattan said nothing. Intelligent alien; if he offered sympathy, Avadhron would likely snap and strike out. He didn't know how much time passed as he labored to regain control. Finally, he was able to inhale deeply, and felt assured he could keep his voice steady. Questions. He needed to ask questions...

"What about these 'tellings' and 'holding' that Kental mentioned?"

"Tellings are just what they call our empathy, our ability to sense."

"And holding?"

"It's a...trick of sorts, related to the empathy. But we don't like to do it. I was, so to speak, linked to the pindouru, to hold it still, and didn't release soon enough as the killing blow struck. I..." His gaze dropped to the table, and he drew his hand across his chest as if in pain, his face distant. "I felt it die."

Now Avadhron stayed silent. Mattan took a long drink and sighed. Leaning close he whispered, "Another thing you should know is that we are able to heal illness and injuries. However doing so drains us, and can even kill us, so we resist its use."

"This is related to the empathy?"

"It is."

He remembered Kental's partner's mauled arm and the look that passed between Mattan and Ismari. "Is that how Gilder was healed?"

"Yes. My sister did it. I was livid at the time, but then, brothers tend to be a bit protective, don't they? She was weak for a few days afterwards." Mattan's eyes glittered as they met Avadhron's. "No one knows this information about us, except Zaidhron—and now you."

"You'd be inundated with requests, and at the risk of your lives."

"Yes."

"And how do you know you can trust me?"

"You have earned my trust, even if you feel the reverse isn't true."

Avadhron snorted. "What else?"

"You know about our past on this planet."

"Our shared past. We were once one race, isn't that right? But your people chose genetic modifications."

"Yes. There were high passions on both sides, and several wars fought. This planet was nearly destroyed. I oversaw the reparation."

"So how long ago did this happen? How long since those tubes saw use?"

"Hundreds of years."

"Are you that old? Is that what they were trying to achieve, longevity?"

"In part, yes. I was a young man during the final war. I thought I could be neutral. I used my studies to hide from taking sides." The Enaisi's voice dropped to a whisper. "Until we lost half a continent."

Chapter Twenty-Eight

Half a continent? Dome above! Avadhron could feel the blood draining from his face.

"I had been off-world, doing research. I returned through the portal to find the planet devastated and deserted. I gained permission to gather a team to try to repair the damage. At the time, everyone was so ashamed, they actually ceded 'deed' of the planet to me, as if that allowed them to pass off their guilt as well."

Mattan paused, tears welled in his eyes. "And guilt they had," he hissed. "The few surviving laboratories and facilities were filled with...I found bodies...from experiments." He stopped and took a breath. "...they were left strapped to tables when those monsters evacuated, crowded in rooms like animals, dissected and tossed aside. And I...I chose *neutrality*." He spat the word out.

Now Avadhron understood. *Your altruism cloaks your desire for expiation?* he had asked Mattan on the mountain that first time here. He had truly hit the center of the target. This man had lived—how long?—with the horror and guilt of his people's crimes, and the guilt of his own willful ignorance and inaction.

Mattan inhaled sharply, one shaking hand rubbing across his eyes. "I'm...feeling unaccountably tired. I'm sure you will have more questions, but have I satisfied your curiosity for now?"

Avadhron nodded, for once unwilling to bait the alien. Overwhelming exhaustion dragged at him as well. He dreaded going to their sleeping tent, dreaded tossing and turning, remembering the horrors of the—had it only been one?—day before. But blessed sleep overtook him quickly, and he didn't remember his dreams.

<><>

A loud clanging woke Avadhron. His first awareness, other than his ears ringing, was that he was frozen. No, only nearly so or he wouldn't be shivering. Would that ever stop? The men in the tent with him groaned. Gilder's voice rumbled, "Ge'up, ye scraggly runt."

"Be off," Kental retorted with a yawn. "Where's m'boots?"

Avadhron's grogginess didn't dissipate as he felt for his own footwear in the dark. He hoped they were his as he pulled them on; they fit anyway. He followed the men out and behind the tents for privacy then again to the

Gathering Tent. Large bowls of water—wondrously, gloriously hot!—and rags had been set out, presumably for washing hands and faces before meal. Not everyone entering took advantage of the offering, but went straight to the tables.

As he washed, Avadhron's fingers ran over the rough stubble on his face. Few men at the camp were clean-shaven; most of them sported a full beard. Zaidhron and many others back at the Great Hall had either been smooth-faced or, as Thuldhan, wore a moustache and chin beard. Which would he choose? For now, he would let his whiskers grow since that was easier.

Breakfast, it appeared, was a thick, creamy, orange-yellow soup, nothing like the broth with bits of vegetable that accompanied the meat they had last night. "Bata soup," someone muttered with a sigh. Avadhron tried it, and his brows rose in delight. Slightly sweet and nicely filling. He ate with guilt, wondering if those at the Great Hall and the Portal Complex had a meal. The picture of so many huddled, grief and hopelessness on their faces, haunted him. He finished quickly and stood, but the room spun. He dropped back onto the bench. *What's wrong with me?*

Mattan stumbled over to join him, his face haggard, carrying two cups. "It wasn't me. My sister admitted she put a touch of loestis in our tea last night."

"What?"

"She knew we were going to have our long-overdue talk and thought it might get...out of hand. So she added an herb to the tea to make us sleepy."

Avadhron slammed a fist on the table and tried to rise, despite the dizziness, to search for Ismari.

"She's already gone, gathering again. I flayed her, and told her you would likely do the same. You have my permission, not that you need it." He slid a cup to Avadhron. "This will take some of the fuzziness out of your brain."

"And what is it?"

"A strong, black tea. It will act as a stimulant." Mattan took a large swallow. "I don't want to delay leaving to hunt if we can help it."

"She had no right."

"So I often tell her. She tends to think rules don't apply to her." The Enaisi sighed. "I had thought perhaps we were starting on a new journey, with you actually giving us a measure of trust. Has she destroyed that?" Mattan's eyes searched Avadhron's—no, begged.

"For her, or you?"

Mattan sniffed and gulped more tea. Avadhron followed suit. This was a much stronger variety than he had yet tasted, with a more astringent flavor. "So when will we leave then? Does Kental wait for us?"

"I've released him to return to his partner, since my sister approved Gilder to resume hunting. I'm not actually sure if she cleared him, or Gilder pestered until she relented. So it will the two of us today. I'll see how you track. And shoot."

"One day? You've given me one day to apprentice?"

"You'll be fine."

"And are you going to hold the quarry for me?"

Mattan shook his head. "This time it will be all on you."

Avadhron glared at the alien and sipped the hot, dark tea.

The day was long. And cold. Avadhron's aim, Mattan assured him, would be better when he was warmer and didn't shiver. The shaking seemed more, not less, but he wasn't sure if it was the result of last night's doctored tea, the freezing temperature, feeling weak from not eating all day, or perhaps all three. Evening meal had been served by the time they returned with their final kill, and only Mattan's ability to sense led them back to the camp in the dark. The Enaisi had truly let Avadhron do the hunting, although the dragging, weary day must have tempted him to pull a few of his alien tricks.

He dropped the sledge. As workers descended on it, he stumbled into the Gathering Tent and fell heavily onto a bench. Despite his hunger, he couldn't imagine standing long enough to hold a bowl and ladle soup into it. He just wanted to rest in a warm place.

Ismari approached, and he scowled. "I know. Serve myself. Just as well, because I wouldn't accept one thing from you anyway."

"I was going to apologize."

"And what would that signify? I don't even trust your brother beyond the length of my arm, the rest of you less. Do you think your mouthings mean anything to me?"

Ismari's eyes darkened, the golden irises turning black. "You are insufferable!"

As tired as he was, Avadhron managed a supercilious smirk. Ismari huffed loudly and flounced away. If he were less exhausted, he might have enjoyed that. Right now, he was more concerned with trying to lever himself up. He must get something to eat. He was saved from the effort by Mattan arriving at the table carrying two bowls.

"Here." The Enaisi placed one in front of Avadhron and dropped to the bench, with a tired smile.

A young woman set cups and a small plate with two translucent, red-veined white vegetables before them, bowed, and left.

Avadhron dove into the soup, not stopping until the bowl was empty.

He would have felt a clod, but noticed the alien had done the same. Following Mattan's lead, he cut one of the vegetables with his eating knife, speared it, and took a bite. It had a firm texture and slight piquancy. "What is this?" he asked after swallowing, lifting the remaining bit on his knife.

"Parik, a root vegetable. We've been fortunate. This area, ages ago, was farmland, and many plants have thrived in the wild despite no agriculture and the devastation. The gatherers have found much more than they thought they would. They're gathering both food and seed. We might make a permanent settlement here."

"And we would continue to use the maglevs?"

"For now."

Avadhron pondered the distance between this place and the Great Hall. Yes, they had the rails as transportation for time being, but days of wilderness rose between the two camps overland. If they had stopping points an easy day's walk from one to the next... An image of a map grew in his mind, sections of land marked off, but not for way points. He frowned and closed his eyes, but the image faded. Was he so exhausted that he was now imagining things? What was it he had been thinking? Ah, travel.

He put his cup down and leaned forward. "Has any thought been given to establishing small settlements about a day's journey apart between here and the Great Hall? They could be way stations for travelers and perhaps grow into villages. We'd have to clear areas for roads and place markers to keep people from losing their way, but I think it would work."

"Not as related to these specific encampments, but yes, the idea is to spread out and start communities. And this is one of the spots where we wish to build with SDC-12, so I can imagine a town will be established here."

After the meal, they joined the others outside, doing what they termed fire-side chores. Avadhron again shaped bones into awls, listening to the chatter. Someone began humming and soon many chimed in, singing an old love song. Avadhron didn't dare move or leave, he tried to ignore the words and concentrate on the bone in his hands. The songs continued as he worked, and he ruined two awls because of his blurry vision.

Mattan rose and walked behind him, slapping him on the shoulder. "Tomorrow will be another long day. Let's retire."

The alien's invitation to withdraw was a relief to Avadhron, though he'd never admit it. Even before entering their tent, they could hear sobbing. They ducked inside and in the dim light from a small hanging lamp, they could see Telkai's hunting partner curled on his bedroll.

"Shall we leave you, Salwin?" Mattan asked softly.

"No, no," the lad managed to murmur, wiping his face. "The

songs...they reminded me of all those who didn't make it...at the end."

"You lost loved ones?"

"My sister and I Crossed, but my parents said they were too old. We were going to settle, then bring them across when we could do for them, to make it easier. My two youngest sisters stayed with them. The baby was only three."

"Do you know for certain they weren't rescued?" Avadhron asked.

"They lived in West Ridge Six, sir. I was told there were no survivors from any of those domes."

"No," whispered Avadhron. "No, there weren't. I'm sorry."

Salwin nodded, his breath hitching, and rolled over to his other side, hugging himself.

Neither man said a word as they removed their boots and crawled into their bedrolls. Avadhron stared at the strange shapes and shadows cast by the faint light, listening to Salwin weeping. He had been right; many others grieved too. But each man's grief had to be borne alone.

Avadhron fought to climb through the rubble, his father's voice calling his name feebly, over and over. He threw huge chunks of wall, digging to find Jhendill. The hole grew deeper, and panic rose as he kept throwing the shining stone out of the way. Finally he saw her, blank face staring at him in frozen horror, arms stretched out to him, pleading to rescue her.

"Chief," Galadhan called. "Chief, do your duty."

"I am trying!" Avadhron shouted, reaching for Jhendill.

"Do your duty," Galadhan repeated, appearing next to Jhendill, trapped in the ruins with her. Flames leaped up.

"I'm trying!" Avadhron yelled. "Give me your hands!"

They both screamed as the fire consumed them, and Avadhron cried out in horror.

A different hand—feminine, but not his wife's—appeared, rising from the blaze, covered in soot and ash, and grasped his. But instead of pulling him down, the hand rose, and he felt himself lifted up—

Avadhron sat up, sweat pouring off him, his breath coming in harsh pants. He flopped back down and rolled over, stifling a sob. Sleep was no respite for his grief.

Chapter Twenty-Nine

Streaks of pink smudged the dark sky as Avadhron trudged to the Gathering Tent to wash. The hot water woke him up but didn't chase away the nightmare. Would that he had never seen Jhendill's lifeless face. But...if he hadn't, would he have been able to accept her death? Would they have been able to make him leave without seeing a body to prove he wasn't abandoning her?

Mugs of steaming tea and broth were the only offerings. The cooks apologized, promising a meal at mid-morning and in the evening. Avadhron waved them off, and when a hunter began to complain, Avadhron's glare shut him up.

A few minutes later another grouched, and Salwin spoke up. "We get more to eat than those at the Great Hall, to keep our strength up. How can you not understand that, Cargil?"

"Keep our strength up? With this? We should have just let everyone die on Teledhar. Bringing them all over here has only killed us."

Salwin dove at the imbecile with a strangled cry, and they wrestled on the ground. Avadhron banked his fury behind duty, a habit forged through years of experience, and rose. He peeled the two apart and, seeing Mattan nearby, tossed Salwin in his direction. Cargil sneered at the young hunter until Avadhron hauled him off his feet and held him face to face. "If you have words for the one in charge of that evacuation you bring them directly to him. Do I make myself understood?"

"And who would that be?" Cargil spat. "The king, I suppose?"

A burst of laughter erupted in the tent, and Gilder boomed, "Glad you track critters better'n you track information. Yore nose t' nose with him."

Cargil's face paled, and his mouth dropped open.

"Go on then," a voice enjoined. "Tell Security Commander Avadhron your complaints. But you'll get no backing from anyone here, you fool."

The offensive hunter tried to wrest from Avadhron's grip but in vain.

"I think most of us, like Salwin, lost family in that last eruption," someone called angrily, and another added in a softer voice, "Or had family the commander and his men saved."

Cargil slumped, and Avadhron let him go. He had no stomach for the broth now. He strode out of the tent and took a deep breath of the icy air, wishing it could strip his mind of his grief the way it stripped his body of warmth. He gazed up at the pink-clouded sky with bits of blue peeking between.

"I truly am sorry for your loss."

Avadhron looked down to see Ismari staring up at him, her golden eyes darting over his face as if seeking something.

"I told you once what your empty words mean to me."

"I just wanted—"

"Leave me, alien. Go hawk your tales and doctored tea to someone else."

"You are insufferable."

"So you have already informed me. Perhaps you should increase your vocabulary."

Ismari hissed through her teeth, whirled, and stormed away.

"It does relieve me a little to know your animosity is toward all of us, and not just me," Mattan quipped, walking up to him.

"I am not in the mood for humor."

"I apologize for the tone but not the sentiment. I find you an honorable man, and have truly grieved that I have not been able to gain your trust or friendship."

Avadhron snorted, then said, "We never did finish that talk."

"Yes, I had meant to yesterday, but..."

"But instead we had to turn our attention to teaching me to hunt. Never mind, I give you a reprieve for now. Today must be a repeat of yesterday."

Mattan offered a tight smile as they proceeded to the tent to gather their hunting gear.

<<>>

Avadhron ate his soup, hoping to finish before weariness overtook him, and he nodded off at the table. Five days he'd hunted with Mattan. They'd never finished their talk; he found he didn't have the energy. Even the drive to hunt morning till night, and the exhaustion from it, couldn't ease the grief. It grew darker each day and consumed him. He hated sleeping and the dreams he had every night. Most of them were nightmares of Jhendill and Galadhan, but a few times he had dreamed of that map. He had no idea what it meant, and that irritated him.

"We're returning to the city day after tomorrow." Kental grinned over his tea.

Avadhron started and peered across the table at the hunter. "Why?"

"We've begun a rotation. Each group of hunters will take a turn going back for just a day's respite."

Gilder gulped a large amount of soup directly from his bowl. "Camp workers too."

148

"Where did you hear this?"

"This morning's maglev arrived with the news," Gilder said, chewing. "The king dinn't wish to overwork us, he says."

"Can we afford a respite with this emergency?"

"I'll leave you to ask the king that, sir," Kental said, chuckling. "I'm just hoping that the worst of winter is past. The sun peeked out today, and it's been thawing so's to get icicles. Have you seen any yet, Commander?"

Avadhron nodded. The long, frozen drips of ice were an amazing sight; another miracle of this world.

Telkai, sitting further down, leaned over. "Icicles don't mean it's necessarily thawing, Kental, only that the sun is shining warmly enough to melt the ice a little."

"Ya must throw water on the fire, mustn't ya, Elder?" Gilder asked.

"In this case though, it truly is warming," the hunter Adara said. "The icicles are dripping and melting, and the snow is slushy on the ground."

"That doesn't mean winter is over," Telkai said.

Gilder scowled down the table. "Yore pardon, Elder, but go sit sommere else if you're going t'keep on cloudin' the skies."

Telkai glared at Gilder for a moment, then looked past him to Mattan. Telkai rose with a sneer, cup in hand, and sauntered away.

"Your friend is a bit more gloomy than usual," Gilder said.

"He is. We all grieve in different ways. Give him time."

"Grieve?" the large man asked.

Mattan inhaled deeply. "We've worked with many of your people on Teledhar as well as here and developed friendships. Some were lost."

"I didn't think about that," Kental said quietly. The table was silent after that.

Avadhron climbed over a fallen tree and caught a branch of another to keep from sliding downhill in the melting, muddy snow, his mind on Telkai and Ismari and how their eyes appeared to turn to black when he had confronted each of them.

"What else—" He pitched forward and grabbed a trunk, the sledge banging into his legs, then continued, "what else haven't you told me?"

Mattan didn't answer.

Lips pressed together, Avadhron dropped the straps and leaned back against a bole, arms crossed.

The alien held up a hand in acquiescence. "There are probably details about us I have overlooked, but you've seen the irises of our eyes darken. It indicates anger."

"I was just thinking about that."

Mattan licked his lips and looked down, whispering, "I know."

"What do you mean 'I know'?"

"We, uh..." Mattan grimaced. "We can read thoughts."

The world came to a standstill. Or was it just Avadhron? He felt the blood leave his face. *A jest. He is playing with me, mocking me.*

"No," Mattan whispered. "It's not some game, and I would never mock you."

Avadhron couldn't find words. He stared at the dark-skinned alien, disbelief warring with a fury boiling up as Mattan continued, "Zaidhron said not to tell you. Not many know. We worried they would become fearful and suspicious. Some, such as you, already don't like that we can sense emotions. If they knew this—"

"Ha! I cannot imagine how this could cause any hysteria or mistrust." Avadhron shook his head. "I would dismiss such a notion as impossible— some prank without humor, but..." He blew his breath out, misting in the icy air. "Have we no privacy?"

"We have a moral code which doesn't allow us to—"

"And you broke it just now, or you wouldn't have known about my thoughts of eyes turning black." Avadhron's lips drew back in a snarl. "What stops you aliens from breaking your *moral code* any time you wish? What stops you from leading our thoughts, or even telling us what to think? How have you manipulated us since you arrived?" The memory of Mattan's arrival burst into his head. "You controlled Zaidhron from the first moment, didn't you?"

"No! We haven't *that* ability. We can read minds, as one reads a book, but we can't change or rewrite what is written!" He grabbed Avadhron's shoulders. "Listen—" Avadhron flung his arms up, throwing off the alien's grip, and stepped back.

With gritted teeth, Mattan hissed, "Listen to me! I am telling you this to gain your trust. Zaidhron said it was a mistake, but I felt it was a bigger mistake to say nothing. Eventually you would find out, and what would you think then of keeping this secret?"

He didn't answer. Couldn't. He wanted to tackle Mattan, punch him, strangle him. No! He should be angry at himself; he had started to trust. This had been his mistake, not the Enaisi's.

"Avadhron..." Mattan swallowed. "If we could control minds, wouldn't I have done so to you, long ago, to ease your suspicions and make you more accepting of us?"

"Are you saying you didn't directly control Zaidhron's mind? From the first moment he saw you, he—"

"I was living, breathing history to him. History come alive!" Mattan lifted his arms dramatically, then dropped them with a sigh. "Yes, he trusts too easily, and I exploited that to create a bond, but for a purpose. As he now knows. When I came through that portal, I saw the condition of your world. I was horrified and frightened for all your sakes. I foresaw the future, and I also foresaw that your drive and insight would be necessary to expedite evacuation."

"You—"

"I did what I needed to do," Mattan yelled, making a chopping motion with his hand. He took a breath and repeated softly, "What I needed to do."

Chapter Thirty

The fervor in Mattan's face and voice stopped Avadhron from pressing the point. He merely picked up the straps to the sledge and continued to pick his way carefully down the slushy trail. He mentally threw cursings at Mattan, hoping the alien was reading his mind at the moment, but if he was, he didn't acknowledge it in any observable manner.

The only communication between the two men for the entirety of the day was using the rudimentary sign language the hunters had developed. Avadhron made several good kills and surprised himself once by coming upon his prey completely unaware and taking it down in one shot. The exhilaration of hunting gripped him and gave him a satisfaction he hadn't expected. As he stood over the pindouru, he wanted to grin at the Enaisi, to share the joy, but he refused to let himself. He wasn't going to give in to any sense of camaraderie with Mattan. He lashed the animal to the sledge and picked up the lines.

"Avadhron..."

"Don't speak to me, alien."

"We must talk."

"Suck sand."

Mattan tugged on Avadhron's arm.

Avadhron dropped the straps and swung at the alien. His fist connected with the Enaisi's face with a *crack*, and the man flew back into the snow and slid until a large bush stopped him. Breathing heavily, he lay, staring up, puffs of mist blowing up into the cold air.

Muscles bunched and his weight on the balls of his feet, Avadhron waited, but Mattan didn't move. Finally, the alien worked his jaw back and forth, prodding the area with his fingers. Slowly and deliberately, he pushed up to a sitting position, his gaze on Avadhron.

I think you dislocated my jaw.

Avadhron straightened with a sharp inhale as the words tumbled through his mind. "Then why didn't you duck if you can read minds?"

Mattan's eyes crinkled in silent laughter. *I wasn't listening. Besides, I don't move as fast as a thought carries.*

"This is mad!"

"It's not the worst," Mattan said aloud, wincing and rubbing his jaw. "At least, probably not from your point of view."

"Oh?"

Give me a moment to speed the healing and dull the pain so I can talk easier. I know mind-speech is strange to you.

Avadhron started to retort but stopped and just snorted. Mattan closed his eyes, frowning, and took a few deep breaths. The lines in his face slowly eased, and after some time, he opened his eyes again with a strong exhale. He rose to his feet and licked his lips. "I have one last secret to share. I doubt you will like it. Do you want to know why most of my team aren't overly friendly to you?"

"I assumed it was my winning personality."

Mattan chuckled. "In the case of Ismari and Ashani, yes. But you see, you are living proof of our past and our shame."

Avadhron crossed his arms. "Explain."

"The children that were dumped on Teledhar were supposed to all be the 'refuse,' the 'rejects.' Inferior to us. But you belie that."

"Because? Is this about my dreaming? I thought only you and Ismari knew of that. You've told the others?"

"No, they don't know. But you see...you once said that you have an excellent sense of when someone is lying. You claimed it was your Sec training, I believe. And perhaps that has been helpful, but it's not the reason why."

"Oh?"

Mattan looked at the ground, the sky, everywhere but at Avadhron. He wanted to grab the alien and shake him, but as he had learned to wait quietly for prey, he would wait now. Was this the final puzzle piece? If so, he wasn't going to move until it was in place.

"You have empathy," Mattan finally said. He raised his hands in a warding gesture. "It's extremely weak, but enough that you have an intuitive sense that is extraordinary. My team has had trouble accepting that. Despite the fact they felt what had been done to your people was wrong, the inbred notion of our superiority is something they are now discovering is more deeply embedded than they realized."

"So they have discovered they are bigoted after all." As he thought about this new revelation, Avadhron slowly grinned. "I'm glad I've been able to disconcert them."

The Enaisi stared open-mouthed, then chortled. "Your sense of humor is really dark."

"So Jhendill says—" Avadhron clamped his lips shut. Grief washed over him afresh.

"I am so sorry," Mattan whispered. "So sorry."

"Suck sand, alien," he growled, pushing his heartache deep inside. "Let's get back to camp." He picked up the lines to the sledge and trudged on as best he could in the melting snow.

A little while later, a thought occurred to him, and he stopped. "Is it just me?"

"What?"

"Not reading my mind then, are you?"

Mattan looked away.

Avadhron shook his head then asked, "Do any others among my people have empathy?"

"Not that we have encountered. You seem to be unique, and we cannot account for it genetically."

Avadhron chuckled morbidly and plodded on. A thought occurred to him. "So Janadhan didn't have empathy?"

"No. Why do you ask?"

"Yet he had visions. Or one, at least, that he told me about." Avadhron frowned, remembering him lying dead on the open ground. "You said...if I recall correctly, that foresight was arbitrary. So could he have had foresight?"

"It's possible."

"Is foresight always accurate? Mine was certainly exact, but is that invariably the case?"

"Why do you ask?"

"He told me he saw himself dying under fallen stone, but he was killed by shards of broken dome, not trapped under rubble. And he thought you aliens placed that vision in his mind."

"As I said, we do not have the ability to control minds."

"So you claim. But was it his vision, or an image you created to sway him?"

"I've already answered that."

Avadhron glared at the alien, and his evasive reply. "Yes, you did answer it, didn't you?"

He put his anger to work in hauling the sledge faster. He soon spied smoke rising just ahead. He still had little sense of time on this planet, but his stomach complained it wanted food. The sky, blue today, although turning darker as the sun set, told him they would probably hunt once more though before evening meal.

They trudged into the camp, and workers descended upon them for the carcass. Ismari stormed toward them, gloved hands clenched, her dark gaze fixed on Avadhron.

"You filthy by-blow!"

Mattan lifted his arms, stepping in her path. "Stop, it's not—!" He cut himself off, glaring at her, then ordered, "Speak aloud, he knows now."

"I don't care what he knows," Ismari hissed, pushing past her sibling. She beat her fists on Avadhron's chest. "Prophet or not, I'm tired of your bullying and thinking you're so superior! Leave my brother alone!"

Avadhron wasn't sure whether to be amused more by her ineffective attack or her rage. She backed up a step, nostrils flared. A burning pain slammed into his gut, and he doubled over with a groan.

I don't need to hit you to hurt you. Even as a thought, the feminine timber of Ismari's voice was recognizable.

Other voices intruded after hers—loud, mental shouting:

No!

Stop!

How dare you, Ismari!

The fiery agony ceased abruptly. Avadhron slowly straightened, shaking and sweating, to see Mattan facing down his sister, teeth clenched. "Don't you dare ever presume to do that again!"

"What did she do?" Avadhron gasped, a hand on his stomach.

"I sent you pain, you thick-skulled—"

Mattan snatched Ismari's arm. "Enough!"

"He hit you!"

"If you felt it when I punched him," Avadhron asked, "why didn't you react when it happened? Why now?"

She flicked her hair out of her face with her fingers and crossed her arms with a sulky pout. "Telkai stopped me. He said you two had to work it out." Eyes smoldering black, she continued, "But nothing has been worked out. You're still as obtuse as ever."

"*You*"—Mattan poked a finger at his sister—"are letting your emotions override your mind."

She spat out something in a different language, spun, and marched to the Gathering Tent, back rigid.

Avadhron didn't need to know the words, the meaning was clear. He glanced at Mattan, who blew his breath out and whispered, "Sisters."

"I wouldn't know."

"Ah, yes. Well, actually I'm one of a few who has a sibling," Mattan said in a quiet, confidential voice. "We were experiments, Ismari and I. Twins. The ultimate specimens. But they found that twins have a stronger bond, and despite our physical 'perfections,' we weren't as *compliant* as our fellows. They blamed it on our intense familial empathy." Mattan's lip curled. "It couldn't possibly be that we merely had a strong sense of *morality*, no."

"So your team, I take it you infected them with your lack of 'compliance?'"

"Infected, corrupted, subverted. We are outcasts, albeit voluntary, along with this planet."

"And along with my people."

"Just so. We're in this together, you know."

"Is that a warning?"

"Merely an affirmation."

Avadhron sighed in resignation, then he noticed the camp workers all stood, gaping at him. He glared back. "Is there something wrong?"

They scattered, suddenly too busy with their chores.

The camp was unusually quiet as everyone sat around the fire doing evening tasks. Avadhron knew he was being stared at, but when he tried to meet anyone's eyes, they looked away. He understood; he shouldn't have punched Mattan. Their people would all be dead if not for the Enaisi. The debt owed to the aliens was immeasurable. He had lost control and let his dislike overwhelm his sense. This compromised his position; Zaidhron would likely relieve him of his duties.

He didn't care. He could hunt to feed his people and learn how to keep them safe from predators with teeth and claws instead of those wielding weapons. How much of the latter would they need with everyone learning how to survive? Thuldhan would be more than capable of taking over.

He concentrated on the bones he shaped into awls.

Ismari sat down next to him and said quietly, "I wanted to apologize. I lost my temper."

"So did I."

"I shouldn't have sent you pain."

"I shouldn't have hit your brother."

"No, you shouldn't." Her voice was peeved.

His desire to rankle overcame him at her tone, and he responded, "It did feel good though."

Her lips pressed together, and her nostrils flared. "Yes, it did."

She rose and strode away, head high and back stiff.

Avadhron smiled inwardly.

Chapter Thirty-One

Avadhron walked up the steps and stopped as he saw people queued up along the hall alongside those sleeping. He continued on, turning down the corridor leading to Zaidhron's conference chamber and realized the line and he had the same destination. He tried to push past the crowd, but several blocked him. He halted long enough to give them a glare, then brushed them aside and entered, ignoring their protests and the sounds of others hissing for them to hush.

A tall, slender woman, arms at her sides and chin lifted, stood in front of Zaidhron, who looked more careworn than Avadhron had ever seen him. A scribe sat by his side, his eyes fixed on the feather quill he twirled.

Despite a disheveled appearance, this female, by her dignified manner and her expensive tunic-over-trous, was high-born and used to getting her own way. Her cultured, smooth voice delivered her petition in a calm, precise fashion. "Your Majesty, it is hard for a man realize the importance of this predicament to a lady in my position. You cannot know—"

He stepped forward. "What's this?"

The woman turned, her mouth open in what surely would be a reprimand at being interrupted. Recognition crossed her features however, and she merely gave a sigh of resignation.

Zaidhron looked up, his expression one of desperation. "Avadhron." His cousin actually sounded glad to see him. "Did you come straight here from the tube, without even bathing?"

"My first duty is you, Your Majesty, unless you state otherwise." He bowed. "I hope I do not give offense." He offered a second bow to the woman. She looked familiar; Viltara clan perhaps, or Jonasel? He seemed to remember her floating about functions he had been forced to attend as a member of the First Table. Fortunately, he had not been invited very often after marrying Jhendill. His heart twisted, and he concentrated on what his king was saying.

"I can smell you across the room, and your clothes could benefit from the use of a sonic. I see you're starting a beard as well. How was the hunting?"

"Good," he managed, then found his voice as the topic took over enough of his mind to crowd out his grief. "We need more campsite workers. Mattan thinks we should establish a permanent camp at Estan and at the Tinshal hub. Until we get the Refugees all settled, we think it best to continue to use the tubes for transportation and communication. We wanted to discuss the idea of having way stations at about a day's walk from each other between the settlements."

Zaidhron's eyebrows raised, and he smiled. "You seem to be getting along with Mattan well then."

"We agree on what needs to be done. Don't take that as any liking on my part." He hesitated, wanting to address his breach of discipline, but not in front of this female. "I do need to talk to you about—"

"Excuse me," the woman said. Her quiet, chiding manner indicated her displeasure in the way a well-born and well-bred lady was expected to behave. "This is my petition."

Avadhron sat on the corner of the table. "Then, by all means, let us hear it."

The king leaned back in the chair, emitting a barely audible groan. "Softly, cousin," he murmured. The woman pretended to not notice the exchange.

"I have need of cleansers and moisturizers for my skin and hair. And special brushes." She lifted her thick, dark brown mane over her shoulder. "*This* is the result of living in this uncivilized manner. Look at this, it's course and there's no brilliancy to it, and my skin is dry and flaking—"

"From which clan do you hail?" Avadhron crossed his arms. "Viltara?"

She drew herself up. "As you should know."

Ha! Thought so. "And has your thane heard your petition?"

"Yes, and he dismissed it." She lifted her chin. "So I am bringing it to the king."

"Is this a matter of life's harm to you?"

"I should think so. I can't go around looking like a low-born, we have an image to maintain. Without the proper care, my skin and hair—"

"Does it cause immediate injury to your body? Do you expect to die soon from this inconvenience?"

"Inconvenience? This goes beyond *inconvenience*! It's bad enough I am told my servants now have other tasks and are not beholden to me, and I am forced to do servant's work myself. I sleep in a small room, crowded in with all manner of untoward boorish types. I am denied the fundamentals of a civilized life. There is not—"

Gritting his teeth, Avadhron whipped up a hand, and the woman stopped, blinking.

"You allow this?" he hissed to his cousin.

"I have stated I will be accessible to my people."

"During this time, you have a greater responsibility. We have to train and settle thousands of Refugees. You need to relegate petitions to assistants. If they cannot resolve it and feel it's of sufficient importance, then it can be passed to you."

"And to whom would you suggest I relegate this, Second at Table?"

Avadhron flashed an evil grin. "Our people may approach *me* at any time." He turned to the Viltara noble. "I reject your petition. You may go."

She drew up, nostrils flaring. "But this is unconscionable! I need—"

"You need a shake up, woman!" Avadhron ignored Zaidhron batting his arm. "You are hereby assigned campsite duty in Estan. You had best hurry to stores and tell them to outfit you for the cold. We will leave for camp at the break of morning's thirteen."

She stared at as one would an errant child. "What? You can't mean it. I am high nobility, Viltara clan! And second cousin to my thane." Her voice never rose, she merely pressed her points firmly, eyebrows raised in expectation that understanding and compliance with her will would follow.

"You are now a campsite worker. *Move!*" The last word, bellowed from the diaphragm as if ordering a trainee, echoed. The woman jumped and rushed from the room, face white. The scribe coughed loudly, his eyes twinkling, then resumed his more or less impassive expression. Zaidhron merely groaned.

Avadhron glared at the ones gathered at the doorway, their mouths agape. "Who is next?" The crowd scattered. He brought his gaze back to his king. "You, Your Majesty, I order to rest."

"You really do need to stop assigning the lowliest of jobs to the highest of nobles."

"Then they should quit acting like spoiled brats."

"I'm glad you decided to go into security and not arbitration. And, pray, who shall assist with these petitions? Your offer, although laudable, cousin, is, since you are at a hunting camp, pointless."

"I don't think so. It cleared the queue."

Zaidhron groaned again, dropping his head into his hands. "Stop."

He put a hand on his cousin's shoulder. "My apologies. I *would* suggest looking for arbiters from among our kin that survived, however, many of them were acolytes of Janadhan and aren't known for their honesty." He ran fingers through his long, tangled hair. "We can discuss this more later, Your Majesty." *As well as other matters, such as security commanders who do not control themselves.* "Please, go rest."

A slight scuffle from behind him made Avadhron twist around. A scrawny lad stood in the doorway, his clothes worn. "If you please, sirs."

He waved the boy into the room. "You have a petition, child?"

"Yes, sir." The little one crept forward by small steps. "I cannot find m'mum, sir. No one will look because we're nobody, see?"

"What clan?"

"We was Tantera clan, sir. But most of our clan died in the earthquake of South Dome Three. Was only m'family left then. And only m'mum and me Crossed. But I can't *find* her now."

"Name, child?" Zaidhron asked softly. The scribe dipped his quill and began writing.

Avadhron crossed his arms, wondering how much time any of the clan workers spent helping the boy. He was low-born, and his clan gone. Tantera would only survive through his mother and him, if they had the will and long lives to build it.

"M'name's Fandel, sir."

"Fandel," the king murmured, "future thane of Tantera clan. And who is your mother?"

The boy's eyes widened, and his mouth dropped open. "I'ndt no thane, sir."

"Not yet." Avadhron said. "Your mother holds that title until she dies, or sooner if she wishes to pass thaneship to you when you are of Age."

"What's your mother's name, Fandel?" the king asked.

"Goshill." The boy frowned. "I don't care nothing about thanes, I just want m'mum."

Zaidhron smiled at the lad. "We'll find her. Where are you assigned to sleep?"

"I'm posted for work in the privs, sir. I sleep nearby, in the corridor."

Lips pressed together, Avadhron met his cousin's blue eyes. "I think, Sire, we have some inequality seeping through, despite our requests that clan affiliations not be a deciding factor in work and sleep assignments."

"That is a possibility. It could also be a disregard due to age, or even just that he was given a task simple enough for a child to manage, or it perhaps merely the lot he drew." Zaidhron rubbed his forehead. "And chore postings are not permanent. We have a rotation system. Nevertheless," The king lifted a hand toward the scribe. "Tolben, a new order shall be distributed to the runners. It is to communicate my displeasure should I find any clan or age prejudice among those in charge of assignments or working to reunite families and clans. Punishment...punishment shall be..." His voice drifted off, his eyes blank. The man was too fatigued to think.

Avadhron finished for him. "Reassignment. To be decided by Second at Table Avadhron."

Tolben bit his lips to hide a grin. Zaidhron tipped his head and slowly smiled. "You seem to make of yourself a formidable threat."

"I try, Sire." He bowed. "And I have a suggestion, if Your Majesty will allow."

"When you're this formal, I begin to worry."

He nodded toward the boy. "I think we should ally ourselves with

Tantera clan."

"Ally? An alliance bespeaks a political or economic advantage to both clans."

"Well, unless we wish to announce a marriage between our clan and his, an alliance is our only option. And I somehow think the boy is rather disinterested in an engagement, I wouldn't presume to speak for his mother, and we have spoken to no one in our clan who might desire a match between our clans so we would be able to make an association claim."

"And what shall we state is the advantage of this alliance?"

"On this world, we have need of every clan in order to build our race. We've been reduced to what? Less than ten thousand?" He pointed at Fandel, who recoiled slightly, as if afraid of being struck. Avadhron stopped and placed a hand gently on the boy's shoulder. "If we can help him—help him grow, prosper, we will save a clan."

"Do you really think it's necessary?"

"I offer it as a possible solution to protect Fandel, his mother, and their clan. No decision, of course, can be made until his mother is found."

"You'll have to come up with a better rationale to formalize an alliance treaty."

"Since we have to find his mother first, I have time yet."

Zaidhron leaned back, eyes narrowed. "Do you want to know what I think?"

Avadhron's brows rose. Surely the king wouldn't just dismiss the proposal. "What is that, Sire?"

Chapter Thirty-Two

The king pointed a finger at Avadhron. "I think that you, my cousin, are a secret idealist."

He snorted. "I'm merely practical. If our race is to survive, we must sacrifice face creams and clan prejudices." He turned to the scribe. "Would you pass word of that woman's"—he jerked his head toward the door— "name and new assignment to the proper person, please?"

"Already writing the order, Your Highness."

"'Commander' is fine." Avadhron hopped off his perch at the corner of the table and knelt in front of the boy. "Your mother came through the portal with you?"

"I...I saw her go through. We was being pushed and hurried, and there was so many people. When we got over here, there was crowds and crowds, we was pushed down hallways. I couldn't see her and yelled and yelled but couldn't find her." Tears trickled down his cheeks. "I just want m'mum."

"I'm certain the mother has been asking about her son," Avadhron murmured. "I want to know why they haven't been reunited yet."

"We still have many who haven't found their families. Don't forget we have thousands to sort through."

He again placed a hand on the boy's shoulder. "We'll find her." Rising, he said, "Now, come with me, Fandel."

"Where are you going?"

"To care for the boy. And for you, Sire, I repeat my order to rest." He glanced at the scribe. "As has been witnessed."

Tolben nodded, then rose. "If the petitions are through, Your Majesty, I will finish publishing the orders for the day." He inclined his head to Avadhron. "And then personally search for Fandel's mother, Commander."

"You have my thanks if you can find his mother quickly." He bowed to Zaidhron. "Sire." He gestured for the boy to follow him.

"Have you seen the outside world yet?" he asked as they walked down the corridor. At least with people working in shifts, not as many folks crowded the hallways; those sleeping neatly lined one wall.

"You mean above ground, to see the dome? No, sir. I've only seen these halls and rooms."

Avadhron halted and stared down at the child. How could he understand their new world was completely different from everything he

162

had known and experienced in his short life? "You lived in an underground encampment in South Dome Three, didn't you?"

"Yes, sir. It wasn't much, but I liked it better than this place."

Avadhron snorted. Of course he would. He had only seen walls, privs, the endless press of people, and not enough food. He led Fandel down the stairs and to the back corridor. He placed his hand on the panel to the entrance to the lift.

As the door slid open, the boy's eyes widened and he smiled, albeit timidly, for the first time. "You must be someone important," he whispered. "No one can make that door work. I've seen folks try. Only the Elders and a few others, like the king and the runners, can use it."

"I'm Second at Table of Ch'shalna clan, do you know what that means?" Avadhron placed his hand on the scanner to the lift.

"No, sir."

"No matter."

They entered the small chamber, and he paused, staring at the panel. Zaidhron and Thuldhan had shown him how to get to several important areas, but not everywhere. But then, how many places did either of them know how to access? If the controls made any sense, one of the top buttons should take them to the mountain entrance, but this was mostly guesswork. He chose the one on the left. As the lift moved, he said, "If I can find the right level, I'm going to show you our new world."

"This isn't it?"

"What you've seen is just a building." The door opened into a dark hallway. Had Avadhron found one of the cordoned off areas? Was his access so complete then? "Wrong floor. Let me try again." He quirked a wry smile at Fandel. "I'm new here too and still learning my way around." He stabbed at the other top button. The lift rose and stopped. This time, the chamber was large and round, with a domed ceiling. Ah ha! The mountaintop entrance. "Come."

The darkened glass doors afforded them a view of the outside, but the snow was piled high enough to cause a problem if they opened. Were they on automatic sensors? A small plate to one side glowed orange. A warning it would be unadvisable to open the doors, or a message that they weren't working?

Before Avadhron could make a decision, Fandel ran forward and pressed his hands on the glass. The doors stayed shut; the boy, however, jumped backwards. "It's cold!"

"It's winter outside. That white fluff is called snow. But see how the world stretches far out? There's no domes here."

"How can we live with no domes?"

"This is the natural way for people to live, on the surface. Our planet was dying, so we had to live in domes."

The boy frowned and looked out again. "There's no quakes here?"

"No."

"You don't need permission to go out-dome?"

"'Outside.' No."

"And you don't need gear or breathing masks to go...outside?"

"No."

Fandel tentatively walked to the doors again and touched them. "What is that white stuff again?"

"Snow. In the winter, it's very cold outside, which is why we are all inside, with fires to keep us warm. But the weather changes. In the summer, you can play out there."

Fandel didn't answer. He just stared through the glass. "Why is it all white and grey up there?"

"Those are clouds. They float in the sky."

A quiet *whoosh* behind him indicated the lift doors opening. He turned to see Telkai, more brooding than ever. He seemed to go out of his way to try to intimidate Avadhron, which was greatly amusing both for the effort and the lack of success.

"What are you doing here?"

"Am I being monitored?"

"No, but certain areas are. I received notice that a restricted area had been accessed."

"This place is restricted?"

"For now. We don't want your people to find their way here and get lost outside."

"I would think locking the doors would be enough."

"We aren't taking any chances." The alien nodded at Fandel. "Who's the boy?"

"Just one of thousands lost, and with little to no idea of the wonders of their new world. He thought—" Avadhron stopped to clear his throat. "He doesn't even understand life, a world, without domes."

"Understandable, given his age. Is he your newest clan-adoptee?" Telkai's voice held a sarcastic edge.

Avadhron really needed to stop and visit Asila. He hadn't seen her since coming through the portal. He ignored the alien and walked closer to Fandel. "What do you think?"

"That's sky? No dome?"

"Yes."

"We can't go out?"

"Not right now. But I promise you before long you'll be able to go outside."

"Will you take me?"

"Most certainly."

Fandel took a step back, hugging his arms. "Will it be warmer?"

"Hopefully. But if not, I'll make sure you have warm clothes."

"Can we...can we go back? I'm cold."

"Let's go." He strode past Telkai to the lift, the boy padding behind. The alien slid in beside them as the doors shut. Avadhron touched the third button from the top on the right-hand side as he said to Fandel. "You will stay with me or one of my men until your mother is found."

"That's putting a burden on your men, isn't it?"

"That's not your concern."

"You feel free with ordering people around, and doing what you please, don't you? Ismari and Ashani are right, you have no regard for anyone."

He smiled. These aliens thought they knew so much.

Telkai snorted as the doors opened. "Yes, we do." He stalked away.

Fandel frowned. "What did he mean?"

Avadhron smirked. "It means the aliens don't honor their 'moral code.'"

Chapter Thirty-Three

Fandel's nose wrinkled. "What's that mean?"

"Nothing you need worry about at the moment. Come with me." He and the lad continued to his quarters. He gestured toward the room, and Fandel peeked in before timidly entering. "What's this?"

"Where I sleep, with several other hunters. But we're not here often, so I'm offering my bunk to you."

The boy's eyes widened. "Me, sir? Sleep in a place as fine as this?"

"As fine as what?" Kental asked from behind them in the door.

"Kental, this is Fandel. He's taking my bed."

The hunter whistled, shaking his head. "Not before a good scrubbing he's not." He bent over, addressing the lad. "I'm off to wash m'self, wish to go with me?" He grinned at Avadhron. "You are invited too, since you rushed off immediately to find the king and still stink of days in camp."

"My thanks, and your excuse for not bathing yet?"

"Went to scc my family." Like Avadhron, the redhead had dropped his pack on his bunk upon returning, then hurried away. "But what do we do with our clothes that need washing?"

"Mattan said we would be allowed the use of sonics for what we're wearing, so they'd be clean after we bathe. A rare luxury I'm given to understand."

"That's a fine treat indeed!" Kental nodded at the boy. "Hunters are the ones with special privileges here, lad, not the nobles."

"I only have these." Fandel looked down at his worn garb, still serviceable but a bit short in the leg.

Avadhron frowned; how many of his people only have what they're wearing? And didn't even have blankets or furs to keep them warm?

Kental grunted. "Let's go bathe."

Coming from a world where water was a precious commodity, only used for drinking and occasionally cooking, the thought of actually bathing was truly strange and new.

Avadhron followed the hunter to a door not far down the hall, the lad trotting behind. They rounded a privacy wall inside the entrance, and the boy gasped. "It's...it's so big! And this?" Fandel crept forward and squatted by one of the pools that lined the humid, circular chamber. His fingers tentatively touched edge and slid lower until they were wet. "It's water?"

It was indeed. Steaming water that flowed into each basin or pool from spouts in the wall, then burbled into channels cut into the floor and to the center where it drained. Smaller basins interspersed with the larger ones. The ripples reflected the recessed lights in scintillating patterns onto the polished black walls and vaulted ceiling. The effect stole away Avadhron's breath.

Ledges protruded from the walls large enough to serve as shelves or benches, and each held stacks of folded drying cloths. Paneled frames stood between some of the pools as partitions.

Fandel gazed about and whispered, "It's pretty."

"That it is," Kental murmured.

"Ready to bathe?" Avadhron asked the boy, unlacing his jerkin. He tossed it over a frame.

"I am!" The redhead pulled off his shirt and dropped it. "Our partners are on their way too. It seems none of us thought cleaning up was a first priority." He began chuckling, then nodded at the lad. "You feel comfortable bathing with a bunch of old men?"

Fandel shrugged, looking down.

"Bet not." The hunter dragged a screen to a side pool, partially blocking it from view. "These small ones are good for washing clothes or children. You can bathe back here."

"You seem to know your way around." Avadhron sat down on one of the stone benches and pulled off his boots.

"I was the youngest of my family. Had to learn quick and move quicker. It's an art."

"What, talking?" rumbled Gilder as he lumbered in the door.

The boy slipped behind the frame.

"Who's the lad?" the huge man asked.

"Name's Fandel. He's the commander's foundling."

"Temporary foundling, until he's reunited with his mother." Avadhron stepped over the lip and down into the nearest pool, easing into the hot water. He hissed slightly at the sensation of his body thawing. After being so interminably cold for days, this was a sybaritic pleasure. He wiggled his warming toes with a sigh.

At the sides of each of the pools and basins, small brown blocks were piled next to rough-textured, fist-sized lumps and little rags. This new world's methods of cleaning oneself? Avadhron wasn't certain what to use, so he waited, but none of the men seemed too interested in bathing. Perhaps they were just enjoying the warmth too.

"How much meat do you think we brought back?" Kental asked, as he reclined.

"You were there, you don't know?" the big man retorted.

"I mean from both camps,"—the redhead waved a hand, flipping water drops at his partner, probably not inadvertently—"in total for the whole time we were gone."

Gilder glared at Kental but didn't rise to the bait. Thankfully. "Hopefully enough to feed everyone and to spare."

"I would assume so." Avadhron slid down into the water up to his neck. *Blessedly hot!* "Or they wouldn't have begun a rotation of hunter teams receiving a day's respite."

"I think the commander is right. We certainly had no trouble finding any beasts. Too many of the critters, thank the Maker."

"Our campsite fellows had their work cut out in keeping up with the carcasses we brought in." Kental grinned. "If you excuse the pun."

"The gatherers weren't quite as fortunate." Avadhron rested his head on the lip of the pool, still delighting in the hot water. "I wonder how much they are able to add in vegetables and herbs to the food supply here."

Two striplings entered with Mattan on their heels.

"Your pardon, sirs, but we're to take everyone's laundry to the sonics," said the one.

"Make it fast, lads," Gilder rumbled. "Afore we all wrinkle!"

"And don't forget those too." Avadhron pointed to Fandel's clothes piled by the frame of the side pool.

One stripling picked up boy's garments, and Fandel stuck his head around the screen, squeaking, "M'clothes!"

"Who is that?" the alien asked.

"Fandel," Avadhron replied. "Don't worry, lad, they're just cleaning them. They'll be returned shortly."

"Yes, sir." The boy didn't look happy but disappeared behind frame again.

Mattan walked to a bench, sat, and began to unlace his boots. "You two wait and you can take mine as well."

The striplings bobbed their heads in acquiescence. The alien stepped to the far side of a screen to undress, then slipped into the pool with an "Aaaah!"

The boys scooped up the alien's clothes and left.

Kental leaned over to peer at Fandel behind the frame. "Know how to wash with water, boy?" He rose and waded to the other end of their pool, and sat close to the where the lad was hiding. The hunter picked up a lump and showed the child what to do, murmuring to him quietly.

"I take it that's the boy whose mother Tolben is searching for?" Mattan asked.

"Yes."

"You certainly do like to give people work, don't you?"

"He volunteered to personally undertake the task. I didn't assign it."

Avadhron grinned. "Has Telkai been complaining about my peremptory attitude?"

"I haven't seen Telkai since we've arrived."

"What has that got to do with it?" he asked laconically.

Mattan sighed and grabbed one of the strange-looking lumps. "You never let go, do you?"

"Never." He nodded at the item in the alien's hands. "What are those?"

"It's from the trunk of the sansil plant. You can scrub with it or use the soap your people have made."

Avadhron picked up a lump. It was rough, almost prickly. He followed Mattan's example and dipped it in the water. Immediately it softened and swelled, soaking up liquid and exuding a sweet scent. He rubbed it on his skin and it lathered. Others did the same, either using the sansil or the blocks of soap and cloths. The dirty foam eddied away and out of the pool. Bathing in hot water was not just a necessity but a joy to be treasured.

"I wonder how soon we can get more folk trained to help at the camp sites," Kental said. "We'll need more gatherers come spring, won't we?"

"I think," Avadhron said, "we should have several camps spread out from the hub encampments, for both hunting and gathering. I've discussed it with Mattan, and he agrees. We just need trained people to man them."

"We have many more capable of joining us," the alien said, "once the Refugees can function here without needing guides or assistance."

"Is it really that hard?" Avadhron asked.

The hunters both grinned.

"Depends. There are some, sir, that need...handholding."

"Especially the nobles," Gilder said, then nodded at Avadhron. "Yore pardon."

He snorted. "I'll be begging for your pardon. We have one noble joining us tomorrow morning. I have a feeling she won't be happy about the matter either."

"I take it she wasn't a volunteer?" Kental asked.

"No, she wasn't, thank you very much, Avadhron," Mattan said dryly. "She is not a good candidate for campsite work. Couldn't you have just shut her up and sent her on her way?"

"She can be my new assistant hunter, once she's used to being domeless. I'd relish seeing her fingers raw learning to use a bow and see her reaction at felling an animal, knowing it will feed her."

"And take the chance she'd shoot you? Or one of us?"

His eyes wide, Gilder asked, "Bells above, what have you done, Commander?"

"He saddled us with a 'pampered noble,' as you call them," Mattan said to the big hunter, glowering at Avadhron. "I'll be surprised if she doesn't burn down the campsite."

Avadhron shrugged. "Send her with Ismari. Your sister can show her what herbs might be beneficial for skin and hair, and she can gather those as well as food."

"Skin and hair?" Kental asked.

"I don't know what she was petitioning for exactly, but she was pestering the king because she was—how did she word it...she was 'denied the fundamentals of a civilized life.'"

Both hunters howled with laughter.

"So you decided to show her what our civilized life is like now?" Gilder asked.

"I wouldn't care what she thought she should have or shouldn't have. The king looked ill. He won't rest unless forced, and probably doesn't eat either, hoping it will give some Refugee an extra mouthful or two, and she's whining about the...*brilliancy* of her hair? Unconscionable."

Mattan tipped his head, peering hard at Avadhron. His dark eyes piercing. "I can see why you reacted as you did. But you cannot make a habit of arbitrarily assigning...distasteful tasks to those who irk you."

He laughed, and the sound echoed in the chamber. "I can do what I please unless ordered by my king. I am under no orders to obey you."

"I am not stating you are, I'm merely trying to make you understand that your people may become resentful if you continue—"

"I would rather have them resentful than dead. How long will Her Ladyship Brilliant Hair last without a quick rearrangement of her priorities? And one"—he lifted a finger—"set to such tasks will deter at least some others. Which reminds me, we need to set assistants to review petitions, so the king can tend to other duties. I proposed it to him, but he will probably defer the idea and continue overseeing all requests and appeals himself." Avadhron narrowed his eyes at Mattan. "Since you are his *friend* and he listens to you, I ask that you speak to him." *Verbally, I hope.*

Mattan shot him a dirty look but that didn't mean he'd read his mind; he could just be responding to Avadhron's sardonic tone. "Any suggestions as to whom we may enlist?"

"I think people need to understand their own thane's decision is final unless it endangers them, not merely discommodes them. For appeals, triads could be established, consisting of a noble who has lived here since last summer, a craftsman, and a chief. Also I'd suggest having one of the striplings in line to be a chief at the First Table attend to learn more about the process, and what needs to take precedence on this world."

"That's not a bad idea, Commander," Gilder said. "If you don't mind the opinion of a low-born hunter."

Avadhron nodded. "Despite her age, I think Tarnill might be useful. She acts as if she's already Confirmed, and she's lived here, and knows the priorities we need to establish. We have two other chiefs' children that should be prepared for their duties. Dandhral's daughter, Felissa, is one year from being installed as a chief, and Vandhrel has sixteen years and a steady head." More so, at times, than his father, Cosdhral—but Avadhron didn't say that aloud.

"You've a steady head as well as hand, Commander," Kental said. "Those are fine ideas."

"Think they'll bring our clothes back soon?" Gilder asked. "M'hands are wrinklin'." He held them up as proof.

Avadhron peered at his own. Sure enough, his fingertips looked wrinkled. *How odd.* Before he could ask about the phenomenon, the striplings entered with piles of freshly laundered garments. Kental scrambled out, snatching a drying cloth for himself and another, which he tossed to Fandel. "Here ya go, lad. Dry off. I'll bring yours over so's you can dress."

After a little sorting and tossing of various pieces of clothing back and forth, they were all clad in their own clean garb. Avadhron had a new appreciation not only for cleanliness but for warmth. The hunters returned to their quarters, Fandel tagging along.

Chapter Thirty-Four

Kental and Gilder proved good "uncles" to Fandel, trying to outdo each other in telling stories of their experiences on this new world. The fascinated boy was well looked after while Avadhron went hunting for his Second. The scribes in their headquarters did not know where Thuldhan was. Twice he lifted his hand to his ear out of habit, then grimaced. He had to find him in the time-consuming, old-fashioned way: asking and searching.

In the end, Thuldhan found him. And had no significant news to pass on. He did approve of his commander's idea of triads for appeals, encouraging Avadhron to submit a proposal for it. He then took him to visit Asila.

The old woman sat in a padded chair in the corner of a room off a medical ward, head tipped to the side, asleep.

Avadhron stood in the door, watching her. "How is she?" he asked the attendant.

"In and out. She doesn't have much longer, Your Highness. But she's comfortable. At least, physically. She still shies away from everyone. A lifetime of being shunned, I think."

"We have no way of knowing why she was clanless now."

The attendant inhaled, but said nothing. Avadhron turned to look at him. He licked his lips then said, "We do, Your Highness, actually. All our records, history—everything was transferred here when we started Crossing."

"I prefer 'Commander.' Then you know her background?"

"She was Tanshon clan, Commander. A niece to the thane. She opposed him, made Claim he was abusing his authority. Several others of their first table backed her, but not the majority."

"So she lost her Claim?"

"Yes, sir. The others lost their clan rank and standing, but as the instigator, her thane made her an example and declared her clanless. She lost her husband, her children, all her family. She has spend over fifty years with no one."

"Tanshon? Isn't that clan gone now? They were caught in the South Dome earthquake, weren't they?"

"Yes, I think so, sir. We lost quite a few clans in that catastrophe."

"Doesn't matter to her, though. She's been alone all these years."

"Subsisting on what she can, from what I can learn. She doesn't say much, actually. She asks for you though."

Avadhron raised his brows. He padded as softly as possible with boots on to the old woman's side and gazed down at her sunken cheeks and wrinkled skin. Scant wisps of grey hair escaped the cap on her head. He pulled the blanket up over her shoulder, and her eyes fluttered open.

Avadhron hunkered down next to her, his knees cracking. "How are you, Asila?"

"You came."

"Why would I not? You are kin now."

"I am clanless. Worse than clanless. All that I lost is doubly lost. All dead. I wanted to be dead."

"You resent me for saving you?"

"What do I have to live for?"

"A bright new world. When spring comes, and the sun shines, I would show it to you."

"Why?"

Could any words give her hope, a reason to live, after all these years? Not knowing what to say, he shrugged.

"And you lost a man because of me, they say. Because of a clanless woman."

Avadhron pressed his lips together and swallowed. It took him a few moments to be certain his voice was steady. "I only lost one man instead of my whole team, and my own life. We would have all been in the shuttle. And even that was not on you, but the medic for whom clan was more important than medicine or saving lives."

Asila shrugged and turned her head away, lips thinned.

After a moment, Avadhron rubbed his hands on his knees, then rose. "I am assigned to a work camp, so I will not be back for some time to visit again. Rest well."

The old woman did not acknowledge him, and he withdrew. The attendant shook his head and whispered, "That is the most she has spoken since being brought here, actually."

"Is she treated well?"

With a snort, the attendant replied, "The king's heir himself carried her through the portal. What do you think, sir?"

"I am not heir."

"You are until his daughter is of Age, Commander."

He waved a hand. "I am grateful for her care, though. Some might wish to withhold it for her lack of appreciation. Let them worry about mine, if it comes to that."

The man smiled, bowing. "Your wishes are already known, but I will reiterate them, sir."

Avadhron nodded and left.

<<>>

The hunters all gathered at a table in one of the large chambers off what had been turned into a kitchen, enjoying their meal amid banter. Fandel sat between Kental and Avadhron, sipping his soup and swinging his legs.

Gilder stopped mid-laugh, his eyes wide. "Her Royal Highness!" He jumped to his feet, jarring the table.

Avadhron rose with the others, turning toward the door. Tarnill lifted her hands. "Please, be seated and continue your meal."

They all sat, but no one resumed eating.

Tarnill's blue eyes landed on Avadhron, then slid to the boy. She spoke into a wrist comm. "I have found them both." She smiled at Fandel. "We have located your mother."

The lad knocked his chair over scrambling to his feet. "M'mum? Where?"

"Tolben is bringing her here. Be seated and eat, child. She'll be here momentarily."

He started for the door despite the order. Kental spun up from his own seat and caught Fandel before he ran out of the room. "She's coming here, boy. If you go looking, where will you be when she gets here? Come back to the table."

Reluctantly, he obeyed the hunter.

Tarnill again stared—glared?—at Avadhron. "I am beginning to see why Father says you cause headaches."

"Would you not have me try to help the lad?"

She waved her fingers in a way that reminded him of Janadhan. "I'm glad you and Tolben took on the task or father likely would have. I am talking about Lady Marinn of Viltara. She is protesting loudly."

"If you had heard her complaining about her flaking skin and the lack of brilliancy of her hair, that we are denying her the fundamentals of a civilized life—that is a quote, cousin. The king—"

"Tolben related the entirety of the tale, Commander. But despite Lady Marinn's lack of...understanding of our situation, your response went beyond what was necessary."

"I am not certain this is the right place to discuss this, but since we are, you did not see how drawn and ill your father looked. He should not be putting his time and energy into these petitions."

"And what is your suggestion then?"

"Triads for appeals. I will submit my official proposal after the meal."

"And Lady Marinn?"

"And what would you do to wake her up, Your Highness?"

Tarnill rubbed her forehead with her fingertips. "I don't know."

"No one does. This is a unique situation. Our only concern should be for survival. Once we have taught our people that, we can—"

"Mum!" Fandel's chair banged back on the floor. Tolben stood in the doorway, smiling. The woman with him fell to her knees, weeping and clinging to the lad. "My son! My baby!"

One happy ending.

Tarnill gazed at the crying pair, then walked over to Avadhron. She leaned close, rising on tiptoe, and whispered, "You are soft at heart, you phony." She pressed her cheek to his, then strode to the door. One hand on the jamb, she turned to look back at him. "I expect your proposal for the triads within one hour, Commander. You may use a computer in the temporary council chamber, which is on the same level as the Hub."

Kental whistled after she left. "She didn't give you much time. Not meaning no disrespect."

"She's as worried for her father as I am." Avadhron picked up his bowl and downed his soup in several gulps and then left.

Being used to the bureaucracy, and the details involved in writing reports, it didn't take long for Avadhron to draft his proposal. Since he would likely be hunting when the clan council would meet, he tried to anticipate questions as to implementation.

He finished, saved the document, and sat back, staring at the holo-screen. How much longer would they be able to use this technology? Before long, he would be forced to learn to use the inks and paper of this world. More learning. But that would wait for another day.

Leaning back and rubbing his face, he wondered if he might sneak a nap.

"You had mentioned earlier that you wished to speak to me." Zaidhron stood in the door, arms folded.

Avadhron rose. "You should be resting, Sire."

"I had some sleep. And I ate, before you ask."

"You would make of me a harridan."

Zaidhron huffed a laugh. "At times you are. So what did you wish to discuss with me?"

"I have done something unconscionable."

A crooked grin spread on his king's face. "What now?"

"I am serious. As Security Commander I should be under good self-regulation—"

"What did you do?" Zaidhron's weary voice sounded like a mother's.

"I struck Mattan."

Zaidhron displayed no surprise. His expression remained neutral, as when he listened to petitioners or took on his role as arbiter. "And why?"

"I could give excuses. Grief, exhaustion, the anger when he told me the last of all their secrets, but none of that justifies what I did. I lost control. As there is no higher authority to which I am accountable except my king, I answer to you for my offenses."

Zaidhron lifted a hand. "It is done, and forgiven. By me, and Mattan."

"Mattan? He told you?"

"Yes."

"And you are just going to let this transgression drop?"

"I have need of my Security Commander, and I am reasonably certain that since you have now done what you have wanted to do since you first set eyes on him, you will be able to restrain yourself in the future. But this is your only reprieve."

"You are too lax in your judgments, Your Majesty."

"So you remind me. See why I need you? Who else is brutally honest with me?"

Avadhron stifled a sigh and bowed to hide his glare. "Sire."

Zaidhron left, and Avadhron did too. He needed to rejoin his team.

Chapter Thirty-Five

Avadhron exited the lift, his attention drawn to his left by sounds of a scuffle. He ran down the corridor, shoving several onlookers aside, and pulled two men apart.

"Will you listen, you useless prig!" one shouted, trying to lunge around Avadhron's arm.

"Scum! Rubbish low-clan!" the other yelled. "Keep him away from me!"

"Enough!"

The noble straightened, adjusting his robe, sneering down his nose. The other man attempted to charge again, but Avadhron held him firmly by the arms.

"What is the trouble?"

"This idiot won't listen to me!" the commoner shouted.

"Why should I listen to inane babblings of the low-born?"

"Because I am in charge of this section, and you will follow the rules!"

"I am from Viltara, my clan makes the rules!"

"Not true," Avadhron spat. The thane of Viltara might be the king's top advisor, but what arrogance to make such a claim!

The noble opened his mouth, but Avadhron jabbed at finger at him. "Quiet!" He turned to the other man. "What is your name?"

"Riltor."

"And what is the problem, Riltor?"

"He is not assigned to quarters in this section. He tried to steal bedding from us."

"I was just taking what—"

Avadhron snarled in the noble's face until he wilted. "Name and rank, Viltara."

"Durdhan. Sept Callana."

So he was of a sept in Viltara, and so far removed from his thane that rank meant nothing. Sad little man trying desperately for importance. "I am reporting you to your thane and to my security. If you try to steal from others even once, I will see to it you are stripped of standing and have permanent priv duty. Do you understand me?"

"But they have blankets and sleeping furs, and they are mere low-born trash! I am from Viltara! It is not right!"

"If you have not yet received bedding, you talk to whoever is in charge of stores and requisitions in your section. Thievery will not be tolerated—by anyone, of any clan. Is that clear?"

Durdhan opened his mouth, then closed it and swallowed. He straightened with an arrogant shake of his head and stormed off.

"Thank you, sir."

Avadhron nodded at Riltor and continued down the corridor to his quarters. Still so much clan division. In the camp, he saw little of such distinctions or bias, but here it seemed as rooted as it had on Teledhar. Could his people ever learn to see past it?

<>

Avadhron blinked the morning sand from his eyes and settled in the railcar with the other hunters. A form approached, bundled in warm clothes, and carrying a pack in her arms. She hesitated, then straightened her shoulders and lifted her chin before entering the car. Her expression one of expectation, she cast her gaze about, waiting for everyone to stand in deference to her rank. When she received only stares, finally she walked farther in and sat, back straight.

The three Enaisi joined them, Mattan looking bemused, Ismari irritated, and Telkai, naturally, disgusted. The ride to the Estan hub was preternaturally quiet. The door slid open when they arrived, and cold air rushed in. Marinn gasped.

Everyone automatically headed to the rear of the car and hauled out supplies. As he hefted a crate, Avadhron said, "You too, Marinn. Pick up something and carry it to the campsite."

"*Lady* Marinn."

"I would worry more about doing your share of the work than about whether anyone cares for rank. I also recommend taking a deep breath and bracing yourself. Once you walk up that ramp, you'll outside a dome, under the open sky."

"I will be fine." She swept past him and grabbed a sack—and almost fell over when it didn't budge.

"Better take one of these, lady." Kental held out a small crate. "And I'd listen to the commander about being domeless. He knows what he's about. Not a one of us was unaffected the first time. Some took quite awhile to get used to it."

"Thank you, but I will be fine." Marinn accepted the proffered box of supplies, her nose wrinkling as if something smelled bad. Was it due to the proximity of a commoner or having to actually lift and tote? Avadhron swallowed a smile.

In the one day they had been gone, the snow melted, leaving only frozen pools of slush here and there. The ramp had been somewhat cleared of ice, making it comparatively easy to ascend, although he slipped several times.

On his trip back down to the railcar for more supplies, he slowed. Marinn leaned against the wall, her eyes squeezed shut, her face white. The small crate had hit the ground at her feet and slid down the ramp.

This he could understand. He softly asked, "Do you wish me to accompany you to the campsite?"

"Thank you, no."

Her brusque reply made one side of his mouth quirk up. "I reacted much as you are the first time I stood under the open sky. Breathe deeply and slowly." He carefully picked his way down the incline to get another load of supplies.

Marinn had not moved by the time he climbed back up. He considered stopping again to ask if she wanted help, but he wagered she wouldn't accept it from him regardless. Wordlessly, he passed her.

At the top of the ramp, Ismari waited, fists on her hips. "Are you just leaving her there?"

"I offered to help. She refused."

"You are the most cold-hearted man I have ever met!"

Because he knew it would annoy her, he inclined his head with a smug smile. *Going to send pain to me again?*

The alien's eyes narrowed, but she didn't reply. Too bad; he would have liked to know she followed their 'moral code' as well as Telkai did. He continued on to the camp.

After finishing his first hunt the next day, Avadhron stopped at the cooking tent, even though he knew the delectable odors would torment his empty stomach. He peered inside. Marinn stood beside a worker, copying his movements on how to hold a knife and chop vegetables.

He called over a cook and asked, "How is she doing?"

"Do you really care, Your Highness?"

Avadhron spared a glance from the lady to the man before him. "'Commander.' And yes, I do care. For our people to survive means a change of attitude and perspective. And an understanding that we must all work together. If she, a pampered noble, can comprehend this and adapt, then I have more hope than I had before."

The cook regarded him, frowning. "I...didn't expect that answer, Commander."

"Let me know how she fares."

The man nodded with a slight smile.

<<>>

In the last few weeks, the weather had mellowed and warmed somewhat, rain replacing the snow. Today offered a clear sky, and the ground remained merely damp, easy for tracking, not saturated and precarious. Avadhron hunkered to examine tracks. Not pindouru. Were they ballan? He wasn't certain, but anyway they weren't too fresh. They shouldn't be in any danger. Twice he had encountered the vicious animals, and both times he had dispatched the creature before it harmed him. Mattan swore he did not hold them either time, stating Avadhron needed to know how to defend himself against the natural dangers of this world.

A breeze gusted, and he inhaled deeply, enjoying the fresh clean air; he would never tire of feeling the wind, blowing through his hair, on his face.

And the trees! So many varieties, most still in bud, some bright green with spring's new growth, others with long, shaggy, dull-green foliage, and scattered among them a few with clusters of perennially blue-green spikes extended along their branches. The sun winked through the sparse canopy, dappling the mould-carpeted ground with light.

Mattan either sensed his delight or read his thoughts because he knelt to tighten the laces on his boots, taking longer than usual.

Avadhron's momentary joy fled as reality flooded back. No one to share this world with. Not his wife, nor his best friend. His people. He had to ensure his people survived. He glanced at the alien. "You ready?"

"We'll not find a good hunt here. Gatherers approach."

He frowned, and Mattan shrugged. "I can sense them."

Of course he could. Why did he keep forgetting that? He became aware of soft laughter and quiet voices.

Ismari, Marinn, and several others came into view, baskets over their arms. Their banter faded as did their smiles. Avadhron was evidently as popular here as he was back on Teledhar. Galadhan would have appreciated that. He could imagine his late Second's ironic smile, and squelched the raging grief that threatened to rise. He swallowed and asked, "Is there much to gather in early spring?"

"No, sir," one of the younger men answered. "But we look anyway. It will be tight."

"Yes," another replied. "My family are in the valley, and have planted crops, and others now are joining them, although not quite prepared. But there is little food to be had until the plants can grow, whether in the wild or in tilled fields."

Mattan nodded. "It is going to be difficult before it gets easier."

"Is it true that another camp has been set up nearer a river, and that they will hunt meat from the water?" the first worker asked.

"They are," the Enaisi said. "Several in fact, not at the river, but near larger streams. They have constructed nets which will catch *fish*. As they grow in skill and the ability to protect themselves in the wild, they can continue east to the river and maybe even the ocean. We are trying to set up way stations so they find ease coming back to the Estan hub."

"There is far more to be done than we have those trained in various needed skills," Avadhron said.

"Dassel and Atesni have turned over coordinating work groups to your people, and are bringing equipment daily to help establish the new camps. It will help."

"A little." Avadhron winced and lifted a hand. "I don't mean to disparage their help. It is great and appreciated, I assure you. But there is so much to be done. Despite everything, my people are still on the edge of starvation." He bowed to the gatherers. "We will not keep you."

As he and Mattan moved past them, deeper into the woods, a woman's voice called out, "Good hunting!" It was Marinn. Had she indeed learned this world's priorities? He could only hope.

"You know," the alien said, ducking under a branch, "they are not just your people. Not really."

"What do you mean?"

"My team has thrown our lot in with you. We may not be of your people, but we have joined our lives and futures to yours."

He stopped and peered at the dark-skinned man. His frame had thinned as had everyone else's, his face gaunt. He could have gone back through the portal to his people. All the Enaisi could have. Yet they stayed, living in primitive conditions, only one step above starving, their stomachs daily pinched with hunger. Grudgingly, Avadhron inclined his head.

Chapter Thirty-Six

Mattan came over to the fire and thudded onto a log, hands dangling between his knees. In the uneven light of the flames, his face seemed more careworn and lined. "Word has arrived from the portal site that we have had yet more deaths, more than usual."

Almost every day reports gave some grim news; they all grew to expect it.

"How many?" someone asked.

"Over fifty in one day."

Murmurs, gasps, and exclamations came from those around the fire, along with questions of who and why.

"Those weak and sick, or old. The combined medical care of your people and mine often isn't enough, especially since food is so rationed. They don't have the strength to fight."

"That much more food for the rest of us," Cargil said.

Shocked silence fell. Avadhron shot to his feet just as several others did. Ismari rose and stepped in front of Cargil while those around them began to shout at the man, cursing him or asking how he could say that? What if it were his family? His mother or son or grandfather or sister? How about if we take your portion and give it to someone more deserving!

Cargil yelled back. Avadhron moved toward him, standing next to Ismari, creating a wall between him and the rest of the workers.

"Do you hear them?" Avadhron asked. "His stupidity has almost turned them into a mob. I need to get him away and safeguard him."

"Yes. Mattan can calm them, but let me take him. I don't wish you to lose your temper—"

"I will not lose my temper."

"You often do."

"Not on duty."

Ismari hesitated then nodded, stepping aside. "I'll trust you in this."

Avadhron took Cargil's arm. The worker struggled, and Avadhron changed to a force-hold, dragging him away, hissing in his ear, "If you do not leave with me, those people will likely do you harm, you fool. Although if they kill you, there would be that much more food for them. Shall I allow them to decrease our population by one more?"

"You can't! You wouldn't!"

"Why not? What makes you so special? Why not let you die so others

182

may live? You certainly don't mind the reverse."

"I'm just being sensible. The sick and feeble only drag us down, weaken *us*. Can't you see that?"

Avadhron was often accused of having no compassion, but this man truly felt nothing. Worse, he could not see the long-term implications of a decrease in their population. He pulled him close, face to face, and growled, "I see that we need every person to keep our people alive. We need more, not fewer Teldheri if we are to survive as a *race*. Can't you see *that*?"

Cargil looked away. After a moment, Avadhron shoved him backwards. "Be off."

The worker disappeared toward the tents. Dome above, how could anyone be so callous? He heard Mattan call to him, and he waited for the alien to approach.

"I wanted to tell you privately, Asila died. I am sorry."

Avadhron pressed his lips together. Her life had been one of loneliness and misery. Perhaps though, just perhaps, her last days had not been quite so bad.

"My thanks for the news." Avadhron rubbed his eyes. Every Respite Day he had visited her. She had softened just a little, almost glad to see him. Once, he had taken her to view the world through the doors of the upper entrance to the complex. It had been bright and sunny, and for a moment, she seemed to take an interest in life. He shook his head as he realized tomorrow was Respite Day, but there would be no visit.

He raised a hand to Mattan and trudged to his tent.

Word awaited Avadhron that Zaidhron wished to see him immediately upon arrival. He strode through the complex to his king's conference chamber. The door was open, but a guard stood next to it. Avadhron's brows lifted, and the guard nodded he should enter.

The king sat alone, writing. Like everyone, he had lost weight, but he seemed more pinched than ever now. Was he starving himself again? Not likely, if Mariss and Tarnill had anything to say about it. Probably just the rationing plus all his worries. And there was nothing Avadhron could do about either. He stepped forward and bowed.

"So, Sire, has something happened which has caused you to realize you need protection, or is the guard to stop unscheduled petitioners from crowding in?"

Zaidhron set the quill on the table and leaned back. "Your Second thought it a necessary precaution, mostly for the latter reason. I gave in when he said he would get you to nag me if I refused."

"I make myself a formidable threat even when not here, enh?"

"A pest, more like." Zaidhron's eyes twinkled, but then he grew more serious. "Please sit, I need to speak with you."

Avadhron pulled a chair close to the table and lowered himself into it, gazing warily at his king.

"You are not returning to the camp."

"I'm not?"

Zaidhron shook his head. "You have learned enough of the ways of this world to safely be outside, in the wild. But now I need you here, in your role as Commander of Security. We have set up shelters all over the plain, and are moving people into them as we can get them readied. There's going to be resistance, and I need a force here that is stronger than anyone's will."

One side of Avadhron's mouth lifted slightly. "So I am a force, am I?"

"You have always known you are. Is there anything to report from the camp?"

"Only that the hunting has become more scarce. The female pindouru have all birthed now, and we need to be careful not to target a new mother, but the males are, naturally lessened. We've had to extend our range to hunt successfully. Each one of the many pounces were in the thousands when we started, and are still significant, but we cannot cull them indefinitely. We've been tracking the wild herds of torchou like the Tinshal camp has had to do since the beginning, because the pindouru aren't native to their area."

"Food will be scarce until the crops come in. Many areas have been, and are continuing to be tilled and sown, and that is one task given to the Refugees. They complain, and yes, it is hard work, but it is that or starve. That is why we need you here. Thuldhan does well, but he is not you."

"So the time for tact is over. You need, as you said, a force."

"You have to admit, you are tactless and intimidating."

"Thank you."

Zaidhron shot him a disgusted look. "Go find your Second and let him acquaint you with all that's happening."

Avadhron rose and bowed. "I am honored to serve my king and my people." He left before his liege could toss an inkhorn at him.

<></>

Avadhron walked across the plain on paths between various crops with Thuldhan, a dagger strapped to his thigh, a sword replacing the half-staff he wore all those years, and a bow slung on his back. Thuldhan also now carried the same weapons. Avadhron peered into the distance. Despite having studied the maps, gauging the reality of walking place to place against them wasn't always easy. Two hours' walk, or probably more to the far side of the flatland. They wouldn't be traveling in a straight line though, but skirting plots and visiting different camps, seeing how things fared in them. This would be an all-day journey.

"This plain...these settlements are not permanent?"

"No. As soon as they are capable, we shall establish villages in the valley and to the south and east, and over the pass to the west as well."

Avadhron nodded. Good. He would wish to see this land returned eventually to its undamaged state. For now, though, the crops grown in divided sections were more important than the aesthetics he craved.

"How is the retraining of Secs coming along? And Training for Ch'shalna youth?" Avadhron asked.

"Fairly well, I think. The trainees and striplings more easily learn the new ways, but even our established Secs can handle the new weapons decently. For them, I fear the whole idea of change is more difficult."

"Sometimes the hardest part isn't letting go but rather learning to start over."

"You might be right, sir. And not just for our Secs."

They walked over trampled grass, and Avadhron winced anew at all the clusters of shelters dotting the landscape as far as he could see, marring its beauty. *Only temporary...*

"So many are complaining," Thuldhan said. "They work until exhausted, get little food, are always cold, always filthy, and usually wet. Nature 'stinks,' I'm told, and killing an animal for food is horrible and disgusting. Did you know dirt is unsanitary?"

Avadhron snorted. "Ah, sounds like a hunting camp."

His Second smiled. "Yes, you've been living like that since...since you arrived."

"Dome above, man, do not tiptoe around me. I cannot abide it. Since the Final Crossing."

Thuldhan cleared his throat. "Some have wanted to have a loosening ceremony for all those we've lost. There's been no time to grieve."

Personally, Avadhron dreaded the notion, but it would be a way for the people to gather and find common ground through mourning. "An excellent idea. Has the king set a date?"

"I don't think so. He and the chiefs have discussed how to accomplish it. It's usually only a small group of those close to the one who died, and we usually have a body. How do we plan something for our whole population? There isn't anyone who hasn't lost someone."

"We have had larger loosenings for dome disasters, so there is some precedent, even if nothing on this scale. We can discuss ideas of how to implement an event so personal to an entire people. Perhaps a day set aside, where families can gather. I'll talk to chiefs and see if they've decided anything."

Thuldhan nodded.

"Besides the complaining and dissension, how are we doing in educating ten thousand people not to kill themselves?"

"It's been a struggle. Some understand all the new dangers readily, but many seem to feel that rules do not apply to them, or that although something bad can happen, it won't happen to them."

"Typical."

"We've had quite a few maddening things occur since beginning to set up these camps. They've put up shelters incorrectly, despite help and advice from more experienced workers. One blew away in a storm, fortunately there were no serious injuries. They hunted the whole next day until they found the remains. We forced them to make do with their structurally compromised home. We cannot manufacture these things. They are all given by the Enaisi, and the supply is gone now."

"How did they have so many?"

"I believe they had a large store of them for their expeditions to other worlds, but I don't know where they kept them. Most are just sections which must be joined, so they can create shelters of various sizes."

Avadhron nodded.

"But it's the...the stupidity of the people, sir. They eat things without finding out if it's safe, they don't watch their children and then become distraught when they cannot find them. We had to threaten one family whose son kept getting lost. I think you know the king decided not to strengthen clan loyalty by weakening family ties as was often custom back home, but we made them understand we would take their son and give him to another family in their clan if they couldn't properly supervise him. We cannot afford to search half a day for a child that has wandered across the fields or into a nearby tent and fallen asleep unnoticed. Forbid that a little one becomes a meal for some animal, or is injured or killed. It happened last summer, but these Refugees don't seem to want to listen to tales of others' tragedies. It won't happen to *them*, you see."

Avadhron nodded.

Thuldhan waved an arm. "They lose their tools, their weapons—they lose themselves. That doesn't often end well. One was eaten by ka'gua. Another was found days after he disappeared, half-dead from exposure and starvation. He didn't make it.

"Some had to return to the Great Hall, they were so frightened by everything. One man went into hysterics during a thunderstorm and could not be calmed down. I, uh, I'm very glad you're back."

Avadhron was too. Learning to hunt and how to survive in the wild had kept him busy, although not so busy that he hadn't grieved every moment of every day. But the one thing he had been Trained to do, and did well, was be a Sec. His duty was to his people. What else did he live for, now?

He sighed, eyeing the few light clouds floating across the deep, blue sky. "These next few months will be the worst. Little food makes for high tempers. We need to keep the peace and help our people adjust." He gazed over at Thuldhan. "One thing though, that you should know. It will never be easy. At least, I hope not. We had it easy on Teledhar. People had no purpose. They had an allotment whether they worked or not, food, shelter—and nothing to do but cause trouble. We need adversity."

"Not too much!" His Second replied, eyes wide.

"Call it challenge then. We are not made for ease, but for struggle and difficulty."

"If you're right, sir, then we should prosper well."

They approached a small settlement, and a skinny lad pelted toward them, yelling, "Commander!"

"Fandel!" Avadhron knelt down as the boy rushed into his arms. "How are you?"

"See? We are at this camp, now. And m'mother is to marry a man from Delangar clan, his name is Mardir, and he is a cousin to Kental. He says we shall be associated clans, Tantera and Delangar."

"I am glad to hear it. And how do you feel about being outside?"

"It's beautiful, like you said. Not so cold now, except at night. But we have furs to keep us warm. I'm learning about plants and how they are our food."

"Good. Show us to your camp, lad, and let us see how your group is faring."

Fandel grinned and pulled Avadhron forward, toward the tents.

Chapter Thirty-Seven

Avadhron turned in the corridor as Tarnill called to him. "Father wanted me to tell you the loosening ceremony has been scheduled for the day after tomorrow, after the morning meal. We will have horns to declare the start time across the plain, and for those still in the complex, they will announce it over speakers. Families are gathering in small groups, and if they have a belonging for any of their loved ones, they are using it as an object for the loosening. Others will just...use memories, I guess."

"That sounds like a fine idea. Good. Our people need it."

"Do you...have anything of Jhendill's? Or for Paldhran?"

"No. And nothing of Galadhan's either." He thought of Rulinn. Dome above, he had never asked about her! "Do you know if Rulinn crossed? She was Galadhan's intended. Her father is Pendhalar."

Tarnill touched the wrist comm, inputting data. Avadhron dismissed his envy at her access to the computers; he had refused a wrist comm for himself, knowing it would have to be done away with in time. Best become used to the way things would be on this world, not cling to the ease of the past.

After a moment, she shook her head. "No, she didn't make it, and neither did her father. I'm sorry."

Avadhron clenched his jaw. So much loss...

Tarnill's expression softened, and she touched his sleeve. "Cousin...how are you doing?"

"I am fine."

"I know you are tough, and hide what you feel, but I truly doubt you are actually fine."

"I will make it, Tarnill. As will our people. We have the strength and purpose to do what we must. To continue on."

"It's all so daunting. Sometimes I don't see how we possibly can."

Avadhron placed a hand on his young cousin's shoulder. "Every little kindness, every task, keeps us going. Don't disregard the courage of a smile or of the scrubbing of a floor."

Tarnill bit her lip, her eyes twinkling. "Are you a secret philosopher, Sec Commander?"

"Forbid, Your Highness!"

Growing serious, she pointed a finger. "Don't forget the loosening. We all need it."

"I will not." He bowed. He would not forget, but neither would he attend.

<<>>

"You missed the loosening ceremony," Zaidhron said. "And you said you would be there."

Avadhron didn't look up at his king as he dipped the quill in the inkhorn. "I said I remembered it, not that I would attend."

"And what is your excuse?"

"No excuse. I just have too much to do, Your Majesty."

"I never thought I'd see you back away from anything, but you have avoided anything to do with the loosening. What are you afraid of?"

Avadhron clenched his jaw. "I am afraid of nothing. Jhendill is gone. Galadhan is gone. Nothing changes that, so why dwell on it?"

"Because—"

"No! No 'becauses!' This is personal, Zaidhron. And my choice." Avadhron took a breath and glanced at the other scribes in the chamber. They all busily wrote, heads down. "We will have this morning's reports ready for you soon."

His cousin's blue eyes pierced, too knowing. And sad. "Anything important?"

"One. Two clans are fighting over a baby. The woman slept with two men, and each claims the child for his clan. Mattan says we can use their laboratories to determine parentage, but Sire, we cannot depend on that forever."

"I fear you are right. The chiefs have suggested that we may need to revise our laws, and invoke even stricter rules for marriage and fidelity. Else what will happen to our clans?"

Avadhron nodded. *Clan first* had ever been the breath, the lifeblood of the Teldheri. Nothing was of a higher priority. He was glad he wasn't a law-scholar and wouldn't be directly involved in drafting any new laws. Enforcing those particular laws now, that he definitely would not look forward to.

<<>>

Harvesting of the early crops coincided not only with the solstice but with the finishing of several large buildings behind the Great Hall. Construction of another facility some distance away would soon be done. It would house administration and security and be the centerpiece of that range of the city. In a fashion reminiscent of the Palace Dome, it included a suite for the king and his family, rather than the small chambers all others had.

Everyone observed the happy occasion, across the plain, in the valley and, he understood, also in the settlements through the pass to the southwest. Those who lived in the "city," as it was already called, would celebrate in the hall or on the plains close by.

The mostly meat diet had given over to mainly vegetables and grains. Starvation still loomed, and likely would for several years, especially if many crops failed, but the spirits of his people had lifted with all the early summer abundance, and promise of more to come.

Avadhron descended the staircase to the Great Hall, the delectable aromas making his stomach rumble before he even saw the trestle tables filled platters and bowls of food.

Without enough chairs or tables, many sat on the floor in corners, or took their food outdoors. Avadhron did the latter, preferring always to be under the sky.

Musicians played tunes on newly learned instruments that did not use technology for sound or amplification: boards with strings, various types of drums, metal discs or pipes hit with padded hammers, reeds cut and tied together, among others that baffled him. Music had never been an interest, although he did enjoy it. And despite the work necessary for survival, these musicians had somehow found time to learn both how to craft as well as how to play these new devices. Their dedication and their sweet melodics earned his admiration.

As dusk fell, Avadhron sat on a log near a fire, just as he had done the summer before. Then his thoughts had been for his future, here with Jhendill. Now his only future was to assure his people would live. He stared into the flames, wondering if that would be enough.

<>>

"Commander?"

A Sec appeared in the doorway of Avadhron's new office in the admin building, two men behind him in rough-spun shirts and trous, boots, and wearing knifes. Quivers and unstrung bows hung on their backs. Hunters.

"These men wish to speak with you, sir."

Avadhron put the quill down and gestured for them to approach. "Your names?"

"Warset, sir."

"Banwin," the other said, bowing.

"And you wish to report something?"

"Yes, sir," Warset said. "There's a small camp not far from ours. It...we think several who were cast out banded together. They don't do right, sir."

"I will need details."

"They steal from us," Warset said.

"We can't prove that, so we can't," Banwin quickly put in. "But we have found trees girdled, sir. We went to them to ask why they would strip the bark all the way around trees, leaving them to die, and they said it made good kindling."

"And that's not right true," Warset said.

Avadhron's fists clenched as he nodded.

"Then they laughed at us when we said we'd tell Security."

"Chased us out of their camp, threatened us with knives, they did," Banwin added.

"They don't do right, sir. They don't follow the laws the Enaisi."

Avadhron rose. "Lead me to them."

"No disrespect, sir," Warset said, "but it's rough country up there. You might want to take a man or two with you."

"I was in the main camp in Estan from the Final Crossing until spring thaw."

"But—"

"As a hunter."

Their eyes widened, and they exchanged glances with small smiles.

"But still, these men are a tough lot. We don't know how many are guilty, and if you need to bring them back for trial, won't you need help?"

"What would you say is the size of their camp? Is it large?"

"We cannot say, but perhaps ten or twelve men."

"All right. I will take back up. Get something to eat, then meet me by the main doors of the Great Hall."

Avadhron provided the names of his two Elites, and they began the trek east across the plain. Several hours later, they skirted the southern edge of the cliff face. A wide swath of ground stretching eastward as far as he could see had embankments on each side, as if once, ages ago, a road existed here. Ahead, both east and south, the land continued fairly level, but the grasses gave way to stands of trees and then to denser wooded areas.

North of the embankment, the western side of that high, sheer cliff was not a continuation of a mountain range, nor was it an escarpment. Indeed, the towering tor seemed almost a massive wall protecting the plain and entrance to the valley. On this side, away from the flatland, the ground rose in a rough, craggy forest, with undergrowth struggling between outcroppings.

"Watch for ballan," Warset murmured.

The Secs nodded, alert for the diminutive danger likely to be found in the woods rather than open fields, and followed the hunters for some time, until Banwin stopped and pointed uphill. "Here, Commander."

"Ka'gua through this area, with all the rocks?"

"Yes, sir. And other critters one needs to be careful of."

Avadhron drew his dagger, and indicated his Elites should as well, peering up the steep, rock-tumbled terrain. Dome above, this would be a difficult climb!

Conversation had been sparse, but all talking ceased now as they concentrated on climbing and keeping watch for the small, deadly predators. Dach'alan stopped once and shook his head. "I cannot get a good grip with a weapon in my hand."

"Sheathe it as you need to, but only then."

Soon they came across a burbling streamlet and followed it upwards, clambering over the stone. Dappled sunlight sparkled onto the water splashing down a series of rocks from high above into the rill below. Avadhron halted, amazed at the beauty found in a small waterfall, mossy outcrops, and ferns growing among them.

"Takes yer breath away, don't it, sir?" Warset asked in a soft voice.

"Indeed."

"Their camp isn't afar off now, so it isn't," Banwin said.

They continued on, sweating in the summer heat. Finally, the ground sloped less, and they could walk rather than climb. The woods thinned, allowing more sun to peek through and, more welcome to Avadhron, the wind to cool them from their exertions. Before long they came to a small glade and found several animals hung from tree branches and pierced with arrows. From the amount of blood pooled under the poor beasts, they had not been dead when strung up.

The bodies of four men sprawled on the flattened undergrowth, mauled and disfigured.

Chapter Thirty-Eight

Avadhron gritted his teeth, sheathing the dagger and drawing his sword. The hunters and Secs readied weapons as well. None needed say aloud what happened. Ka'gua had smelled the blood. Wordlessly, they retreated.

"We will have to try to bury the bodies of the men and animals, but not without help. The ka'gua might come back." He scanned the ground. Spoors led away from the scene. He raised a hand in a hunter signal, and they began to follow the track, weapons remaining ready for feral beasts or savage men. Not fifty paces farther on they found another body, this man's wounds too great to survive, despite escaping the scene of the slaughter.

Avadhron peered around, still no ka'gua. They must have had sated themselves. For now. More blood continued in a trail. He gave the signal to advance carefully.

The five approached the camp, slowly and quietly. Pride of his Elites filled him; although they had not served in camps, they knew what to do. Thuldhan had taken Fadhalan and all the Elites for Training in the mountains above the Portal Complex, familiarizing them with their new world, weapons, and dangers. The hunters seemed impressed, and that took some doing.

The camp snugged under an outcropping. From the amount of tents—and he used that term loosely, as these were rough shelters of furs atop some sort of framework—not many lived there.

Two men lay by the fire, moaning and weeping, and a third man attempted to bandage their wounds. Another two sat, watching dispassionately, one with brown hair and beard, the other dark blond, or so it appeared. Hard to tell from the grime.

"Blast you, help me tend them!"

"Why?" the blond sneered. "They got themselves in that mess with their sport."

"Best use a knife and put an end to them," said the other. "They're bleeding out. We should move camp before those fiendish reptiles smell it and come after us."

Using hand signals, Avadhron ordered the hunters to stay back, in the trees, bows ready in case they were needed. His Elites would flank the camp, arrows nocked, moving forward as he announced his own presence, sword drawn.

This was his first true encounter as a Sec on this new world, with new weapons. Also, the first time he and his Elites had to work as a team without ear comms to coordinate. He waited until he felt everyone was in position, then took a breath and stepped out from the trees.

"Hold," he ordered.

The two hale men jumped up, drawing daggers. The one tending his companions, sat back, mouth open.

When the brown-haired man shifted his weight, Jhuliss called, "I wouldn't."

The man glanced to one side then the other, licked his lips, and dropped his weapon, spreading his arms wide.

Avadhron said, "You are all under suspicion of crimes against the laws of the Enaisi. You will come with us to the city where you will be tried."

"Who are you to tell us what to do?" the blond scoffed.

"If you don't recognize these black Sec jerkins you are a fool," Avadhron said. "Put your weapons down and kneel, hands behind your heads."

The man lunged at Avadhron, thrusting with his dagger. Easily parrying the blade, Avadhron struck the assailant in the face with the hilt of his sword, knocking him to the ground. The man held his jaw, glowering.

"Kneel," Avadhron ordered.

The one acting as medic gestured toward the two men. "I can't. They're hurt. I need—"

"You all need to kneel."

"But they're wounded!"

"They made it to camp, they can make it to their knees. And quickly, so we can bind your arms. Who knows when the ka'gua might decide to have another meal."

That brought compliance, albeit slowly from the two injured men. One had a slice taken out of the side of his face, the other's arm and shoulder had been mauled. Their wounds might be painful, but neither looked serious enough to be life threatening, unless infection set in.

Both should be capable of travel, and treatment would be better at the city.

Once the men had been secured, Avadhron asked Warset, "How far is your camp?"

"Not far enough away from this place for our comfort, but a right bit. You think of staying with us overnight?"

"If you would allow it. Much easier than a journey back at night."

"We would be honored. Some of our hunters could set watch on the prisoners, if you wish, so you Secs could get some rest."

"I thank you."

They arrived later than they thought, the two wounded men slowing their pace. But the camp welcomed them, doubly when they saw their treacherous neighbors had been arrested, those who survived at least. Dach'alan and Jhuliss were taken aback at the cordial reception; it wasn't the usual response back home—back on Teledhar, that is. *This* was home now.

The workers eagerly brought them food and tea, all of them profoundly offering thanks. When Warset and Banwin described the area that had been desecrated by the sport with animals and the subsequent attack of the ka'gua, the whole camp agreed they would undertake to bury all the bodies the next day, setting guards to protect against the vicious reptiles.

"Although if the critters get hungry, they might leave us with less digging," Banwin said. "It would make the task quicker, so it would."

"Something must be done about those who don't do right," Warset said. "What do you think should be done, Commander?"

"I have been giving that matter thought for quite some time. After what I saw today, I think I am right about what we must do." He stopped, frowning down at something moving in his mug. With a finger, he fished out the bug and flicked it away. "Since our people do not understand the importance of caring for our new home, it seems my clan shall have to become custodians of this planet."

"What are you saying, Commander?" Jhuliss asked.

"We enforce the laws, do we not?"

"Yes, sir," both Elites chimed.

"We have laws given to us by the Enaisi regarding this planet. If we wish it to nourish and provide for us, then we need to watch over and protect it. And stop those who would disregard their laws."

"But how shall we do that?" Dach'alan asked.

"We'll have to give our people additional training." The image of that map he had seen in his dreams, and once while awake, hovered before him like a hologram. This time more vivid than ever, with demarcations that now he clearly understood. Another prophetic vision? Foresight of what he must do? It settled his decision. "We shall give some of our Secs boundaries, and they shall range them, assuring the land is properly tended and not abused."

"For what areas?" asked Dach'alan.

"For everywhere people settle."

That's adding quite a burden to our personnel," Jhuliss said. "Do you think the king will approve?"

"I think he must. And so will the Enaisi. It's their rules we'll be enforcing after all. We're Ch'shalna. We are honored to serve our people. And our new planet."

His Elites inclined their heads.

<>>

Avadhron and his party approached the admin building with the offenders, their arms tied behind their backs. A crowd followed the Secs and hunters, some curious, many angry.

Zaidhron stood at the entrance with the chiefs and the Enaisi. All had forbidding expressions. Mattan's crossed arms and black eyes said more than if he spoke.

After a bow, Avadhron supplied the king with the men's names, and gave an account of the crimes they had witnessed, and the hunters attested to more offenses, such as the tree girdling, and dumping filth improperly in the woods.

Zaidhron stared at the five men. "And what shall we do with them?"

"That is for Your Majesty to decide." Avadhron bowed.

"I am asking for your opinion. These men have survived in the wild. If we let them go, as has been the rule in the short amount of time we've lived here, I don't think it will be much punishment." Zaidhron's eyes narrowed. "And I doubt they would learn from it if they did survive."

"This isn't the proper place for a trial," said the blond Tagnen.

"As king, that is my decision," the king replied. "Your crime is one that affects all of us. It shall take place publicly, under the open sky."

"It was just a small spot in the woods, a few animals."

"It was not. It is a pattern of destruction, displaying a complete lack of respect for both the beauty and danger of our new world and the laws the Enaisi. If everyone adopted your actions, how would this planet sustain us then? We were given lease of this planet by the Elders, with rules and conditions of how we must behave and care for it. You have broken that. I could rightly turn you over to them as a punishment. What do you say, Mattan?"

The alien's face displayed no emotion, nor did his voice. "I could send them back through the portal to Teledhar."

Avadhron's brows rose at that harsh answer.

The captives' glowers melted into fear.

"You wouldn't dare!" Tagnen exclaimed. "That's murder!"

One person called out, "We could just stone them right now. Take care of it."

Avadhron raised an arm, and bellowed, "Enough! Justice is the purview of the king only."

Zaidhron turned to Mattan. "You ceded the planet to us with

conditions. What would you have us do to these who violated that agreement?"

"As I said, I could return them to Teledhar."

"Is that your recommendation?"

"An offer."

"You make it seem like we killed someone," Tagnen shouted. "What's wrong with some sport? Who cares about a few trees or animals?"

The crowd cursed and shouted. Avadhron again raised his arm, and his tacit command brought silence. If only that had happened more often back on Teledhar.

"I have decided," Zaidhron said softly, his face pale. "They find nothing wrong with playing sport with living creatures or stripping trees and leaving them to die. Then let us do the same to them. Strip them bare, and send them off. But not together. Each one will be sent alone into the wild in a different area."

Amid all the reactions, the cheering of most of the crowd, some gasps and yells, and the hysterical cries of the sentenced men, Avadhron and his Elites dragged the scofflaws off to wait under guard until they could be taken away.

<<>>

Avadhron plodded across the trampled grass toward the admin building. The king stood in the doorway.

"Is it done?" Zaidhron asked.

"Yes. An experienced hunter is accompanying each of my Secs as they take them to the designated spots and let them loose."

"And?"

"They are to follow and see how the offenders fare, but not interfere. If they live, we will track where they are until Secs are ready to take on those areas to range, then give that information to them."

"How soon will you have your people ready to begin these ranging duties?"

"Some have already started. I chose from among those who came over last year, and they are being sent to the various camps. They aren't enough, but it's a start, and will serve as a warning."

"You don't let the sandstorm end before acting, do you?"

"Safeguarding this world won't wait. I've made arrangements for hunters and gatherers to teach my Secs the wild and how to survive. They're intelligent and learn fast. We're going to designate boundaries and consider the logistics on how many of these ranging Secs will be needed to start. As the settlements increase, so shall our number of Secs."

Avadhron rubbed his hand across his eyes. "When I have the details prepared, I will present my recommendations to you and the chiefs." He nodded toward the building. "I'm going now to work on it. Treyor said he would provide me with detailed maps."

Zaidhron followed him inside. "There is no need to present anything to us for approval. Only to show us what you are implementing. We back you, Commander. Wholly."

He inclined his head and reached for the latch of the door into the chambers of the new Sec headquarters. He heard his name and turned to face his king, standing on the stairs. "I'm glad I have you, Avadhron."

He bowed. "I am honored to serve, Your Majesty." He had that to live for. At least.

Thank you for reading *Unlikely Prophet*. If you enjoyed it, I'd love for you to leave a review at your favorite retailer.

~L.S. King

ABOUT THE AUTHOR

L.S. King has novels published in two series: Deuces Wild and the Sword's Edge Chronicles.

Besides having short stories published in *Deep Magic*, *The Sword Review*, *Dragons, Knights & Angels*, *Digital Dragon Magazine*, and *Residential Aliens* (the fact that several of the publications which have released her stories are now defunct has nothing to do with her, honest), she also authored a column for writers, has worked as a submissions editor and a copy editor on several magazines, and was a founding editor of the semi-pro online magazine *Ray Gun Revival*, currently on hiatus.

<\>

Check out her website: http://loriendil.com
Follow her on Twitter: @Loriendil
Friend her on Facebook: @AuthorLSKing
Facebook fan group: Loriendil's Lair
Subscribe to her blog: http://loriendil.wordpress.com/

www.ingramcontent.com/pod-product-compliance
Lightning Source LLC
Chambersburg PA
CBHW051505170626
46811CB00002B/654